BLACKFERN GIRLS

Elizabeth Yon

Bannerwing Books
www.bannerwingbooks.com

For the Saturday Scribes

Wine, camaraderie, and gleeful mayhem forever.

CONTENTS

ACKNOWLEDGEMENTS

A thousand thanks to Saturday Scribes: Eleanor Curtis, Rose Voth, Terry Carnila, Dorothy and Tony Rawski, Ron Curtis, Susan Keith, Anthony Mangos, Karen Semanek, Marie Jorkasky, Morgan Marisic, and Marissa Carney. They listened to readings, served as beta readers and editors, cheered me on, and inspired me through the entire process of writing these stories, and they deserve medals.

Thank you, Jack Yon, for making it possible for me to write, and for all the lovely things without count that you do for me every day.

BLACKFERN
GIRLS

THE UNDERTAKERS

1.

I was eight years old the summer I went to Bitterberry Farm. My mother and I left the city in a funk of hostile misery and drove for hours through the heat shimmer of an August afternoon. The air conditioner was broken, and a whiff of exhaust worked its way into the old car, a nauseating stink that coated the back of my throat. The radio broadcast a garble of voices in scratchy bursts like alien transmissions. I reached for the dial to turn it off.

"Leave it."

They were the first words my mother had spoken since forcing me into the passenger seat. I glared at her, but pulled back my fingers and flung myself back against the ripped upholstery. She slid a sidelong glance at me. Her eyes were bloodshot and weary, with a deep-down glint of mean.

"I don't want to miss the weather report." Her eyes had turned forward again.

"Can't hear it anyway, with all that static."

She ignored me. My knee bounced up and down, and I gripped and released the loose seams of the seat, twisting them, hoping they would tear. The fight was building up in me again, like steam in a boiler.

"Why do I have to go to the farm? It's gonna be boring. It's gonna ruin the rest of the summer!"

"You can use some time away from the city. You'll have your cousins to play with."

I scowled. "I hate them!"

1

"You don't even know them. For Christ's sake, stop whining about it."

She lowered her window, letting in the roar of hot air and traffic to drown me out, and lit a cigarette. Her fingers trembled, and the first plume of smoke streamed from her pinched nostrils like a malevolent genie.

We were not a close family. I had met my aunt and her daughters only twice – once at my grandmother's funeral, where nobody spoke, and again at a dismal, suburban Blanchard reunion where the crowd divided into those who nibbled picnic food in silence and those who became loudly drunk. I remembered Aunt Melanie crowing about the farm she and Uncle Ted had just bought.

"I got it back, just like I always said I would," she'd said, flushed and spiteful, like she'd really put one over on somebody who deserved it. "Bitterberry is finally back in the Blanchard family."

Ted, leaning in a dim corner with his sixth chilled longneck for company, had muttered, "All on the Tarrington dime, not that anyone asked."

Tarrington was his name. Aunt Melanie used a hyphenated version that kept him in his place, the cumbersome and pompous sounding Blanchard-Tarrington. I didn't think anyone had heard him – there was a pretty respectable boozy din going by then – but his wife shot him a look that turned her face into a hateful Medusa mask.

Later I asked my mother what Aunt Melanie had meant.

"Bitterberry's the old Blanchard homestead," she told me, and I pictured pioneers raising a log cabin. "Things went to hell, some backwoods scandal, and they had to sell it. I don't remember the details. It was back when your great-grandmother was a girl."

"Then Aunt Melanie didn't grow up there?"

Mom snorted. "None of us ever saw it except in old pictures. Mel was always running her mouth about the place, wanting to hear Granny's stories about growing up in Blackfern County."

"Is it nice?"

"It's the ass-end of nowhere, that's what it is."

That's where we were heading, where I was doomed to spend the last glorious weeks of the summer. The Ass-End of Nowhere.

We traded the rush and glare of the highway for country roads where wildflowers nodded at the asphalt's edge. A vacant blue sky sizzled over fields of hay. A spicy, prairie perfume flooded through the open windows and washed away the reek of the car's exhaust.

There were no houses in sight; and soon the hay gave way to corn, a kingdom of deep, shadowy green. We had exchanged the familiar urban tumult for plant rustlings and the drowsy click and whirr of insects, everything pressed to dreaminess by the weight of the sun. My eyelids drooped and my stomach growled.

"Are we in Blackfern County?" I asked.

My mother's hands jerked on the steering wheel, as though she had forgotten my presence.

"County line's just ahead. See the sign?"

I sat up straighter and peered through the bug-spattered windshield. A sign rusted on a roadside post, but I didn't need to read it to know we were rolling across an invisible boundary. The sunny fields halted at the toes of a forest out of fairy tale, and as I caught my breath, we slid beneath its dark spell.

2.

There is a story about a girl who leaves her home to go to the witch's house in the woods to earn bread. The house in the story is tall, crooked, and shabby. It breathes and walks like a living thing, and it has consumed more than one young girl. My first sight of my aunt's farmhouse was a powerful reminder of that tale. It stood in a plot of field grasses that clumped and flowed like hair. Goldenrod and enormous candelabras of tiny white asters grew among the grasses, along with weeds I later learned were poke and nightshade.

"I don't want to stay here. Mom? It's falling down." I kept to the facts, and didn't mention the cautionary tale of the witch's house. "They don't really live in there, do they?"

My mother pressed her lips together until they disappeared. The car bucked over the twisted ground. "Don't be such a little snot," she said. "It's not that bad."

I sucked in my breath at the daring of such a lie.

"It's bad," I whispered.

The house stretched up out of the weed tangle like pulled taffy. It leaned in several directions at once, a jumble of additions, extensions, and angular nooks assembled with the care of a bumper car pileup. Its clapboarded hide had once been white; but the paint had flaked and peeled from it in patches, leaving large sections of weathered grey. Its tin roof was a patchwork of faded blue and rusty scarlet. We pulled up by a dilapidated shed. There was no other car in sight.

"Maybe she went into town for something," my mother muttered, craning forward over the steering wheel to look up at the house.

She shut off the engine, and the car gave a groan of relief. We sat in the hot silence, listening to the tick of the cooling engine. Without looking at me, she opened her door and scrambled out. She stood with her hands on her hips, stretching and looking around as if she had come to buy the property.

"Come on, get out. You may as well stretch your legs."

I crawled out, my shirt and shorts stuck to the back of me, and the red imprint of the cracked leather seat branded on my legs. I wanted a Coke and some fries. I wanted to go back to the city. A sultry breeze blew the scent of miles of green in my face like a taunt.

"There's no one here, Mom. Let's go home."

The words were no sooner out of my mouth when the screen door opened with a shriek. A woman came out onto the sagging porch and put up a hand to shield her eyes. Where my mother was skinny and angular, Aunt Melanie was as curvaceous as a screen goddess. Her honey-colored hair flowed past her shoulders in sensual waves. Though the color was the same, my mother's hair was straight and lank, pulled into an exhausted ponytail that needed washing. The comparison was not favorable, yet my aunt's glamor left me cold. For what seemed an eternity she only looked at us, then she came across the hard packed dirt to my mother.

"Sharon. You're late. I thought maybe you changed your mind." She turned to me. "Hello, Francine."

My mother put out a hand toward me, her fingers making a get-over-here gesture, and I sidled closer to her. "Everyone calls her Frankie," she said.

"Hmm." My aunt looked down at me with cool, considering eyes. "Well, come in before the baby wakes up and wonders where I am. I made some sandwiches and lemonade."

The screen door opened into a large kitchen. Six red vinyl chairs and a Formica-topped table clustered at its center. Sunlight streamed in the window over the chipped porcelain sink and struck walls of bare, whitewashed planking. The floor, under its red and white skin of cracked linoleum tiles, canted toward the door, so that we struggled uphill over a massive chessboard.

In a laundry basket in the far corner, a baby lay in a snowy drift of blankets, waving its arms and gurgling. Aunt Melanie went to it and smoothed the black fluff of its hair, fussing with the blankets. Mom went over and stared down at it with all the tenderness of the thirteenth fairy at Beauty's christening.

"How old's this one, Mel?" she said.

"Fourteen weeks. Would you like to hold her?"

"No thanks, I'm out of practice." Mom went to the table and dug her cigarettes from her purse. "Maybe Frankie wants to hold her."

I shook my head, and Aunt Melanie put the baby back in its nest and bustled away. I shot a look of enraged embarrassment at my mother, but she paid no attention.

"Sit down." My aunt spoke with her back to us as she busied herself at the kitchen counter. "The girls are out somewhere. They'll be back soon. Their stomachs bring them in. Francine will share a room with them." She turned with a platter of sandwiches in her hands. "Sharon, we should talk."

My mother froze in the act of lighting a cigarette, the match guttering in her cupped hands and throwing campfire shadows over her face. Her eyes narrowed in suspicion.

"What's to talk about?"

"Don't be stupid." Aunt Melanie spoke without heat. She set the platter on the table.

Mom bent her head and set fire to her smoke, inhaling right to the basement level of her lungs. She shook out the match and sat back, crossing her legs. Smoke streamed from her nostrils beneath a reptilian squint.

"You got an ashtray?"

"I don't smoke."

They stared at each other for a long moment, long enough for me to understand that they were fighting, and then Aunt Melanie sighed and turned to the sink. She pulled a saucer from it and set it in front of my mother.

"Use that." She dragged out the chair opposite her sister and sat, back straight and hands folded in front of her.

Mom's mouth lifted at one corner. She flicked ashes onto the damp saucer.

"Where's Ted?" she asked. "I thought he'd want to be here, to wring his hands over how Tarrington money has to fix yet another Blanchard fuck-up."

"Do you always use that kind of language in front of Francine?"

Mom leaned across the table, quicker than a sucker punch, the cigarette in her fingers only inches from Aunt Melanie's face.

"Yeah, I do. We live in the real world, Mel, where it's hard. You want to make something of it?"

Aunt Melanie turned her head aside to avoid the smoke that rose between them.

"There would hardly be any point, would there?" she said.

Mom sat back again, squashing the cigarette into the smudge of melted ash on the saucer. She no longer looked fierce, but only tired.

"No. I guess not. Seriously, why isn't Ted here?"

Aunt Melanie stood and went to the refrigerator. It was the old, fat kind with rounded edges. She opened it and took out a pitcher of lemonade.

"He's not here because he's gone, Shari. He left me."

She turned and looked at mom, whose eyebrows had risen in surprise to the top of her creased forehead.

"Jesus, Mel. It took him long enough."

They stared at each other for a shocked second, and then both burst into peals of laughter.

The late-day sun dragged its golden train across the room like a fleeing bride. My mother and aunt huddled at the opposite end of the table from where I sat eating thick-sliced ham and pickles. They talked in hushed voices. Occasionally, they paused and looked at me before leaning their heads together again, and so I knew their conversation must be about me. I assumed that my mother was warning her sister about my behavior and giving her permission to knock some manners into me. I strained my ears to no avail.

"It's not polite to whisper," I said in a loud, self-righteous voice.

Aunt Melanie's face turned toward me in astonishment, and my mother gave a bark of laughter that held no amusement.

"Look who's talking about being polite," she said.

I read violence in the coil of her muscles, and slid to the edge of my chair in readiness for flight as the screen door sang out in pain. Two girls tumbled in. One was tall and brown, the other slight and blonde; and both were barefooted and dirty. Their chattering voices dropped from their mouths into sudden, awkward silence. They stood gawking at my mother and me until Aunt Melanie broke the spell.

"Girls, this is your Aunt Sharon and her daughter Francine."

I interrupted. "Frankie. My name's Frankie."

My aunt went on as though I hadn't spoken. "Come and eat your supper, and then I want you to take Francine up to your room and show her where she'll be sleeping."

The girls went straight to the sink to wash their hands, and then stood at the counter, wolfing enormous bites of ham like a couple of starving dogs. Aunt Melanie cast a glance at the sleeping baby and returned to her seat by my mother, where they resumed their inaudible conference. I watched the two girls, grabbing and chewing, swallowing lemonade in hurried gulps. Their eyes never wandered in my direction; and when they were finished, they padded from the kitchen. The taller girl paused in the doorway to say, "Come on."

I remembered them from the reunion, though we hadn't spoken then. They had pretty, fairy names: Ariel and Poppy. I would have made fun of them if I'd had the chance, even though Ariel was bigger than I was and celebrating her tenth birthday. I could be mean when I was jealous. They hadn't strayed to the fringe of the gathering where I lurked; and anyway, my mind had been occupied with more hedonistic things. There had been an immense sheet cake under a heap of pink icing roses, and I had wanted one of those roses. Birthday cakes were not entirely unknown at my house, but they were unpredictable; and they certainly never arrived wearing frilly, white piping and roses. I took my slice of cake with its precious sugar bloom under the stairs, where I removed the flower with the precision of a surgeon and laid it at the edge of my plate to savor last. It had a metallic flavor that stuck to the roof of my mouth and was so sweet it made my teeth ache.

Now, in the girls' attic bedroom, the three of us stood looking at one another, too shy to speak. Three iron beds dressed in white chenille stood in a line against one wall. Against the opposite wall towered a wardrobe of dark, polished wood with an oval mirror in its door. Two low dressers flanked it. Aside from these meager furnishings, the room was bare and scrubbed down to the raw, silvery planking of the walls and floor. A breeze slipped over the sill of a wide dormer window and stirred the ribbons on the pink cushion of the window seat. The taller girl made an impatient gesture and broke the ice.

"I'm Ariel. This is Poppy." Ariel shrugged in the direction of her younger sister. "We saw you at the reunion last summer. We have another sister now, but she's just a baby. Her name's Bit."

Ariel rolled her eyes and huffed. She stood too close to me, forcing me to look up at her.

"It's short for Bitter, like the farm. You know, Bitterberry." Poppy said this so softly I almost didn't hear her. Her gaze skittered between Ariel and me.

"She knows the name of the farm, stupid." Ariel gave Poppy a withering look. "She's going to live here, too."

I shifted from one foot to the other and took a step back. "I'm only staying for the rest of the summer," I said. My voice rose at the end, turning the declaration into a question.

Ariel laughed, and her eyes narrowed. "Is that what they told you?"

Voices murmured up toward us from outside, and she went to the window.

"Come here, Frankie. Look."

I crossed the room and knelt beside her on the window seat. Below us, the damaged shed sagged beside my mother's car. Mom and Aunt Melanie hauled a bulging suitcase out of the trunk, along with some boxes from our corner grocery in the city. On top of one of the boxes, I saw the covers of some of my favorite books. I looked at Ariel, who looked smugly back at me.

"Do you always pack everything you own when you go away for the summer?" she asked.

"What do you mean?" My mouth was dry. I looked at Poppy, who stood wringing the hem of her sundress and staring at her dirty toes. "What does she mean?"

"You weren't supposed to tell her," Poppy said. She looked at Ariel from under her sun-bleached brows.

"Tell me what?" I grabbed Ariel by her skinny shoulder. "Tell me what?"

"Get off me." She shoved me backward on the window seat and stood. "Your mom is giving you to our mom. You have to live with us now. I guess that almost makes you another sister." Her smile was an angry grimace.

"You lie!" I jumped up and took a step toward her with my hands balled into fists. Surprise registered on her face. Poppy whimpered.

"It's not a lie. I'm sorry, but it's not."

Ariel didn't look sorry, but neither did she look as superior as she had. She walked away from me and studied herself in the mirror. Her reflected eyes found mine.

"Don't worry. You'll like it here when you get used to it. There's secret, magic things here, if you're not afraid."

The sound of a car engine turning over interrupted us. I flew to the window. My mother was in the car, and Aunt Melanie stood speaking to her.

"Mom! Mom!" I waved frantically from the window. "Wait!"

She looked up briefly, and said something to Aunt Melanie who stepped back from the car. Then my mother drove away.

I raced to the door of the room, but Ariel got there first. She blocked my passage and grappled with me as I tried to push past her.

"Stop. Frankie, stop. You can't go down there."

I barely heard her. "Get away. Let me go." I shoved at her.

Her arms were wiry and strong. We wrestled in panting desperation until she was able to fling me down on the hard floor. She dropped on me, crouching over me on all fours like a wild animal. Her hair fell over her shoulders in a dark cloud.

"Let me go," I yelled.

"Shut up!" She hissed the words in my face, and her eyes were hot blue sparks. "Shut up, or I'll make you."

Poppy began to cry softly with her hands over her mouth. I fell back against the smooth boards and looked up at Ariel through stunned, tear-blurred eyes. She stared down at me for a moment, assuring herself that I was going to be quiet, then looked up at Poppy.

"Stop blubbing. Go look out the window and tell me if you see Mom." She glanced back down at me and laid her finger on my lips. "Not a peep, okay?"

I nodded, and she rolled off me to sit with her back against the foot of one of the beds. I sat up warily and rubbed my bruises.

"Mom's in the shed," Poppy said. "She's putting some boxes in there. I don't think she heard Frankie yell." She came over and knelt beside me. "Are you okay?"

I ignored her. Ariel leaned against the iron bedstead as though exhausted, but her face showed angry determination.

"Why did you do that?" I asked. "What's wrong with you?"

"You were going to get us in trouble, Frankie. Big trouble. We weren't supposed to tell you about all this. We're not even supposed to know about it, but I heard our moms talking on the phone." She gave me a hateful glare, as though the situation were my fault.

"We can listen on the phone in the barn," Poppy said. "It still works - "

"Shut up, Mouth!" Ariel lunged at her sister, who cowered against me.

I pushed them apart and stood. Something bad was happening here, and I felt cold prickles walk over my skin.

"Why would you get in such big trouble just for telling me? I was going to find out anyway." My voice had a strangled quality, and my throat felt tight and narrow.

The sisters looked at each other. Poppy was white, her eyes huge and round, her lips pressed into a bloodless line. Ariel was grim, thinking. After a long silence, she sighed and said, "I guess we'll have to tell her. She won't keep her mouth shut if we don't."

Poppy nodded.

Ariel stood and faced me. "We're going to show you something, and you have to promise not to breathe a word about it to anyone. You have to swear on your life."

3.

I swore. We left the attic and, at the wide second-floor landing, passed through a door I had thought concealed a closet. A narrow, twisting staircase fell away from us in darkness. There were no handrails, but the walls crowded in close enough for us to touch on both sides as we descended.

"This goes to the canning kitchen," Ariel whispered. "We can go out through the back yard without Mom seeing us. We have to go to the barn."

"Won't she wonder where we are?"

"No." Ariel didn't elaborate.

At the foot of the stairs, she put her eye to a knothole in another closed door. The stairwell filled with the sound of our shallow breathing.

"Okay, it's empty. Come on, and don't make any noise."

She lifted the latch and eased the door open. Poppy slipped through and scampered across the galley kitchen. Her bare feet slapped on the concrete floor. She waited at a screen door where white moths jostled and fluttered. I went next, jogging past the old gas range. Huge, gleaming kettles stood on the stovetop; and rows of jam jars stood atop white towels on the butcher-block counter. The kitchen smelled sweet and tart at once, a hot sugar and berry smell. I paused to look up as a breeze from the open door stirred the pots hanging from the iron pot rack.

Ariel was behind me, looping a canvas tote over her shoulder. "Get moving! She'll be back any minute."

I scooted through the door and down the limestone steps. Ariel swung under the pipe handrail and dropped into the ferns that skirted the foundation. She pried open a section of scabby lattice work and reached under the house, dragging out a plastic bag that she handed to me. It bulged with some soft weight like sand, and I hefted it in the dim light; but the plastic was blue and opaque. Ariel pushed the lattice back into place.

"Here, gimme that," she said, snatching the bag from my raised hand.

The three of us ran across the tangled wreck of a garden toward the barn dozing under the angry, red scald of the sunset. The high grass slashed at us as we pressed through it in single file, Ariel in the lead. The barn was a massive, grey structure of scoured wood slumped atop a fieldstone undercroft. Part of the roof was gone. Swallows watched us from the dark bones of the rafters, swooping down like a hail of arrows when we approached. The great rolling doors wore a rusty chain and padlock, and we entered the barn by squeezing beneath a loose plank in its side. The splintered wood, smooth and rough at the same time, caught at our hair and clothes.

"It's easier to get to the well if we go through the barn," Poppy explained. "There are too many sticker bushes to go around." She gave me a solemn look and added, "Snakes, too."

"Dad was going to brush hog it all," Ariel said. "He started to - that's how they found the well - but the bushes grew back over the trail he made."

Dust hung like a mist inside the barn, phantasmal in the faded light that filtered through the holes in the roof. The place was oven hot, and the air was thick with an ancient fug of hay and animals. We crossed a large open area to a hole in the floor with a rough trap door that leaned open against the wall. A steep slide of steps that was more like a ladder descended into the cobwebbed darkness below.

"We have to go down to get out," Ariel said, and slipped over the edge without a pause.

In the undercroft, the light was even weaker. We crept through the dark, slapping at spiders, real and imagined. Old farm machinery hulked out of the shadows, rusty and menacing. The dirt floor smelled moldy and cold.

"I don't want to be down here." I stopped and looked over my shoulder at the ladder.

Ariel scowled. "Don't be a baby. Here's the door. You want to see what we have to show you, don't you?"

She pushed open a low door, and twilight flooded in. The sinister tomb of the undercroft transformed into a dirty junk room. We filed out onto a sort of lawn, as wild and weedy as that in front of the house, and peppered with big stones. The woods jostled at the edge of the small clearing, thick and dark with wild rose and berry bushes.

In the shadow of the tree line, a wooden frame about four feet square lay in the grass. The wood was soft and crumbled to sawdust in places, but newer, weather-warped planks covered it, held down with cinderblocks. Poppy picked her way over to it and waited. Her face was set in a mask of resigned suffering.

"Do we have to?" she asked her sister, who chose not to hear her.

Ariel turned to me. "That's the well. Mom and Dad covered it so we wouldn't accidentally fall in, but the boards are loose and we can pull them up. The thing we need to show you is in there. Are you ready?"

I wasn't ready for anything. Dread had bloomed in my belly and crept up my throat until I felt that I was trying to climb out of my own skin. I followed dumbly along as Ariel walked to the side of the well and bent to heave a block aside, her scrawny arms straining with the weight. She grasped a wide plank and looked over her shoulder at me.

"Kneel down by the side of the well. You have to lean over it to see in, but don't lean on the wood. It's rotten."

"What's in there?"

Ariel blew a strand of hair out of her eyes and looked up at Poppy. "Don't just stand there; get your end of it."

Poppy bent like an automaton and grasped the plank. Together, they lifted it away. Blackness sprang up the sides of the well, as though the pit contained the coming night. A smell came with it. The odor of death and decay, fat and gassy, climbed the air and blotted out every clean, green scent. It rose on a column of damp, wound about with tendrils of mildew and a chill underworld reek of stagnant water and toadstools. Poppy gagged, throwing her end of the plank to the side as she staggered backward to collapse in the grass. I recoiled from the lip of the well as though slapped, my hands over my nose and mouth.

"God! What is that?" I looked up at Ariel who had pushed the plank further to the side and stepped back, her face twisted in disgust. "Something's dead down there."

I don't remember if I had ever smelled decomposing flesh before, but I recognized that monstrous stench with primal accuracy. Ariel pulled a flashlight and a length of dirty clothesline from the shopping tote.

"Yeah, something's dead down there." She tied the clothesline to the handle of the flashlight and clicked it on. "I'll lower this down so you can see."

She stepped closer to the well and swung the flashlight over the edge, feeding out the clothesline without looking into the pit. I crawled to the edge, one hand still clamped over my nose. I breathed in shallow sips through my mouth, and the nightmare perfume slid over my tongue in greasy ribbons. I looked down the well.

At first, I couldn't make anything out. The white glare of the light swayed over rough stone and thrusting roots, and the tumble of earth and debris at the bottom was a seething nest of shadows.

Then a shape leaped out of the stinking gloom. It was a boot, a thick-soled work boot clotted with earth and clumps of dead grass. It jutted upward and lay against the side of the well, as if kicking at it, maybe fifteen feet down. As the light ceased its swinging, I saw that the boot was attached to a denim-clad leg. My gaze scrabbled madly over a loose, twisted terrain of torso and shoulder and fastened on the staring fright-mask of a face that had gone to bone and ruin. The thing's head was wedged against the wall opposite its booted foot. It canted at a weird angle so that it seemed to be trying to look over its shoulder at the suspended flashlight. Something stirred in the empty eye socket, and I threw myself back from the well in a spasm of terror and revulsion.

"That's a person!" I stared up at Ariel, electrified in parts of my body and numb in others. "There's a dead guy down there."

She crouched beside me and stared into my eyes. "I know. It's my dad."

She began to wind in the clothesline, and the flashlight made soft, echoing thuds inside the well as it bumped upward.

"Your dad? Uncle Ted? Did he fall in?" I asked, all the volume shocked from my voice. A sudden cramp of fear rippled through me. "Does Aunt Melanie know he's in there?"

Ariel wound the clothesline into a neat loop, and the flashlight swam through the grass toward us. She picked it up and let the light spill through her fingers. I thought she wasn't going to answer me. Her jaw worked, the muscle bunching and relaxing; and I realized she was in the grip of some powerful emotion. Her face was as closed as a fist, the muscle in her jaw jumping under the skin, while she calmly stowed away the clothesline and flashlight and smoothed the canvas of the tote. When she turned to me, her face was still.

"She knows, Frankie. She knows because she put him there. I saw her do it."

I didn't think I believed her, but my body turned cold and rigid just the same. I was untethered from the humid woodland around me and floated on a dizzy swirl of half-formed thoughts and the conflicting impulses to run away and collapse in tears. Poppy, forgotten in her nest of grass, leaped up as though galvanized. Her normally placid face was blotchy with anger.

"That's not what happened, Ariel!" She pointed a finger at her sister. "You tell her how it really was. Mommy didn't kill Daddy!"

"She as good as killed him! And she did so push him down there. I saw it, I tell you." Ariel kicked at the ground, and then moved to the edge of the well. "Help me cover him up."

"Tell how it really was," Poppy repeated. Her chin trembled, but her voice was hard and she made no move to help her sister.

"Fine! I'll tell it, you little baby." Ariel reached for the end of the shifted plank. "Frankie, get the other end of this."

I helped her cover the well again, dropping the boards over the crawling black and shutting the smell inside. It was like closing a door. Already, I was unsure if I had seen a dead man or only dreamed it.

Ariel walked into the deepening shadow of the oaks and sat down. She didn't wait for us to join her, and she didn't look at us, just began her story all in a rush. "I was playing on the old tractors in the barn, and we're not allowed in there, so when I heard Mom and Dad coming I hid where I could see them and was real quiet. They were coming to close the well up good, because there was just a sheet of old plywood over it. They were fighting about the house again."

"Mellie, this place is a money pit and a hazard. I can't do the work, and you know it. As soon as we get it cleaned up a little around here, we're putting it on the market." Ted stopped on the hill and massaged his hip.

Melanie marched on, stomping through the weeds that the old brush hog had chopped and flattened into a composting stew. It stained her work boots and flecked her calves with green, and filled her nostrils with a sharp, summer smell. At the top of the hill, in the shadow of the barn, she turned to watch her husband resume his lurching trudge. His limp had always hurt her heart, but now, watching him stagger through the thick vegetable crush, she felt ice forming crystal by crystal where her love had been. There was only so much to go around, and she had girls to raise, a home to reclaim.

"I'm not selling this farm, Ted. We can use the college fund - "

"And leave the girls without an education?"

Melanie's head pounded. The sun was so hot, and the humidity rose from every blazing green thing and fattened the air until it was heavy and smothering. Sweat ran down her spine, pooled under her milk-heavy breasts.

"The girls need a home first, Ted. They need a connection to their own roots."

Ted laughed, a mean shout that held no mirth. "Their roots? Hon, your family's about as rootless a bunch as ever shared blood." He reeled up beside her and leaned in, his lips at her ear like a lover's. "I'm not putting one more penny into this forsaken hell patch."

The lumber to cap the well lay in a neat stack at the edge of the woods, splintery planks they'd found in the barn. Ted walked toward it, adjusting his tool belt to relieve his aching hip. Melanie clenched her hands into fists and wondered if she would cry again. She'd wept rivers over the last few weeks; but the tears seemed to be as rationed as love, because none would come. Instead, a red hatred rose up. She turned and looked at the well, at Ted bent to grasp the first plank, and her vision narrowed and grew sharp on the strop of her rage. She saw the papery grey cells of the hornets' nest in the pile of lumber. She saw the poisonous black dart of a single, white-faced killer, but her anger would not let her speak.

"Ow! Jesus, Mellie, I'm stung!" Ted jerked upright, his hand clapped to his neck as though he'd been shot. With his teeth, he tore the leather glove from his other hand and fumbled in his shirt pocket for the epinephrine pen he carried. It fell from his fingers and vanished in the thick grass. More hornets were stirring. "Mel, help me!"

She watched him go down on one knee and sweep at the grass with a wooden hand. She went to him and knelt beside him. She found the hypodermic and tossed it into the woods.

"Dad needed his medicine, and she threw it away." Ariel's voice was flat. We knelt in front of her, and Poppy reached out and touched her sister's face. Ariel closed her eyes and slumped against the oak. "After he was dead, she rolled him over the edge of the well and covered it up."

In the spectacular horror of viewing my uncle's corpse, I had forgotten my own crisis, but now it rushed upon me with a new sense of urgency.

"Why would she do that?" I asked. "Is she crazy?"

"Yes!" Ariel hissed, her eyes snapping open. "She's totally nuts about this farm, and Dad was going to make her sell it."

I glanced over my shoulder at the well. I felt that Uncle Ted was listening, that he was still aware of the world above him, and his interest in it was awful. The electricity that had zinged through me when I looked down the well had drained away, and my teeth chattered.

"Why did you leave him down there?" I asked.

"We can't get him out, now can we? He's too heavy." Ariel scooped her sweaty hair off her neck and looped a rubber band from her wrist around it.

"We tried to pull him out with the rope," Poppy said. "But then we found a better way."

"Shut up and hand me the bag." Ariel stood and shoved Poppy toward the plastic grocery sack that lay in the grass behind us. "There's no point telling her about it, she won't believe us. We'll have to show her."

The bag was knotted at the top, and Ariel looked at me from under her brows as she picked at it.

"Remember," she said, "you promised to keep the secret. I don't know what Mom would do if she found out you knew. She might throw you down the well, too."

"I'm no snitch," I said. "And I'm not afraid of Aunt Melanie."

It was a brazen lie, but it seemed to impress Ariel. She stopped fiddling with the knot and stared at me.

"You're a pretty brave kid. That's good, because we have more to show you."

She gave the knot a final tug and upended the bag. A ragged, yellow cat slid from it and fell to the ground at her feet. It was stiff, frozen into a curl that looked like sleep. Its one open eye was milky green, and its tongue poked out like the leather tongue of a shoe.

"Poor kitty," Poppy murmured at my elbow.

I couldn't look away from the dead cat. "What happened to it?"

Ariel shrugged. "I don't know. We found it in the weeds by the mailbox. Maybe it got hit by a car or something. The important thing is that it's fresh."

I watched as she used the plastic bag as a glove and picked the cat up by its tail. She marched over to a large, flat boulder that lay half in the woods, and laid the cat on it with the care of a hostess setting out dinner. Poppy touched my arm and smiled at me. She rummaged in Ariel's canvas tote and found two fat candle stubs and a box of kitchen matches, which she carried with great solemnity to the rock. While Ariel set them in place and touched a flame to them, Poppy yanked a handful of wildflowers from the weedy verge and laid the bundle beside the dead cat. The two joined hands. Ariel looked back at me.

"Come on. Hold hands. We have to say a prayer now."

I stepped forward and clasped hands with them. A bouquet of hot beeswax and bitter herbs rose up, masking any smell the cat might have contributed. We stood in prayer-like attitude, all of us gazing down on the dead cat, until I began to fidget. The light drained from the sky, and in a dreamy lurch of time, it was dark. The transition was seamless and complete. It scared me, to be out under the belly of the night like that, with no light but candle flicker and the brief flare of fireflies. A new world of furtive, somehow threatening, sounds awakened. The forest that had drowsed in the daytime heat opened its eyes wide and looked at us with hungry amusement.

"There's something in the woods," I whispered.

"I know," Ariel said.

"Do it now." Poppy forced the words out between her teeth.

Ariel took a deep breath. "We brought you this cat," she called into the dark. "It's a good cat, and hasn't been dead long. We'll trade it for the man in the well."

She freed her hands from mine and Poppy's, reached into the pocket of her shorts, and brought out a dainty, pearl-sided pocketknife. The blade gave a wicked flash when she unsheathed it.

"I wish it," she said, and made a nick on her finger.

A bead of blood welled up, and she squeezed it over the cat. It plopped onto the yellow fur. She passed the knife to her sister.

"I wish it." Poppy repeated the blood offering, and held the knife out to me. "Go on. It doesn't hurt."

When I hesitated, she said, "Do you want me to do it? You'll have to say the words, but I'll cut your finger."

Ariel stared at me, her eyes hard and remote. I was adept at reading such things, and I saw terrible thoughts sliding behind them, like sharks in deep water.

"No," I said, "I'll do it."

I took the knife and jabbed my finger.

"I wish it."

Blood fell. The woods became silent.

Perhaps a minute ticked by in which I became aware of the cold rush of blood in my veins and the crackle of my hair as it tried to rise on my scalp. Something was coming. I wanted to shout that I didn't believe, to tear myself from our fragile circle and run away, to break the dreadful spell that had fallen over us. I wanted to stop the momentum of the thing that raced toward us from the heart of the forest. A pressure built in the air that finally equaled that of the fear bursting within me, and I stood paralyzed. Poppy moaned, and Ariel fell to her knees, dragging us down with her.

"Don't look," she said, her voice strained. "Keep your head down and be quiet."

The heaviness of the air was almost unbearable. I bent forward over my knees, my face only inches from the grass, as the thing slipped from the woods and approached our rough altar. I had an impression of a vast form standing behind me, and several hoarse, snuffing sounds sketched themselves on the silence. In a sidelong glance, I saw a long, black boniness of arm extend like a shadow between Poppy and me. It had a sinewy claw at the end, digits tipped with curving nails like thorns. The claw petted and squeezed the dead cat, scattering the flowers, and then seized it and whisked it from the stone faster than a blink. The candle flames bent after it and drew out long and blue before parting from their wicks. The night came back to life with the sounds of crickets and tiny rustlings. The air was sweet and light again, and we sat up, blinking at one another. I swiped a hand across my face and found I had been crying.

"Is it gone?" I breathed.

Ariel made a chopping motion to silence me and tilted her head in a listening attitude. Poppy's face was tense as she, too, strained her ears. Questions jostled in my mouth, and I opened it to see which one would spill out first.

"Listen!" Ariel snapped the word at us.

A sound came to us, like the scrabbling of a rat in the walls of an old building. It was a soft sound, and it came from the well. We huddled together, staring at the old boards that covered the pit. We heard a slithering sift of earth and the *plink* of a pebble against the stony walls. A breeze dropped from the trees and glided through the grass toward us, carrying with it what could have been a sigh.

Poppy, clutching my arm hard, quavered, "Daddy?"

"It was just the wind." I said it mostly to convince myself.

Quiet filled the clearing. None of us could bring herself to approach the well, and we sat in the dampening grass for several agonizing minutes, waiting. When it became apparent that Uncle Ted was not going to climb from his grave, Poppy burst into tears.

"It didn't work," she said. "The cat wasn't good enough."

"Stop your bawling." Ariel stood and began to rummage in the shopping tote for the flashlight. "It almost worked. I think I know what we need to do next time."

I leaped up. "Next time! You're going to do it again?"

"Frankie, we've already done it, like, three times." She switched on the light and played it over the dark trees behind me. "This was the best, though. Next time, it'll work."

"Well, I'm not doing it."

Ariel stopped waving the flashlight beam and directed it under her chin. Her face, lit from beneath, was white as a skull, with black pits where her eyes should have been.

"You will so do it, Frankie. You'll do it and keep your mouth shut about it, or I'll leave you here right now. Wonder if you'll still be here in the morning?" She stepped closer. "In fact, if we gave you to the woods, I bet we'd get Dad back right away."

Poppy pushed her way between us.

"Stop it, Ariel." She looked at me, her expression hurt. "Don't you want us to get Daddy back, Frankie? He'll be your daddy, too."

They turned away from me and began to pick their way toward the barn. I followed as closely as I dared, thinking about what Poppy had said. There was no way I wanted to see Uncle Ted creeping out of that well. I was sure that he wouldn't be the kind of daddy any of us wanted.

4.

The house was dark and filled with an expectant, crafty silence. The sisters hesitated at the bottom of the stairwell that led up from the canning kitchen into the blackness of the second floor.

"What time is it?" Ariel asked.

Poppy looked at the foggy, blue glow of her Cinderella watch. "It's just past nine o'clock. We're not very late."

Ariel let out a breath and turned to me. "Okay, we're going up and straight down the hall to the bathroom to get cleaned up. Mom is probably sleeping. Don't make any noise."

One by one, we crept up the stairs, Ariel pointing out the creaky spots to avoid. The second floor hall was a dark throat, a pale glow at its end from the nightlight in the white-tiled bathroom. Four open doorways, pasted to the walls like rectangles of starless night, towered over the strip of threadbare runner before us, two on each side. Ariel put her finger to her lips, and then she and Poppy went swiftly along the middle of the corridor, quiet as thieves. I counted - *one Mississippi, two Mississippi, three Mississippi* - before following. The sense that a trap was waiting to be sprung in the dark weighed on me, and I wanted to see if anything happened to them as they passed those doorways. They made it to the bathroom and crowded together, beckoning me. I stepped into the hall and scurried toward them.

"Francine."

The voice pounced from the first door to my left and froze me in my tracks. Ariel and Poppy eased the bathroom door shut between us. The faint illumination from the nightlight winked out.

"Come in here, Francine," Aunt Melanie said.

A light clicked on in the room, a gentle, low wattage blush designed to be sleeping-baby friendly. Aunt Melanie sat in a rocking chair in the soft halo of light, nursing little Bit. The lamp, which featured a smiling bear seated on an alphabet block, stood on the table beside her. I went in, dragging my feet, wondering why she had been sitting in there in the dark.

"Close the door," she said. I did as she told me and leaned against it. Aunt Melanie made a frustrated cluck with her tongue and held out her free hand, waving me in with impatient flutters of her fingers. "Come here, closer. I don't bite."

I trudged closer, my eyes on the baby and my aunt's round, white breast. Bit was like a celebrant at an altar, her eyes shut and her tiny fist lying against the curve of flesh. The room was warm, and I could smell the baby, a combination of powder, milk, and a strange humidity for which I had no word.

Aunt Melanie's hand closed on my arm, and I jumped. "Francine, I want you to know that I'm glad to have you here. Things are going to be different for you now. I hope you'll be happy."

I held very still. I didn't like to be touched. Her hand slid down my arm and clasped mine. I let my fingers lie in her grasp, unresponsive, ready to snatch them away.

"Where did you and the girls vanish to for so long?" I didn't answer. "Did they show you some of the farm? I don't want you children playing around the old buildings, they can be dangerous." She gave my hand a little shake. "Francine?"

"Is my mother coming back?"

She squeezed my fingers. "Not for a while, sweetie. It may be a long while. I'm going to take good care of you, though."

"I don't want to stay here." I spoke to the tops of my sneakers.

Aunt Melanie dropped my hand. She cradled Bit against her and leaned back in the rocker, looking at me from under half-closed eyelids.

"Go and get your bath, Francine. It's late. Tell the girls I expect all of you to be in bed when I come up there."

She began humming softly to Bit, and I went to the door and pulled it open. Her voice followed me.

"This place will be good for you, Francine. You're a Blanchard. You'll see."

I hurried down the hall to the bathroom. It was empty, my cousins already gone to the attic, and I closed the door and locked myself in. I stripped my clothes off, tearing my tee shirt, and flung them from me. I climbed into the big claw-footed tub, opened the taps, and let the rush of the water mask my sobs.

5.

Morning came with birdsong and a breeze that smelled of hot foliage and sunlight. I lay on my back, the sheet kicked away, and stared up at the sharp slope of the ceiling where the heat was already collecting in a suffocating cloud. There was no traffic noise, no stink of summer-stewed garbage from a neighboring alleyway, no shouting for me to get my lazy ass out of bed. The serenity, with its black heart of death and madness, was terrifying. I closed my eyes against it and thought of ways to escape.

"Frankie, are you awake?"

Poppy crouched over me, rocking the mattress, her face only inches from mine. I looked at her from cat's-eye slits in my lashes. She was already dressed, her blonde hair pulled into a ponytail. I pushed her away.

"Come on, Frankie," she said, pulling at my arm. "Get up. Ariel's making breakfast, and she doesn't want to wait. We have to go hunting today."

I sat up. "Hunting?"

I envisioned the three of us slinking through the woods, armed with Elmer Fudd blunderbusses. The idea of having a gun appealed to me. I'd seen a handgun once, and even held it for a minute, the weight of it coiled and expectant in my hands, before the bigger kid took it back and stuffed it in his waistband. A gun was power.

"Yeah. Mommy's making us pick berries, so we're going to hunt for another dead animal while we're in the woods." She grabbed some clothes from a box on one of the dressers and threw them on the foot of my bed. "Sometimes it takes all day to find one - a good one, anyway. Hurry up."

I pulled on my clothes, and we went down to the kitchen, Poppy skipping on the stairs and swinging around the newel post, ecstatic at the thought of finding some smelly dead thing. Breakfast was on the table, a stack of cold Pop Tarts and a couple of juice boxes. The dirty canvas tote from the night before lay there, too. Ariel rummaged in a cupboard under the countertop and emerged with three dented metal buckets. Her dark hair hung around her face in twisted hanks that made her look like a wild girl.

"It's about time," she said. "Here, take these and let's get going. You can eat while we walk."

"Where's Aunt Melanie? Isn't she coming?"

"Yeah, right. She's already working in the canning kitchen."

I picked up a Pop Tart and looked around as I bit into it. "What about the baby?"

Ariel became very still, and a strange look passed over her face. "What about her?"

"Well, where is she?"

"Oh." She tossed the tote at Poppy and headed toward the door. "She's with Mom. Come on, and don't forget your pails."

The berry bushes grew everywhere in the woods around the farmhouse, weirdly lush despite their lack of sun. They crowded together under the trees, the dusky fruit fattening on the shade and on the cold nurture of the moss-furred fists of limestone that thrust up from beneath their roots. Poppy bounded ahead, peering under bushes and stirring the shadows with a stick. I dragged along behind, my mind churning around the indigestible nugget of the thing I'd seen in the woods, its awful power and loathsome demands. I stripped berries from their prickly stalks and quizzed Ariel about it.

"Is it a monster?"

"Don't be stupid."

"A ghost?"

"Nope, too solid."

"Then what?" I stopped plucking berries and turned toward Ariel, my pail swinging on my wrist. I dropped another handful of the tiny, black orbs into it. Some of them had bled onto my fingers, ugly, dark smears. I lifted my fingers toward my mouth, but Ariel slapped my hand away.

"Don't. You can't eat them. They're poison until Mom cooks them. Do you want to get sick and die?"

I gave the question some serious thought. Maybe I'd just cram a bunch of them in my mouth and chew, letting the juice run down my throat. That would show them. Would it hurt, being poisoned? I imagined Aunt Melanie and my mom weeping at my funeral, sorry for all they'd done. Of course, my aunt was a crazed murderer, so maybe she wouldn't cry at all. And Mom hadn't wanted me anyway. I gave up the idea.

"Why would anyone cook poison berries?" I asked.

Ariel wiped the sweat from her face with her bare arm. "She sells the jam. It's super expensive. The berries only grow on our farm, and you need the Blanchard secret recipe to make the jam."

"Is it good?" I looked at the berries in the pail with more interest.

"I never tasted it. It's not for putting on toast or anything. It's a special kind of jam, for really sick people. It can make them better, as long as they keep eating it."

"Oh." Medicine. My interest died, and I returned to my previous line of questioning. "So, what is the thing in the woods, if it's not a monster or a ghost?"

Ariel set her full pail on the ground and began helping to fill mine. "I don't know for sure," she said, "maybe some kind of witch. Or a goblin. Goblins live in the woods and have magic powers."

I couldn't refute her logic, and gave the woods around me a wary scan. "How do you know it can bring your dad back from the ... well?"

"Shh!" Ariel gave me a vicious pinch and glanced back down the path toward the farmhouse. "Do you want her to hear you?"

"But ..."

"I know what I'm doing," she hissed. "Just keep your mouth shut."

Her bossy, know-it-all attitude was like a goad to me. I put down the pail of berries and squared up in front of her. "Uncle Ted's not just dead down there, Ariel," I said, "he's all rotted and gross. He's like a zombie."

She sucked in her breath, and I thought she'd clobber me. I balled up my fists and got ready, but instead, Ariel said, "He'll be okay when he comes back. We just have to trade the right thing, and he'll come back as good as new."

"How do you know that?"

"I figured it out. What we were doing wrong." Ariel dodged the question. Her gaze wandered over the woods until it found Poppy, crawling into the underbrush, her stick probing before her. "I know what we have to trade. We'll do it tonight."

"I'm not."

Ariel wasn't even looking at me, so it scared me badly when she reached out and grabbed me by the arm, hard enough to leave a bruise. I kicked over my pail of berries as I flailed against her, but she didn't seem to notice. Her eyes were electric blue pinwheels in her tanned face.

"Yes, you are," she said. "We'll all have to work together. If you don't help ..."

Her threat went unvoiced, for just then a triumphant Poppy erupted from the forest tangle, holding aloft a dead crow on the end of her stick.

"Hey, you guys, look what I found!"

6.

By the time we trooped back to the house for a late lunch, it was nearly suppertime. Poppy patted the canvas tote, stopping to hold it open so I could see the prizes inside. In addition to the crow, she had found a chipmunk - somewhat the worse for having been mauled by one of the cats that slunk about the place – and a dried crisp of a newt with its eyes eaten away by ants.

"I know where there's a possum, too," she said, "but it stinks. We'll have to get it on the way to the barn tonight. We can give them all a nice funeral." She gave me a blissful smile.

"That's disgusting," I said. "What makes you think the thing in the woods wants a bunch of old rotted up animals? It could get them itself if it wanted them."

Poppy's smile crumbled. "No, we're helping. It takes them and makes them alive again, only then they're like ghost animals. It likes it that we help find them."

"If they're ghosts, they're not alive."

"Yes, they are, Frankie. It's just different, because they can't die anymore. And they can play and be friends forever."

"You're full of shit."

Poppy went rigid at the swear word. She closed the tote, her expression suddenly distant. "I saw them. I wouldn't lie."

I felt a little bad about hurting her feelings, but I didn't get a chance to apologize. Ariel caught up to us, a full berry pail in each hand.

"Put that under the porch," she said to Poppy, nodding at the tote. "I have to take these in to Mom. Meet me in the kitchen."

The kitchen smelled like Rocco's Pizza and Subs, only better because there was no base note of ancient grease in the perfume of tomato sauce and garlic that met us. Bit was back in her blanket-padded laundry basket in the corner, reaching up sleepily to count her bare toes. Aunt Melanie turned from the counter, her hands made cartoonish in gingham oven mitts.

"I swear, you girls are like wild animals. I never see you unless there's food." Her scrutiny fell on me. "Francine, I hope you like lasagna."

I nodded. I'd only ever had the frozen kind, or sometimes, when Mom didn't feel like turning on the oven, the kind that came in a can and looked like someone had thrown up. I'd never seen a homemade lasagna, and Aunt Melanie was setting out a bowl of fresh salad and a basket of hot garlic bread, as well.

"Did you make all this?" I asked.

"Oh, I love to cook. I don't always have time to set a big table, but my girls never go hungry." She watched me ogling the feast. "Wash your hands and sit down."

We crowded around the sink, passing around a bar of lemon-scented soap. Ariel jostled me with her pointy elbow, splashing me in the face with stinging lather.

"I don't know why she wants to impress *you*," she hissed under the thunder of the water in the old pipes. "We'll talk later, *Francine.*"

I sat down at the table, my heaped plate in front of me, and waited until the others dug in with their forks. I lifted a small bite to my mouth and chewed. Gastronomic heaven opened before me and angels sang. If life at Bitterberry Farm included regular offerings of such gourmet grub, I was ready to revise my opinion on staying. I looked up to find Aunt Melanie's gaze on me, watchful and considering before it slid away, and I understood. The food was a bribe, bait in the trap, and I wasn't so sure that it wouldn't work.

"Look at us," my aunt said, reaching out to stroke Poppy's ponytail, "all the Blanchard women together on Blanchard land. It hasn't been easy, but we're all home now."

Poppy grinned around a mouthful of lasagna. Ariel scowled, but kept silent. I ate with cautious gluttony, thinking that not all the Blanchard women were here. My mother was missing, and although I couldn't have said that I loved her, I wondered if I should feel some sense of outraged loyalty at her omission.

Ariel seemed to read my thoughts. "Aunt Sharon's not here. And you know who else should be here? Dad."

The silence ticked like a bomb, and then the kitchen timer shrilled and I dropped my fork with a clatter. Aunt Melanie threw down her napkin and pushed back her chair.

"We are not going to have this discussion, Ariel. I have to get back to my jam-making. You girls can clear away when you're finished."

She picked up the laundry basket full of sleeping baby and left the room. For a moment, we sat and stared at one another, and then I pushed away my plate and leaned back in my chair with a hearty belch. Across from me, Poppy laughed, her lips ringed with a faint smear of tomato sauce like a clown's mouth.

"Don't be such a hog," Ariel said. She stood and began clearing away dishes, and Poppy leaped to help her. "Now that she's gone, we can talk. Frankie, I need you to steal something from Mom's room."

I brought the legs of my chair down on the linoleum with a thump. "What? No way."

"It's in her nightstand, in a locked drawer," Ariel said. "I know you can get it open. I know you're a thief."

"Ariel!" Poppy turned to look at me, aghast.

"What? You heard as well as I did." Ariel stood in front of me. "When our moms were talking on the phone, yours said that you stole some money at school. From your teacher's locked desk drawer. She said you were a shoplifter, too. Don't act like you don't know what I'm talking about."

I was dumbfounded. I'd been suspended from school for three days after being caught with the fifty bucks from Mrs. Frazier's desk, and Mom had been furious that she had to go in and talk with the principal. But I'd never been caught lifting anything from the neighborhood shops, and I thought I'd hidden well my stash of ill-gotten gains. I couldn't believe she'd known all along, and now Aunt Melanie knew, too. Was that why Mom had left me at the farm? If the worst that can happen to a thief is being found out, it was done, and I'd weathered it. I shrugged and leaned back in my chair again.

"So what? I'm still not stealing anything from Aunt Melanie's room. Why don't you do it yourself?"

"Because," Ariel said with exaggerated patience, "I can't find the key. I don't know how to pick a lock."

Neither did I. I'd broken the lock on Mrs. Frazier's desk drawer with a screwdriver I'd brought from home.

"What's in the drawer?" I asked.

"You'll see if you can get it open."

I thought about the tiny locks on the drawers of the antique dressers in our attic bedroom. They weren't much more than flimsy latches that had probably barely required a key to flip. Aunt Melanie's nightstand couldn't be much more of a challenge. I let the legs of my chair down softly.

"Do you have a nail file?" I asked.

There was nothing in the drawer but a bookmark, a hairy stick of gum, and a bottle of pills. I looked at Ariel in disgust.

"Is that what you wanted?" I pointed at the pill bottle rolling toward the back of the drawer.

She reached in and grabbed it, looked over her shoulder with a mixture of guilt and excitement, and shook three of the pills into her hand before returning the bottle to the drawer.

"Hurry up and lock it again. Let's get out of here."

In the attic, Poppy and I sat on our beds and watched Ariel line up the little, pale green pills on the dresser. She dumped a jumble of plastic hair baubles from a saucer that had lost its cup and looked around the room.

"I need something hard to smash them with," she said. She pointed at a marble egg on one of the nightstands. The egg was a pure, lovely lavender with a white rabbit painted on it.

"Daddy gave me that," cried Poppy.

"I'm not going to hurt it. Give it to me."

Ariel put the pills into the saucer one by one and crushed them with slow pressure from the egg. I felt jumpy. I'd seen kids get high by snorting stuff like that, but I'd always been afraid to try. I didn't like the idea of not knowing what was happening around me.

"What are they for?" I asked.

"Mom takes them when she has a migraine. They knock her out." She looked up from her grinding. "She has a glass of wine every night when she gets her bath. I'm going to put this in the wine."

"Why?"

"Because, dummy, we don't want her in the way tonight if we're going to get Dad back."

I thought about it. "What if you give her too much?"

"I won't." Ariel didn't sound confident. She stared at the powder in the saucer, then tossed her hair. "Besides, you can't die from headache medicine. She'll just sleep extra long." She lifted the saucer as though it were explosive. "Come on, you guys can keep watch."

We crept down to the kitchen, made furtive by our mission. Poppy and I stood in the doorway, ready to give the alarm if Aunt Melanie made an appearance, and Ariel took the wine bottle from the fridge. She held it up and sloshed it around.

"There's not much left in this one. Do you think that's more than a glassful?" She thrust it in front of our eyes. "I'd better pour a little out."

She let some of the red wine trickle into the sink before carefully scraping the powdered pills into the bottle with a butter knife. She put the stopper back on the bottle and shook it. Sounds drifted toward us from the canning kitchen.

"Hurry up," Poppy squeaked. "I think Mom's coming."

When Aunt Melanie came into the kitchen, we were washing up the last of the dishes, and the wine bottle waited on its shelf in the fridge.

7.

We stood around her bed, looking down on the sprawl of her limbs and the stupefied gape of her mouth. Her breath came deep and even, punctuated with purring little snores. It struck me that in this state, Aunt Melanie looked a lot like Mom, the only difference being that she wasn't on the bathroom floor.

"She's conked out good," Ariel said. "The sun's setting. I'll get Bit. You two get the flashlight and stuff."

"We can't take the baby up there!" Poppy was scandalized. "What if something happens to her?"

"Nothing's going to happen. We can't leave her here alone, can we?"

"Why not?" I said. "She's asleep, and we won't be gone long."

"We're taking her with us," Ariel said, and her voice chilled me. It was the sound of an implacable will grating against a weaker resistance, and I think I knew then what she planned. With lethal practicality, she had calculated the cost of resurrecting Uncle Ted and found it cheap. "Come on, Frankie," Poppy said. "Let's go get the animals from under the porch."

The sun had gone by the time we reached the well. The dark was so complete it had body, cool and big enough to lean against. Things popped out of it like targets at an arcade, and I stumbled and thrashed through the obstacles, unable to identify the most mundane objects. I yanked the flashlight from the tote I carried and switched it on, momentarily blinding myself before directing the beam outward.

"Hey, watch it," Ariel growled, turning her face away. The sisters had found their way by starlight, and stood calmly by the well. "Get over here and help Poppy pull the boards up. My hands are full." She clutched a squirming, fussy Bit against her.

I dropped the tote on the grass and put the flashlight on top of it, and the beam of light spilled out in a diminishing stripe that climbed weakly over the rotted well frame. The hair all over my body stood up, and I felt as if I might do anything - run into the woods, burrow into the rubble of the barn, leap screaming into the thorny embrace of the wild roses. Instead, I trudged to the well and helped Poppy open the pit. I was ready for the smell this time, and still it made my stomach roll. I avoided looking into the black mouth of the well and stepped away. If Uncle Ted knew we were there, he made no sign.

"Now we're ready," Ariel said. She walked to the flat altar rock, Poppy trailing along.

"Where's our offering?" Poppy asked, looking around for me.

Ariel stared at me. "Come on, Frankie."

I shook my head. "Answer her," I said through numb lips. "What are you going to give it this time?"

Ariel bent over the rock and placed Bit on it. The baby whimpered at the touch of the cold stone, and Poppy leaped forward.

"What are you doing?" she shrieked. She reached for the wriggling baby; but Ariel pushed her aside, hard enough to throw her to the ground.

"We have to. I figured it out. We have to give it something alive. Another *person*, don't you get it? A person for a person."

"No!" Poppy got to her knees and crawled to the rock, stretching out her hands for Bit.

Ariel grabbed her sister by the ponytail and pulled her head back, making Poppy wail in pain. "Don't you want Dad back?"

Poppy's voice bubbled with tears. "No! If we have to give it Bit, I don't want him back!"

Ariel flung Poppy to the grass again, and faced the woods. She took out her pocketknife and pulled up the blade.

"I'll trade this baby girl for the man in the well," she called. "I wish it!"

She slashed at her thumb, and turned the knife toward Poppy in warning. The night went still. I felt the dark regard, and the momentum, of the thing that rushed toward us. I picked up the flashlight, every instinct telling me to run and leave my cousins to their fate. The weight of the light in my hand decided for me. It was a heavy, baton-type flashlight, like the kind I'd seen security cops carry. In two steps, I was behind Ariel. I swung the flashlight. The sound of the impact when it met her skull shocked me so much that I dropped it, and the light went out. Ariel fell in the grass beside the rock, and Poppy scrambled to lift a crying Bit in her arms.

"Let's go," I shouted. "It's coming."

"You killed Ariel," Poppy cried, hugging Bit to her scrawny chest.

I grabbed her by the shoulder and pushed her ahead of me, into the barn and through the pitch black of the undercroft to the ladder, with Bit howling at the top of her lungs. I never told Poppy that I'd looked back just once, or that I'd seen Ariel stirring on the grass, not dead at all.

8.

We went back at dawn. Aunt Melanie still slept, curled into a sweaty fetal ball, but breathing normally. We left Bit in her crib, exhausted from screaming. We had barely a nerve left between us, but we had to bring Ariel back to the house. The early sunlight melted down through the trees in great misty smudges, and I breathed it in, liking the clean smell of it.

The clearing looked smaller, somehow. Less important. It was just a patch of wiry grass and rocks. Our tote lay near the trees, torn and empty. The flashlight was gone, and so was Ariel.

"It took her," Poppy whispered.

I looked around, expecting to see her hiding somewhere. I thought of shouting for her, but the quiet was so peaceful I couldn't bring myself to break it. Poppy went to the well and looked down.

"Frankie," she said, "he's still here."

"What?"

"Daddy. He's still in the well." She looked up, confused and sad. "He looks different. Do you think he tried to get out and couldn't?"

I moved to her side and looked down into the well. The earth of its throat was torn, stones dislodged and roots pulled out like old wiring. Uncle Ted lay crumpled in the soft, lemony haze of a sunbeam, his position shifted, but just as dead with his wrecked face turned toward the muck at the bottom of the shaft. I didn't know what the truth was, and I didn't want to know.

"Animals must have got in there and moved him around," I said, and the words sounded good to me. "That's all. We'd better cover him back up."

Poppy looked into the woods. "What about Ariel? Should we look for her?"

I didn't want to go among those trees. I didn't want to look down on Uncle Ted anymore, either, in case it hadn't been animals that had moved him and he was just taking a rest before trying to climb out again. I grabbed a plank and dragged it across the well mouth.

"Don't worry about her," I said. "She's probably just mad. She'll be back when she gets hungry."

Without even trying, I had spoken the truth.

There were plenty of dark days to follow. Men from Wickeford Mills, and from other farms in the area, combed the ridges, day and night, for weeks. Helicopters buzzed the thick wilderness, but they never found Ariel. Aunt Melanie, who believed she'd come down with a particularly nasty virus that night, cried until her red-rimmed eyes took on the bloody, grief-maddened aspect of a banshee. I wondered how she could be so heartbroken over Ariel after what she'd done to Uncle Ted, but I was no judge of love. I'd barely thought about my mother since looking down that well, only of what would happen to me. Watching Aunt Melanie grieve unlocked something in me – a desire to be loved so much that my loss would be unendurable.

All through the autumn and the long, bitter winter, Poppy and I waited; but Ariel didn't come home. We began to breathe easier, our secret safe in the frigid grasp of the Johns Woods. On my birthday in November, I came home from school to a cake alight with pink candles. I had to share it with Poppy, whose birthday was a week after mine, but I didn't mind. My name was piped on the top right beside hers in pretty, green script, and there was an icing rose for each of us, froths of whipped sugar that melted on our tongues and tasted clean and sweet.

"Do you think she'll come back and haunt us?" Poppy whispered in the dark that night.

I understood her feelings of guilt, but a fierce territoriality rose up in me. I was the big sister now. However it had come about, I'd found a home at Bitterberry Farm. I didn't think even Ariel's ghost could dislodge me.

"It doesn't matter," I said. "If she comes back, we'll deal with it. She can't really come back, though. I mean, she can't be one of us anymore."

One day in spring, I got off the school bus alone at our mailbox. Poppy was in bed with measles, which I'd already had. The new leaves were on the trees, a fine and tender green with the light caught at their hearts so they glowed; and the dogwoods had unfurled white pennants in the half-dusk at the fringe of the woods. I pulled open the mailbox and looked inside, thinking about how my new life had sprouted so keenly from the ashes of the old one. There was a cat in the mailbox, long dead and dried to a yellow rag. I sprang back from it and turned in a circle, staring into the woods.

I almost missed her, she was so slender and pale, like a young dogwood. Ariel stood among the trees, the long, dark snarls of her hair like shadow around her. Her skin was white as birch. Her eyes were blue as flame, fixed on me in a ferocious appeal.

"What do you want?" I asked, glad that my voice didn't quake the way my insides were doing.

I thought of going closer, of asking if she was okay, but she repulsed me in a way I felt in my guts. I could see she wasn't okay, with her crazy eyes and stick thin arms. Looking at her was like looking down the well for the first time. She didn't speak. She only smiled a sharp, savage smile and put her hands over her stomach. Her purple tongue, like the tongue of a hanged girl, came out and licked at her lips.

"Are you ... hungry?"

She gave one slow nod before she stepped back, and was gone. I walked the long, muddy lane through the trees with my head down, as fast as I could without running. Was she like the thing in the woods, existing on the carcasses of wildlife? If I refused to feed her, would she wither away? It came to me that she was my responsibility, that I'd caused this and no one could help me, not even Poppy. I reached the porch and put my hand on the screen door latch. I glanced behind me at the woods, grey and melancholy now as the changeable spring sky threatened rain. Ariel stared from the profusion of new leaves, her white face beseeching and feral. My personal ghost.

I had to make a decision, and I weighed my guilt against the possibility of a lifetime of sugar roses. In the kitchen, I heard Bit screech with laughter, and the sound freed me. I turned my back on Ariel and went inside, leaving her there in the wild gloom. Just another lost girl.

THE SKEPTIC

Present Day

They are going to wreck Sparrowgate. "Tear it out of the ground like a rotten tooth," says Ford Waterhouse, "foundations and all." The timbers and plaster they'll burn, even the gorgeous wainscoting, and the smoke-darkened moldings stacked a foot high to the ceilings. They'll cart the foundation stones away and scatter them across the hills, bury them in the laurels of the forest. Nothing will be salvaged, nothing used again. Sparrowgate will be excised from the landscape, and no one will speak its name afterward.

"There's still blood in the floorboards," Ford says. "They never could get it out. And a chill on the air that no fire can warm away. It can't be lived in, and believe me, plenty of folks have tried."

Ford believes in ghosts. He studies them, teaches classes on their detection and exorcism, pursuits I scoff at even though he's a well-known author on the subject. I tease him about his expeditions and lectures. *Where's your medicine show going next?* Or, *Got any new snake oil for the rubes?* He looks at me with sad eyes and shakes his head.

"I wish you could believe," he says. "I wish I could make you understand."

We don't speak often. We both travel a lot, Ford on the colorful paranormal circuit, and me because I'm restless. A few times a year, he calls, checking on me. I drop in to visit him, compelled by my sentimental heart. Old feelings never seem to grow duller for me, however unreciprocated. We stay in touch, linked by the old blot of horror that is Sparrowgate. They can tear it down, but it

33

will stand forever in our minds, the only structure in the dark country of Memories-Best-Forgotten.

"It's scheduled for demolition in the spring, as soon as they can get the equipment back on Carver Hollow Road."

I don't want to talk about it. Ford has called for me for weeks, his pleas unheeded. Only my old longing for the place, stirred up violently like sparks from ash, induces me, at last, to answer him. Hating the weakness of my curiosity, I ask, "What's wrong with the road?"

Carver Hollow is a lonely dead end that tracks into the Johns Woods with only Sparrowgate along its seven-mile stretch. The county plows don't bother with it; and where the forgotten hay fields lie open to the sweep of the wind, the snow drifts in like eternal sleep. But there is no snow yet, still two weeks from Christmas, despite the brittle quality of the air.

I feel the hesitation before Ford says, "You realize the house has been empty for several years? The road is in bad shape, and the bridge over Sugar Camp Creek washed away two summers ago. The only way back now is on foot."

I am shocked, the way I suppose we always are when the vagaries of passing time are suddenly superimposed on the unchanging pictures we carry of childhood homes or faces. As the silence between us spins to awkward length, Ford clears his throat.

"You never talk about it, but I assumed you knew how things were with the house. I thought you might have gone back, you know, just to look around." He is tentative, feeling his way over hazardous terrain. "I mean, it's been empty so long. People just couldn't live there ... you understand?"

"Yes, you said."

My tone is curt. What do I care about silly, superstitious people? I could have told them how it happened, the terrible thing that tainted Sparrowgate, and that it had more to do with bad whiskey and weak minds than with demons. I'd told Ford as much in the days after it happened, while he lay stricken amid the professorial jumble of his office, wrapped in a cat-frazzled afghan. I told him it was human dysfunction, not haunting or some medieval idea of possession, that had wrought such darkness. I tried to soothe his shattered nerves, but all he could say was *I'm so sorry, I'm so sorry*, over and over until he was hoarse.

A vague fear touches me, a stirring like the hair-raising creep of the air before a massive storm. In a flash of clarity, I understand what Ford is planning before he speaks.

"Listen," he rasps, excitement and terror robbing his voice. "This is our last chance to try to set things right. Once the house is gone, well, I just don't know. We can go back now, while it's all still there, and ... and fix things."

"Ford, we're too old for this nonsense."

I've just turned sixty, and though I don't feel much different from when I was younger, the years have surely left their mark. Perhaps I am vain, but I find myself avoiding mirrors, afraid my grandmother's face will look back at me. Ford is seventy-two, an old man, and never mind how distinguished in his field.

"We won't even be able to get across the creek," I say, "let alone hoof through the wilderness to the house. If it's as bad as you say, it's probably falling down."

I hate the bitter taste of the words. In spite of its death sentence, the thought of Sparrowgate sagging and broken open to the elements is painful.

"I didn't say the house was in bad shape. Oh, a little down-at-the-heels, but solid. And the creek is frozen, easy to cross."

"You've been out!" My voice is accusatory even to my own ears.

He chuckles. "I'm still fit enough for hiking. Of course, it might mean camping, too. There's no electricity." The mirth drops from his voice. "Come with me. Just the two of us, no camera crew, no students. We're the only ones who need to be there now."

Devil's Night, 1966

I was a cynical twelve-year old. It had been a few years since I'd seen behind the curtain of the family business, and all the shadowed, fairy tale magic of ghosts and goblins turned to cheap flummery designed to rook the marks. Table knocking, spectral voices, and clammy, phantom breezes. Ectoplasmic eruptions, devil lights, and the head-lolling mediumship of my mother in the darkened parlor. They came from near and far to be fleeced, the curious and the grieving, a steady trickle of seekers that swelled to a torrent each October. Halloween was the night of nights at Sparrowgate.

The members of the Waterhouse Paranormal Studies Group weren't like the others, though. They'd heard of my mother, but Ford had taught them to be skeptical of self-proclaimed mediums. What really interested them was the house, or to be more precise, the land.

"The area is rich in quartz and limestone, which is often present in neighborhoods of frequent paranormal activity," Ford had told my father over the phone, a conversation I eavesdropped on from the extension in my parents' bedroom. "There's a great deal of local anecdotal evidence, things like strange sounds and apparitions in the woods and fields around Sparrowgate, and not to frighten anyone, stories about the house, too. It's been on my list of study sites for a while now, and given your wife's, um, abilities, now is the perfect time to investigate." When Daddy didn't sit up and pant for a visit from what he thought of as academic ghost groupies, Ford was quick to dangle the carrot of easy cash. "Look, I've got a grant. It's not huge, but I can compensate you for your trouble. My team is small, and we'll only stay Halloween night."

Mama came on the line, enthusiastic and breathless. "Oh, Mr. Waterhouse, we'll be thrilled to have your group stay, even several nights if you like. I've spoken with many of the spirits here, and you're right. Sparrowgate is a portal. I'm happy to act as medium for you, and my daughter is a gifted clairaudient ..."

Daddy spoke, cutting her off. I imagined them with their heads together over the telephone receiver, and Daddy suddenly turning his shoulder to her before she could scotch the deal with her Madame Cassandra routine. "I think something can be arranged. You understand, this is our most active time of the year. We'll have to turn away other clients to accommodate you."

In the background, Mama called, "Tell him about Juliet, dear. Her gift is very strong."

Daddy went on to secure a much larger chunk of Ford's grant money than the investigator had intended, but I hung up, not caring if they heard the click on the line. I was furious with Mama for mentioning my name. Anyone could hear voices if they concentrated, voices made up of ambient sound and imagination. I'd made a game of it, secretly proud of my acute hearing. It was a personal amusement, not something to add yet another layer of razzle-dazzle to Mama's spiritualist silliness. I thumped the mattress in a temper, swung my sneakers to the gold shag carpet, and stormed downstairs to share my feelings.

I could have saved myself the effort. Mama was over the moon about the Waterhouse group's interest, and there was no reasoning with her, no leading her back to reality.

"The spirits are real! Jules, baby, don't be mad, it's not all tricks, I swear," Mama said, her words crowding up the staircase in an agitated rush, trying to catch and soothe me before I slammed into my room. From outside my locked door, her long, tomato-red nails made kitten scratchings. "Honey, come and talk to me. I know you have the gift, too. Mr. Waterhouse and I can teach you how to use it."

I dropped the needle on my new Animals album, and *I Put A Spell On You* growled out at full volume. I fell back on the bed, retreating behind the wall of sound. There was no gift. Despite Mama's dead-eyed channeling of various spirits, her hollow-voiced proclamations and warnings flung out at random, her obsessive sage-ing of the rooms until the house smelled like a hippie pot den, I maintained staunch non-believer status. Daddy, busy running wires under the carpets, his cigarette hanging at the corner of his hard mouth, had cautioned me often enough. *Never fall for your own patter, Sugar Bear. Sooner or later, it'll eat into the profits.*

The days of belief, days when Mama's spook show shenanigans had scared and awed me, had evaporated like the ghostly mists Daddy puffed down on the clients from concealed vents in the séance room. Now, when one of Mama's spirits spoke to me, shambling after me in her loose-limbed body, I knew it for what it was: a combination of harmless eccentricity and practice for the next performance. I understood that Mama more than half believed her own patter – in fact, was well on the way to believing it wholly – and that Daddy, an ex-carny with a lizard eye on the profits, exploited her madness.

I lay on the green and brown daisy print coverlet and listened to the open space at the end of the album, a calming, empty-air white noise that seemed at times to contain a conversational whisper. *He's coming, he's coming*, soft shush of the needle over the vinyl, and then a little skip as the whisper elided into a hiss, *He's gotta eat, he's gotta eat.* Or maybe, *Beasts gotta eat.* I couldn't quite make it out, straining my ears and playing the game until it wasn't a game anymore and the hair began to rise on my arms. The thud of Daddy's fist on the door sent a jolt of bright terror through me, and I sat up half sick with adrenaline.

"Jules, open this door. We need to talk."

I opened the door to Daddy's characteristic workday fragrance of sweat, cigarettes, and the strange flash-of-ozone smell from his workshop. He wore his usual uniform of jeans, steel-toed boots, and a white tee shirt stiffened in spots by a satiny crust of egg white from his experiments in the creation of more realistic ectoplasm. His unapologetic swindler's face, the audacity of the cootchie dancer tattooed on his bicep, the squashed pack of Raleighs rolled in his sleeve and sitting at his shoulder like a hoodlum's epaulet, were like gravity, putting my feet firmly back in the practical.

"This is a business meeting, kid. I've hooked a big one with this Waterhouse guy, and I need a partner." He drew the half-smoked butt from behind his ear, fished a match from his pocket, and struck it alight with a dirty thumbnail. In the sulphurous flicker, he was a charming, but disreputable, devil, and I was instantly ready to agree to any scheme he might propose.

"Well, come on in, then."

We sat on the edge of the bed, shoulder to shoulder, and stared at the floor together. After a moment of smoking and thinking, Daddy said, "Jules, your mom's pure nuts, God help us, but she's brilliant at what she does. She believes all that shit, and so others believe in her. It's psychological, or something. Now we got this egghead and his cronies coming to eat it all up with a spoon, and, yeah, they're paying a wad, but I think there's more to be got from them. You diggin me?"

"You think they'll want to come back again?"

He inhaled his cigarette down to his fingers before grinding it out on his boot heel. "Yeah, I do. Even better, if we give them something to sink their teeth into, they might just see us right through the whole winter."

Winter was slow business, and I'd been wanting a new bike for Christmas, a blue Schwinn Deluxe Breeze 2-Speed that stood gleaming in the window of Shepphard's Hardware in town. I thought about it, and Daddy inspected his fingernails and let me think.

"You promised Mama you wouldn't use any tricks on the Waterhouse Group," I pointed out.

"No *physical* tricks, Sugar Bear. No *illusions*. I never said nothing about mind tricks."

"And I can help you with that?"

"You sure enough can." He was grinning at me now, smelling a sale. "All that baloney your Mama wants to feed them about you being able to hear spirits, well, who's to say you can't? Who's to say you can't hear 'em real good, and they might say all kinds of interesting things."

I didn't like it, but with Daddy sitting right there, smiling at me, confiding in me, I heard myself say, "What's in it for me?" Just like he'd taught me.

"That's my girl," he said, cocking a finger and thumb at me, *bang*.

Daddy and I struck a deal, and although it meant that I would have to be a part of the show (Daddy always called what he and

Mama did *the show*), I was proud of my ability to bargain for a stack of new albums and a guitar in addition to the coveted bicycle.

"You promise?" I asked, slanting a wary gaze at him.

Daddy looked wounded. "My word is good. When I give it, it stands. Now that we've reached an agreement, how about you take a look at this." He pulled out a script he must have crafted while Mama and I were having our argument. He'd had it in his back pocket all during our negotiations.

"You knew I'd help," I said. Suddenly my amazing horse-trading skills seemed as false as the phosphorous hands that sometimes emerged from Mama's spirit cabinet. "How high would you have gone?"

He laughed and pinched my cheek. "A sure thing is the best thing, Jules. But don't get mad; you did pretty well for yourself." He smoothed the paper out on the bed. "Now look, these are just suggestions. This is your game. You don't have to do any of the physical stuff; your mom's got that covered. We're not claiming you're a medium, just a clairaudient. Keep it simple and pure. That's the ticket with these university types."

I glanced over his bulleted lines. "Daddy ..." I hesitated.

"What's wrong? You don't think you can pull it off?"

I shook my head. I could do this. I'd just play the listening game, like I'd done with the album.

"No, it's just, well, these aren't really the kinds of things I hear." He stared at me, and I rushed on. "I mean, you know how if you listen to sounds sometimes you can make a voice out of them?" He shook his head, and I felt the heat of a blush rise out of my collar. "Well, you can, if you really try. It's just pretend, but you can make out words. Some really weird things, too ... creepy."

"And you can do this anytime?"

I nodded, wishing I hadn't said anything.

"You ever mention this to your mom?"

I nodded again.

"Well, that explains a lot." Daddy stood, smiling down at me. "Hey, if you think you can do this more, you know, authentically, I trust you. The Waterhouse people will be here tomorrow, so get your act smoothed out. Not too much, now," he cautioned. "If you need any help, you just come get me. Good to have you on board, partner." He dropped a kiss in my hair and left whistling.

Daddy didn't have to warn me about overplaying it. I had a deep dislike of Mama's histrionics and no desire to emulate them. I went off to practice in different rooms, listening for the tonal quality of each space, how the sound flowed around the objects and furnishings. The dining room had a cavernous voice, all hard maple surfaces and no rug to buff the edges off sounds that chimed against glass and china. The drapes there were a softly hissing taffeta, too cool and slick to muffle sound, and one of the windows rattled a bit in its frame, a fragile alto that most people didn't seem to hear. The séance room, swathed in velvet and fully carpeted, was a box of plush, round exhalations, so quiet that the candle flames beat against the air like moths' wings. The slide of the melting wax was like someone talking in his sleep. In the hallway, I identified a voice like the low boom of the sea, felt on the sensitive machinery of the ear and in the chest rather than heard. I moved on to the kitchen and found Mama sitting at the dinette table with her head in her hands. I stopped in the doorway, struck with sudden guilt.

"I'm sorry I was mouthy, before," I said. "Mama? I didn't mean to hurt your feelings."

Mama wagged her head slowly back and forth, the heels of her hands to her forehead, and her face turned toward the tabletop, eyes closed. She sniffled a bit. I stepped over to the table, so filled with remorse for making her cry that I barely realized I was walking on tiptoe and holding my breath.

"Mama? I'm going to help with the Waterhouse group. Okay? I'm going to be a clairaudient for them."

I reached out to touch her shoulder and stopped. A little electric tingle scurried up my arm, and I felt my scalp prickle. Mama was still sniffling, only now I could hear that it was a kind of laughter shuddering behind her closed lips. The tips of my outstretched fingers went white with cold.

"He's coming," Mama said. I recognized the voice of the control she used during her séances, a voice lively with mischief, that she insisted belonged to a spirit called Rumkin. I'd heard it often, and wondered how people could be gullible enough to fall for it, but now it sounded different. It sounded real. "He's coming. Little girls should run."

"Mama? Stop it."

Rumkin slammed Mama's hands flat on the table and looked up at me with glittering eyes. "You know better, you know better, you know better," it sang. "Too many mediums richen the broth. He's gotta eat."

My lips were numb. I would have screamed for Daddy, the way I used to when I was a little girl and Mama, channeling Rumkin, followed me around the house babbling nonsense, but it caught like a bone in my throat. Instead, I asked, "What are you talking about?"

Rumkin nodded approvingly. It drummed the tabletop with the fingers of both hands, tapping out two distinct rhythms. "One can hear, one can see, one can speak. That's the ladder."

"I'm no good at riddles."

Rumkin looked away from me, watching Mama's drumming fingers.

"Mama? Rumkin? I don't understand."

The spirit seemed to have fallen into a reverie, mesmerized by the rhythmic motion of the hands in front of it. "Blood or whiskey," it finally said, giving a woeful sigh. "He's been down so deep, but he's coming now. If you won't give him blood, better use the whiskey."

Mama's eyes had rolled back in her head so that only a sliver of their deep blue was visible. A shudder passed over her body, and she stood as though jerked to her feet on marionette strings. Her chair fell backward with a crash. I shrieked and danced away from her, but Rumkin was faster. It snatched me by my shirt and leaned toward me, staring into my face with Mama's unseeing eyes.

"Don't let him come. The seer." It shook me. "The seer." *Shake.* "Three is the ladder."

A final shake, and I heard the thin plaid rip as Rumkin dragged me toward the cabinets. Mama's other hand shot out and wrenched open the door to the liquor cupboard so hard that one of the old hinges snapped. Bottles trembled against one another, a faint ringing like tiny bells, and then Rumkin was knocking them aside to shatter on the countertop and floor. A reek of booze rose up, so powerful my eyes watered. Rumkin seized on a bottle near the back of the cupboard and drew it out with a triumphant cackle. It thrust it into my hands.

"Use the whiskey. Make him quiet." Mama's hand twisted in my torn shirt until the fabric felt like a tourniquet on my arm. "MAKE HIM QUIET," Rumkin shouted. A spasm released Mama's fingers, and I was free.

I turned and fled for my room, clutching the whiskey to my chest like a priceless treasure, past Daddy who had appeared in time to catch Mama as she toppled forward.

Mama lay on their bed, waxy as a funeral lily. Daddy sat beside her, warming first one of her hands in his, and then the other, rubbing them briskly but with great tenderness.

"Rest now, Sandy. No more spirits, okay? Save something for the show. I'll get you a sleeping pill."

"No!" Mama clutched at him, struggling to sit up. "If I'm drugged, there's no one to manage Rumkin."

"Okay, okay. Lie down. I'll stay with you." He ran a hand through his hair so that it stood out in all directions. His face was tight and tired, and for a moment I saw what he would look like as an old man.

Mama's eyes found me where I leaned in the doorway, ready to retreat if Rumkin made another appearance. She lifted a languid hand toward me.

"Come sit by me, Jules. It's gone now."

Daddy tried to overrule her, but Mama shushed him. "You've got a lot to do. Let me talk to Juliet, and then I'll take a nap." When he hesitated, she patted his thigh. "Go on. I'm fine now."

He stood, and I took his place. Mama waited until he'd left and closed the door before taking my hand.

"I'm so sorry, baby. Are you hurt?" When I shook my head, she touched my shoulder where Rumkin had torn my shirt. "Do you remember what it said?"

"No," I lied.

Another time, I might have rolled my eyes at her, pointed out that Rumkin wasn't real and so hadn't actually said anything. But I was still shaky from the incident in the kitchen, and Rumkin seemed less like a con and more like some bizarre relative whose visits are dreaded. Mama relaxed against her pillows and closed her eyes.

"You're a skeptic, Jules. That used to worry me, that you would never develop your gift, but now I think it's a good thing. I don't want you taking part in the Waterhouse session tomorrow. Stay away, stay in your room."

"Why, Mama? I thought you'd be happy about me working the show." When she didn't answer, I plucked at her sleeve. "I can help you, so you don't get ... overtired." *Crazed*, that was the word that had filled my mouth, the word I'd swallowed whole.

She looked at me from under her lashes, a look both weary and wise. "This is a house of illusion, Jules, but some things are real. Under the glamor, under the patter, there is another house, with other inhabitants. Today, you saw a little bit of it. Now, I want you to forget about it."

Present Day

Ford's old Volvo sits in the middle of Carver Hollow Road, perched on the dirt hump above ankle-turning ATV ruts that end in a scribble of frozen earth where the bridge used to be. Sugar Camp Creek is silent, locked in ice, and the hemlocks throw their shadows over the edge of the embankment with Gothic drama.

Somewhere high in the grey that hangs swag-bellied into the forest, a crow calls; and the lonesome sound sums up how I feel, standing by the car at the end of the world. I don't see Ford at first, and his absence is an opportunity to turn back. I look behind me at the ravaged road. A fog has crept in, erasing the way, an insubstantial bulk that squats on the road and digests the fringe of the woods.

A scraping sound, and the dull, emphatic *clack* of a stone falling on ice draw me to the creek; and when I look over the embankment, I see Ford dragging a backpack up the opposite side. I haven't seen in him in nearly a year. He has always been lanky, but now he is thin in a way that suggests illness. He reaches the top of the short slope and huffs out a breath, stretches with his long hands in the small of his back, and sees me. I raise a hand and wave, unwilling to break the quiet.

"I was afraid you'd stand me up," he says, and although his voice is not loud, it carries clearly on the cold air.

With it comes the scent of snow, and I look up at the pewter ceiling of cloud and see one perfect flake waltzing down. Almost immediately, a second, and a third, join it, and then the air is populated, though sparsely. Ford is looking at me as though afraid I'll vanish, his smile slipping a little. I sigh and step toward the trail he's flattened in the dun-and-speckle weeds.

"I'm coming. Can't let you go alone, you might need a medium." I mean it as a joke, but it sounds ominous in my ears.

Three miles further on, Sparrowgate hulks into view, broad-shouldered and blank with that drowsing introversion that abandoned houses adopt. Black-eyed dormers stare out at the frisking snowflakes and the two tiny people trudging down the long drive, and the house's dream state shivers. Echoes stir – I hear them, like the sound of silk dragged over flesh, and a tremor runs along my nerves. Ford is quick to notice my half-step hesitation.

"Do you feel something?"

I give him a long-suffering look. "I was kidding with that medium crack. What's to feel, except sorrow, and even that's worn thin by the years." I toss him a sharp glance. "Are you afraid?"

He walks on, and I think he isn't going to answer, but he says, "Yes. Jesus, yes. This place, it made my career, you know? It very nearly ended it, too. Dear God, the nightmares I had after ... well, it was nothing compared to your experience. That's what I want to put right."

We go up the front steps together and stand at the door. Ford pulls his glove off with his teeth and fumbles in his coat pocket for the key, offers it to the lock. It skitters across the ornate blackened escutcheon and falls to the peeling planks of the porch. Ford curses, and I hear the tightness in his throat. I bend down for the key, raise it to the lock, turn it.

"Ford, we don't have to go in. You don't owe me anything; there's nothing to put right. This is just an old, bad memory. Let it go."

In answer, he reaches out and turns the knob. The door swings in with the appropriate haunted house groan. Darkness rushes away down the entry hall, retreating from the snowlight. Ford steps inside, where the air is even colder, and turns to extend a hand to me.

"I can't let it go anymore, Jules. This is the last stand."

I look past him at the shadowed honeycomb of Sparrowgate. I can hear them clearly, here at the threshold, and I want more than ever to leave and never look back. I ignore Ford's hand and walk past him into night.

His camp is in the old séance room, naturally. It doesn't look any different from the other rooms now, its tall windows naked and the carpet ripped up, exposing the red pine planks of the floor. My gaze goes right to the stains where they creep out of the wood in faint, rusty ripples, the ghosts of terrible blood angels thrashed irrevocably into the fiber of the house. Seeing them makes me feel thin and watery, as though I will melt into their voracious patterns. One delicate wash in particular draws my eye, paler than the rest and silent, while the others crackle and hiss. There is a message written there if only I could read it, but seeing was never my talent.

"Don't look at them," Ford says, and throws a painter's cloth over them, kicking the folds out of it until most of the floor in the small room is covered.

I am shaking inside, and Ford is staring at me. *Why did you make me come back here?* I want to scream at him. *Why did I listen to you?* Instead, I look around the bare room and gesture at the wood laid in the fireplace, more heaped in a messy tumble beside it.

"You'll burn the house down if you try to start a fire in there. The chimney's probably stuffed full of bird's nests."

Ford lets out the breath he's been holding. "I've been out here many times in the last few years, since it was abandoned. I keep the chimney in here as clear as I can. You can see sky if you look up it."

"I'll take your word for it." There are folding camp chairs in their nylon bags lying against the baseboard. I nod at them. "How about setting some of those up?"

When we are settled in front of an ambitious blaze, a rickety card table between us, Ford offers me cocoa. He knows I have an insatiable sweet tooth. Always, when we are together, he has little gifts of candy or cake for me. I can't think about such simple pleasures now. I feel frozen inside, a cold that cannot be thawed by the cheerful fire snapping on the hearth.

"I'll just have a sip of yours, if you don't mind."

He pushes the fragrant mug across the card table to me, watches as I lean into the steam. "Can you hear anything, Jules?" he asks, and for the first time, I notice that his hands are trembling.

"What's wrong with you? You don't look well. This was a mistake, coming here. We should go." I stand up, but Ford only smiles and shakes his head.

"We can't go. Look out the window. We only just got here in time."

I rush to the windows and stare out through their time-rippled glass. The snow that had been so inconsequential is now falling thick and fast. The woods catch it and spin it into a web of fog and crystal. The road is gone. Sparrowgate floats in a white void, and its voices sob and moan like the wind.

"Jules, can you hear anything?" Ford repeats his ridiculous question, hammering at me.

I turn to look at him, huddled in his camp chair by the fire in what may very well become his tomb. How could I not have seen how frail he's become, his skin like parchment showing the blue veins beneath, his eyes burning in the hollows of a skull? I am not strong enough to drag him miles through the snow, and no one will come this way until spring.

"Ford, what have you done?"

He waves the question away. "It should be quiet. I've worked so hard to release them, and there is only one left."

Halloween, 1966

The Waterhouse Group arrived at sunset, three of them in a white panel truck. The empath, Minette LeClerc, was slim and stylish, with a cloudy purple scarf knotted about her throat (the canary in the coal mine, Ford later told me). The recording technician, Josh Candless, lurched about like a bear in brown corduroy, bearded and walled away behind black-framed glasses. Ford, tall and athletic, looked more like a rock climber than an academic. The air around him sang like the best of summer nights, crickets and the low throb of strobing fireflies, the joyful sliding scale of a shooting star. I hovered nearby, entranced, as Mama met them at the door.

"Welcome, everyone, welcome to Sparrowgate. I'm Cassandra Pinkney. My husband won't be joining us this evening, business called him away."

This was a typical bit of subterfuge. Daddy was in his workshop, but he'd be hidden behind the spirit cabinet when the show began in earnest, just in case a trick or two was needed to keep things interesting. Mama noticed me lurking in the gloom of the big staircase, and a pained expression flitted over her face, but she reached out to me, drawing me into their circle.

"This is my daughter, Juliet."

"Ah, the clairaudient," Ford said, and bent his dark gaze on me. He was only 24 years old, but he had Rasputin's own eyes. I felt boiled down to an essence by their perusal. The idea of running a game on this man seemed suddenly ludicrous.

"Um, no, I mean, not really," I stammered. The scrutiny continued, and I blurted, "Everyone calls me Jules."

He smiled. "I see," he said, and I was left in no doubt that he did see, very clearly. "The ability to hear what others cannot is rare, Jules. I'm very happy to meet you." I floated on his smooth, faintly British baritone, pulled toward him like sand drawn under a strong tide.

"Where can I set up the equipment?" Candless interrupted, and the intense beam of Ford's gaze lifted from me as he turned toward his colleague. "Sun's about gone, and the wind's picking up. I want to get everything hauled inside before we get rain, too."

"Right this way," Mama said, and led him toward the séance room.

Ford made to follow, but was stopped by Minette's white hand on his arm. There was a possessiveness in that hand, a certain ease in its delicate caress, that I found I didn't like. Ford looked down into Minette's face with more affection than I felt a working relationship warranted.

"There is something here, Ford," she said, her voice a quick undertone. "It's watching." She glanced at me. "The girl can hear it."

The girl. Humiliation and rage swept over me at the words. I didn't fully understand the emotional maelstrom swirling inside of me. I only knew that in that instant I hated Minette LeClerc. I stepped past them, pausing to look into her wide eyes.

"That's Rumkin," I said. "It'll probably talk to you all night. It likes blondes."

I noted the surprise on their faces before I bolted up the stairs, Ford's deep laugh flying at my heels.

The house was a blaze of candles. Mama never allowed the house lights during her sessions, claiming that the cold, electric glare created a barrier between the spirit world and us. It was, in reality, one of Daddy's simple disorienting tactics. Deep pools and swags of shadow filled the rooms, their edges shifting in constant, inky fluidity with the stirring of the candle flames, making the familiar strange and tricking the senses.

I sat at the top of the stairs and watched as they brought in the recording equipment, trundling it along the hall to the séance room. Candless cursed the lack of light, and I thought Ford would demand the abandonment of the Halloween theatrics of the candles, but he seemed content to leave things as they were.

"Well, give me the damn flashlight, then," Candless grumbled. "I can't see my hand in front of my face."

The men disappeared into the séance room, their voices fading to murmurs. Mama and Minette stood together in the hallway. Minette glanced about, her shoulders tense, and drew her sweater closer around her.

"How can you live here?" she said. "It's oppressive. The atmosphere is so ... hostile."

"I'm accustomed to the ways of the spirits," Mama said. "They want only to speak, to be heard. What you feel, what you perceive as hostility, will dissipate and become peaceful when they are able to speak. You'll see." Mama's face was calm, her voice dreamy and nearly toneless. She was already into her act.

Minette paid little attention. She was taut and thrumming with nervous awareness, a vibration that shivered on the air like a tiny moan that I could hear. She reminded me of a rabbit that had ventured too far from safe cover and now cowered in the grass, every sense searching wildly for danger. Her distress, obviously genuine, irritated and amused me. She wasn't part of the show, but she would have been great at it.

"I should walk the house," she said, her voice tight with reluctance. She cringed away from a fluttering banner of shadow, her hand going out to grip Mama's. "Will you come with me?"

The two women moved away, and I sat alone, hoping Ford would emerge from the séance room and see me there in the dark.

Hoping he would talk to me. Instead, another voice slithered over my ear.

Scared the pretty one, it said. *Sweet, like candy, but we don't like her.*

I gasped, my breath puffing out in a cloud of vapor on frigid air. "Rumkin?"

My whisper was barely a sound. The spirit had never spoken without Mama as its vehicle. How could it? I rose stealthily to my feet and pressed myself to the wall, as though I could sneak away from the presence at my ear.

Flesh like sugar. He's gotta eat. An idiot giggle. *Take a rung from the ladder. Use the whiskey.*

A flurry of hard knocks from behind the wainscoting tumbled down the stairs. The men ran into the hallway, Candless waving a boxy instrument. Ford's gaze flew upward. He couldn't have seen me there, flattened into the black as I was, but his eyes found mine before sliding away to fix with frightening intensity on something over my left shoulder. A sense of doom, of time run out, iced my body. I turned and ran.

"Wait! Jules, wait!"

I heard Ford's quick sprint on the stairs behind me, and the heavy thud of Candless's sneakers. I ran along the upper hall toward my bedroom, but before I reached it a terrible peal of laughter broke over my head, and the squeal of it unhinged my knees. I crashed to the floor clutching my ears.

Eeeeheeeee! It shrieked, swooping close to my face before winging down the corridor. I rolled onto my back and stared up at the unlit chandeliers that marched along the ceiling in winking splendor, their crystals catching the crazily swinging beam of Candless's flashlight as he and Ford jogged toward me.

Ford fell to his knees beside me. "Are you okay, honey? Can you sit up?"

I was sick and shivering. "Did you hear it?" I asked.

"No, but I saw it. Okay? I saw it." He smoothed the hair out of my eyes and lifted me against his chest. "Is that your room?"

I nodded, listening to the steady drum of his heart. It was the most beautiful sound I'd ever heard.

Ford looked up at Candless. "I'm going to help Jules to her room and get her settled. Get everyone together. We're going to go to work. Now."

Candless lumbered away, and Ford helped me to my feet and steered me through the doorway into my room. I clung to him, fighting the fog that had crept into my head.

"Lie down, Jules," he said. I fell onto the bed, and he swung my feet onto it and pulled a throw over me. Breaking Mama's rule, he switched on the rose-shaded bedside lamp, and a weak glow suffused the room. "What did you hear? Did it speak?"

I grabbed at his sleeve. "You're the seer, aren't you? You saw it. I heard it. Mama can speak for it. We can't all be here together. It can climb up now, from wherever it's been." My voice rose on a little thermal of hysteria. "Rumkin said not to let you come here."

"Is that its name?" The wind howled and flung itself against the house, and Ford looked out the window at the tossing trees. "It'll be okay, Jules. I'm trained to handle this kind of thing. Go to sleep."

He left me there, in the blush of lamplight. I listened to his footsteps retreating down the hall, and I sat up. I heard him descending the stairs, and I bent over to look between my feet at the dim space under the bed. The bottle Rumkin had given me stood there, its contents an amber flare in the murk, the black bird on the label fixing me with an evil eye. Like everything, it had a sound: rough and thick with aggression. *Blood or whiskey.*

Their voices lifted through the old plank floors - Mama and Minette, Ford and Candless - meaningless mutters as they took their places around the table in the séance room. Daddy would be watching from his place behind the spirit cabinet. If I concentrated, I could hear him shifting his weight into a more comfortable position in the cramped space, and the sizzle of the sweat that slipped over the stubble on his face. I could hear each throbbing heart, the rasp of their feet on the carpet, and the muted tinkle of the charms on Mama's bracelet.

I reached under the bed and pulled out the bottle of Old Crow, hoping it wasn't too late. From the hallway came the sound of footsteps, slow and heavy, with the wood cracking under them. No one else could hear them. I stared at the label on the whiskey bottle as they stopped at my open door.

"Rumkin? Is that you?"

I knew the answer. I'd gone beyond my own disbelief and into the land of terror. I listened to the sound of its harsh breath, like an animal smelling for its prey. An unfamiliar voice replied.

"No."

I unscrewed the cap and held the bottle up, sloshing a little over my hand and wrist. "This is for you, then," I said, and tipped it to my lips.

The thing in the doorway entered the room. The liquor walked down my throat in boots of flame. A freezing bolt of darkness struck me in the heart.

Nothing was ever the same after that.

Present Day

I flit from the window to kneel at Ford's knee. I put my hand there, and he shivers. The room is cold and growing colder, despite the fire.

"Where is your phone?" I ask, struggling to keep my voice even.

"There's no service out here, Jules." He reaches out as if to stroke my cheek, but he doesn't touch me. "You break my heart, do you know that? You always have. All these years, I've only wanted for you to be happy. I wanted to stop the voices for you."

Waspishly, I say, "Well, you haven't. They're all still here."

I intend to make a sweeping gesture that encompasses the room, the entire house, but instead I tap my own skull. Can a gesture gone awry be an acknowledgement of madness? The pain of it is instantaneous and searing, and a tear slips down from the corner of my eye. I dash it away and glance at the snowfall that has become an impenetrable, white flocking with a noise like radio static. Sleet.

"We're in trouble here, Ford. We have to get back to the car."

He looks at me, silent for so long I begin to worry that he's suffered a stroke. Then, with a sigh, he says, "It's cancer. The doctor says I only have a few months at best. So, you see, I had to do this."

He takes a stoppered vial from his vest pocket and sets it on the card table where it glows like absinthe in the gloom. A single air bubble rises through it with the soft sound of a door closing forever. It may as well have the skull and crossbones on it. Ford strokes it with an unsteady finger.

"I won't be going back," he says.

I am stunned. Grief like a cold sea washes over me, along with the impulse to throw myself into Ford's arms. Death is in the room with us. Perhaps it has waited here for us for 48 years, the ones who got away that bloody night. One frosty pearl of fear glides down my spine.

"Ford, this is crazy. Do you hear how crazy you sound? Look, maybe I can make it to the car and go for help." I stand and try to gather coats and gloves, a hat. "Give me the keys."

He doesn't move. I am angry, frightened the way I was all those years ago.

"Damn it! You can't just come out here in the woods and die, like some old wolf. Do you want to take me with you? Give me the goddamned keys!"

My voice is a sob. The ice is rattling against the windows, blown by a screaming wind, and I know that even if he relents, I can never make it.

"Jules, do you know why I was spared that night?"

He stands, and despite how the illness has gnawed at him, he is still handsome. I stop pawing at the coats and gloves – they are suddenly so heavy. I know something that I don't want to know, and it squeezes my heart in a cruel gauntlet.

"Because I loved you," I say. "I loved you the first minute I saw you."

The voices, the echoes of Sparrowgate's horror, cease. The implications are unbearable, and I cry out as though stabbed. Ford comes to me, his face filled with sorrow and the poignant light of hope. He points at something behind me.

"Look, I want to show you something."

I turn and see a sheeted shape. It's familiar, this tall, slender object with a sound like a lullaby. I know what it is – it's my mother's cheval mirror.

"No," I say, shaking my head. "Don't."

Ford is already reaching past me to pull the drape away, and I must look. I raise my eyes and see us reflected there, a gaunt old man and a skinny twelve-year old girl with blood in her hair, blood smeared on her face, blood dripping from her hands. I stare at the girl, at my real self, and something shatters and falls away from me. Some chain I'd forgotten I wore.

"The last one," Ford says. "It wasn't your fault, not any of it. I was arrogant. I thought I was strong enough to stop what dwelled here." He reaches out and strokes my matted hair. "You can go now, Jules. If you like, we'll go together."

LOCAL HONEY

1.

Frost glistened on the windowpane, and Sylvia Peach dreamed into its patterns a cold forest of fairy tale creatures winking in the lantern light. The mid-April dawn kindling over the village held no warmth, no springtime promise. The clouds belonged still to winter. Their only concession to the calendar was to threaten rain, like a barrage of icy needles, instead of snow. Sylvia pressed her palm to the glass, melting the fantastic forest. The cold seared her flesh and shot along the bones of her arm to lodge near her heart. She leaned over the floured lump of bread dough on the board before her and peered through the hole in the frost. In the dark yard next door, she could see the Berrybright sisters struggling with their frigid laundry, wrestling it from the baskets and bearing it above the frozen mud to the waiting lines in almost ceremonial solemnity. They were blue and pinched-looking, the bloom drained from their faces by the relentless chill.

"Will spring never come?" Sylvia whispered to the frost.

A soft rustle behind her caused a chill of a different kind. "It is coming, and summer hard after it. Coming like a storm."

Sylvia turned, the lump of dough seized and held to her chest as though it were a shield. Her father sat at the table, his hat on his head, his boots caked with mud that smeared the clean floor in a dark scuffle of foreign meaning. He gazed at her, and through her. The emptiness of his eyes was terrible. She moved her lips to speak, but no sound came. Her father seemed to hear her anyway.

"I won't visit again, Syl. I feel a pull, here -," he touched his abdomen, just below the breastbone, "- like I'm unraveling. And

53

there's a sound, like little bells or chimes. A sound ..." He cocked his head to the side, listening, and Sylvia saw the thick rope of blood that crawled from under his hat and wound down his neck. The air was cold enough to hang her breath.

"Do you have something to tell me?" she asked, and her voice was steady despite the painful thud of her heart. "Daddy? Before you go?"

His dreamy eye swiveled toward her, his gaze sharpening until it pierced her with an awful awareness. "Yessss," he sighed. "The dead are a wolf's feast, Syl. The living, too, as long as winter remains. But summer is coming, and a new way comes with it. Be careful, girl." He stood, and the rope of blood uncoiled over his shoulder and dripped to the floor, mixing with the black river mud.

"Wait. Don't go." She held out a white-dusted hand toward him. "I don't know what any of that means."

He paid no heed. He strode from the room, passing through the stout and unsuspecting body of his wife as she appeared in the doorway, and was gone. Mrs. Peach scowled at her daughter.

"Sylvia, who are you talking to?" When the girl did not answer, Mrs. Peach set her lips in a thin, determined line. "I won't tell you again to stop this nonsense. Jasper will never marry a girl who acts like a halfwit."

Sylvia tossed the bread dough back onto the board in a puff of flour. "Jasper's the halfwit, Mama, and ugly, besides. I wouldn't marry him if he was the only man in Wickeford Mills."

"He might as well be, where you're concerned," cried Mrs. Peach. "I don't know where you get your high and mighty ideas, but you've scarcely anything to recommend you. You've no looks and no money, and your tongue is sharp. If Jasper Coltsfoot finds something pleasing in you, I am nothing but thankful."

"I don't want to get married, anyway," Sylvia shot back. "Dr. Finchwhistle says I'd make a fine nurse."

"August Finchwhistle is not responsible for the welfare of your sisters, Miss! If you haven't the ambition to better your circumstances, you might at least think of Junie and Rabbit. Your brother is old enough to make his own way, but you girls – well, I'll be lucky to keep this roof over our heads long enough to see Junie settled." She stopped in mid-tirade and mused, "That Wes Meadowsweet will be looking to remarry soon. Ann's been gone over a year now."

"Mama, Junie's only thirteen." Sylvia wiped her hands on her apron before tugging it free and crushing it into a ball. "Wes has children only a few years younger."

Mrs. Peach brought her gaze back from the future to the cold kitchen and her eldest daughter. "Well, I don't mean she should go to him just yet. These things take time to arrange. I was no more than fifteen when I married your father, you know. Younger than you, my girl, and quite ready to take up housekeeping." She turned to feed the stove, and gave the wood a vigorous stir with the poker. "We're to have supper tonight at the Coltsfoot farm," she said over the noise. "Edna and I believe Jasper will ask for your hand."

Sylvia, who would be sixteen in another month, made the most of the clanging of the poker and fled through the tiny vestibule and out the door, pausing only to snatch her cloak and muffler from their pegs. Mrs. Peach whirled about at the icy touch of the air. "Sylvia," she bellowed from the open door. "The baking!"

Sylvia did not look back. She dashed across the lawn and vaulted the low stone wall into the street.

The dead were numerous that spring, and restless. They wandered along the street, peering in at the goods in the general store. They roamed aimlessly over the rotten ice by the river. Dead children played near living ones. Sometimes, they waved to Sylvia, but few approached and she was glad. She did not know where they were meant to go, or why they stayed in such numbers. She did not understand why some who had died during the terrible winter were absent. Her father's words rang in her head, *the dead are a wolf's feast*; and she lifted her eyes to the wooded hills beyond the village where the cemetery lay hidden and unvisited. The winter's dead were not there. Instead, they lay wrapped and stacked like funeral garments in the root cellars, for the frozen ground would not accept them.

She hurried along the High Street to Dr. Finchwhistle's surgery. The little white frame cottage had always looked so cheerful, its front door framed by the arch of a rose arbor, but the winter had laid its grim pall over it. Among his dying patients, Doc had numbered his son, Charlie. Sylvia stood at the gate and stared at the weather-bitten wreath of black crepe that hung on the door, hoping she would find the doctor sober when she knocked.

"You'd better not be passed out or raving, Doc," she muttered under her breath.

"He's only a little drunk, Syl. He has to go to Founder's House to tend Mr. Johns."

The quiet voice at her elbow gave her a start. The dead were peculiar in their etiquette. They would not be summoned by plea or command, yet they attended dream gabble and careless whispers with promptitude.

"Lucy! Where have you been? I looked everywhere for you yesterday."

Lucy shrugged. "I don't remember. Maybe in one of the looms."

Sylvia felt a pang of sorrow for her friend, who spent long days inhabiting her mother's looms, hoping to feel Mrs. Weaver's hands caress her pale hair as they used to do. As far as she knew, Lucy's efforts were unsuccessful.

"Look, I have to check on Doc, but if he's going to Founder's House, he won't have time for lessons today. Meet me in the smithy loft?"

Lucy smiled and was gone. Sylvia turned to knock at the surgery door, but it swung open before she could raise her fist. Dr. Finchwhistle, black bag in hand, staggered a little at the surprise of finding her there.

"Miss Peach, you are an early riser." He swiped a hand over his face as though to erase the weariness from it. "I'm afraid our little class won't convene today. Abram Johns is threatening to die."

Doc pulled the door shut behind him, and Sylvia fell into step with him as he strode back up the High Street toward Founder's House. She had sniffed the air of his passage at the gate, and been satisfied when she detected only the scent of his tobacco. Doc's drinking, a genteel booziness that had never interfered with his work, had nearly consumed the man since Charlie's death.

"Can I help you with Mr. Johns?" she asked, already knowing the answer.

"No, no. He's at the end, Sylvia. I can only try to ease his passing." He peered at her, his nearsightedness giving him the expression of a sleepy mole. She knew his spectacles were about him somewhere, and that he would not wear them if he could get away with it. It was his one little vanity. "If you like, this evening we can discuss tinctures and poultices for putrid throats. It would be a handy thing to learn, for Rabbit."

Sylvia thought of her youngest sister, whose name was really Rebecca. The girl had always been so tiny and frail that the play name stuck until it took precedence. Rabbit had suffered such croups and inflamed throats through the long winter, there had been times when Sylvia saw her spirit rise like fog to the surface of her skin, tethered by wisps as fine as spider silk.

"I wish I could, Doc. Mrs. Coltsfoot is having us to supper." She dropped her voice. "She and Mama want me to marry Jasper." She did not know why she told him, only that she felt compelled to share her misery.

Doc stopped as though transformed to stone, and Sylvia walked on without him for several paces. When she turned to ask if he'd forgotten something, the alarm on his face arrested her.

"Sylvia, this is hardly my business, but ... do you want to marry Jasper?"

"No!" She shook her head until her hair flew about her. "He's about as interesting as a fence post. And he has bad teeth."

"My dear, have you seen young Mr. Coltsfoot recently?" When she shook her head again, Doc went on. "There has been an odd change come over him. I can't put my finger on it, precisely, but it makes the hair stand on the back of my neck. I noticed it after his father was killed. A strange alteration in temperament in the boy, and one he appears to wish to hide. An almost savage interest in people, where before he was indifferent. I put it down to grief and the responsibility of taking over the farm, but now I'm not sure it was that at all." He tugged at his beard, groping for the right words. "I saw him in town a few days ago. On my oath, his face is like a mask, imperfectly applied over ... well, he's simply frightening."

Sylvia snorted laughter. "Jasper Coltsfoot? I know he's a big lummox, but he could never be frightening. He has the temperament of one of his sheep."

Doc stepped forward and put a hand on her shoulder, cutting off her laughter. "Listen to me, Sylvia. There have been many strange things afoot this winter, not the least of which was the tragedy at the Coltsfoot farm. You be careful around that boy."

Her father's words. *Be careful, girl.* She swallowed her mirth as a shiver walked over her skin. Doc pulled his watch from his vest pocket and tutted at the face he could not see without his specs.

"I'll have to leave you here. Remember what I told you, at supper tonight."

He turned in at a white picket gate. Sylvia looked up at the dour face of Founder's House. The second floor windows presented a shuttered pensiveness, but a tiny square casement in the downstairs parlor was open to the chill and drizzle. The soul window. Abram Johns, the founder of Wickeford Mills, would be lying in a makeshift bed near it, ready to flit through it into the smoky air as soon as he could get free of his dying flesh.

The open throat of the smithy flared and smoked in the grey morning fog like a dragon's maw. Its stone, barrel-vaulted length opened at each end to release the heat and din, making a tunnel large enough to drive a wagon through beneath the crooked, timber garret atop it. Sylvia stopped at the arch and peered into the firelit gloom. Henry Smith, wearing his great leather apron and a black scowl, brought his hammer down upon the iron on the anvil. The sound of it buffeted the girl like a physical blow. Henry flicked his gaze toward her, and she pointed to the ceiling. The hammer rose, Henry gave her the barest nod, and the hammer fell. The glowing metal screamed, and flakes of fire scale flew from it as though exorcised. Sylvia retreated to the narrow stair that clambered up the side of the smithy and made her way to the storage loft.

Doc might think Jasper changed, but Sylvia knew it was true of Henry. His young wife lay with the shrouded dead, a charred thing from nightmare. Sylvia had once nurtured a not-so-secret infatuation for the handsome blacksmith, when she was Junie's age and full of dreamy notions. When Henry married Ava Summerhill, Sylvia had thought her heart would break. It hadn't, mostly because the older girl, fey and lovely as a midsummer morning, had charmed her. Ava had taught her to wear fireflies like living gems and to plait crowns of wildflowers. But the winter had been long and plagued with shadows, even during the bleak days, and Ava had feared the dark. She had feared it enough, one frigid night, to embrace the fire in her husband's forge.

Sylvia moved to the window overlooking High Street and sank down on the dusty plank floor there. "Oh, Ava, where are you?" she whispered.

Outside, the fog thinned and swirled along the ground. Old Mrs. Greenbriar crept along the facades of the shops, flat as a silhouette, before vanishing with the tatters of fog; but Ava did not appear.

"Maybe her spirit got all burned up, too. Maybe there's nothing left of her." Lucy stepped from the air and knelt at the window beside her, looking out as Mrs. Greenbriar unwound like a sock with a loose thread. "What are you looking at?"

"Nothing." The dead seldom saw each other. It was another mystery to which Sylvia was privy, yet did not understand. "How can you say that about Ava? Burning can't destroy the spirit."

Lucy lifted one thin shoulder in a shrug. "Not the burning, Syl. She killed herself. Maybe, because of that, she's just gone."

"Do you know that?"

"No. I don't know anything. Only ... lately, I hear a strange sound that comes and goes. It reminds me of Ava's wind chimes. Do you remember how they tinkled? It makes me think of summer, so that I can almost feel it and smell it. I hear it right now, closer than before."

Sylvia stared into Lucy's wide, green eyes. "How long have you heard this sound?" she asked, thinking of her father's last words.

"I don't know. What day is this?" Before Sylvia could answer, a spark of mischief lit Lucy's eyes. "I heard something I do remember, though. I heard that Jasper Coltsfoot is sweet on you, and fixing to ask you to marry. Tonight? Yes, I think it's tonight." She clapped her hands, laughing. "Oh, Syl, you'll be a wife, with a big farm and your own carriage! Ain't you excited?"

Sylvia groaned and turned away from the window, slumping against the wall. The floor beneath her, heated by the forge below it, soothed the chill from her limbs, but could do nothing about the ice around her heart.

"No, I am not. I wish everyone would leave me alone. I feel nothing for Jasper." She made a frustrated sweep with her arm toward the window. "There is no one of any interest in this whole village. They are all dull and unromantic."

Lucy's eyes burned like foxfire in the dark hollows left by her final illness. "What are you hoping for, Syl? Do you think romance is real?"

Sylvia pondered the question. What she wanted seemed like so much girlish nonsense. She was under no illusions as to her own beauty, or lack of it. She was as tall as her older brother, Edward. Her hair sprang out from her head with the wild yearning of young vines, and no number of hairpins would subdue it. Where other girls her age were softening into bumps and curves, she was hard and lean. *Straight as the road to Hell*, her mother lamented. If she were wise, she would marry stupid Jasper Coltsfoot and be done. There were worse fates, she supposed. A warm, silvery sound intruded on her angry musings.

"Listen," Lucy gasped, pressing her face against the window. "It's the sound I told you about. Can you hear it? Something's coming."

Sylvia rolled to her knees beside Lucy, and gazed out at the muddy, rutted mess of High Street. The morning fog had withdrawn from the village center and gathered into a bank of cloud that climbed into the woods. Where it touched the edge of town, it roiled and bulged, disgorging a pair of fog-colored horses as though performing a magic trick. The horses wore hundreds of tiny bells on colorful ribbons threaded through their long manes and tails. They high-stepped inside an enchantment of tinkling music and drew behind them a hut-like scarlet wagon painted all over with jewel-toned summer blossoms. On the driver's box, under a swaying fringed canopy, sat a woman swathed in a worn duster, her face hidden under the wide brim of a man's hat. She guided her horses with a light hand, leaning forward comfortably with her elbows upon her knees. Sylvia's breath rushed from her at the sight, fogging the window. Both girls reached to clear it, their heads close together.

"Is it a traveling show?" Lucy asked.

The words had barely left her lips when a second enclosed wagon, this one painted deep indigo peppered with stars, emerged. Bell-bedecked horses pulled it, too; but Sylvia's gaze fastened on the driver. His knees were folded nearly to his chest, and he was thin as a last hope, though broad in the shoulders. She could see the knobs of his wrist bones jutting from his dark cuffs, and the long fingers that held the reins with delicacy. He wore a black coachman's hat. One handsome peacock plume nodded from the hatband, a satin iridescence of blue and green. Sylvia studied his pale face and felt her heart speed.

"... and get a closer look." Lucy put her hand on Sylvia's wrist and shook her. "Miss Mooncalf, do you hear me?"

Sylvia came back to herself and to the ache in her bones elicited by her friend's touch. "What?"

Lucy grinned at her, and she blushed. "I said, why don't you go down and get a closer look. Fine-looking young men don't travel through here often."

"Don't be foolish," Sylvia growled, turning away to watch as the wagons came on, cracking the scrim of ice beneath their wheels. The big, dappled horses arched their necks and snorted steam onto the air, picking up their feet as though dancing until they drew up before McCreary's General Store. When she turned back, ready to accept Lucy's advice, the dead girl was gone.

Down on the High Street, Sylvia skipped across the partially frozen mud, her skirt bunched in her hands so that her boots and knit stockings showed to the world. A press of shivering children, and curious townsfolk jostled about the painted wagons, and she shoved her way through. There were words in fancy script emblazoned on the sides of the wagons. LOVE & DARK glowed on the indigo field surrounded by stars. HONEY rippled like a banner over the scarlet-backed riot of flowers. Someone in the crowd spoke the simple word, and Sylvia's tongue curled with the memory of thick, amber sweetness. She gazed up at the impassive woman driver.

"Are you from a traveling circus?" she asked.

The woman looked down at her, showing a face as smooth and white as the summer moon, but sharp like a fox's face with long, dark eyes. A coppery braid glowed like a low fire against the black duster. "No, child," the woman said. "We are from no circus, though we have traveled long. We've come home at last, to take up our true work once again."

Her voice slipped through the chatter of the crowd like the breeze before a summer storm, soft but honed along its edge. It lodged in Sylvia's ear and vibrated there like an echo.

The girl blinked and opened a mouth full of questions. Before she could voice even the first of them, a babble rose at her back and the crowd shifted. Angus McCreary stepped out onto the wide porch of his store and addressed the air above the painted wagons.

"Strangers, welcome to Wickeford Mills." He looked about him for encouragement. Seeing several nods, he tucked his thumbs beneath his suspenders and went on. "If you're in need of provisions, I'm happy to accommodate you. I daresay I've got anything you might need."

The copper-haired woman took in the shopkeeper from his balding pate to the hem of his long, pinstriped apron, and smiled. "I am sure that you have," she said. "Mr. Love will give you a list to fill, if you please. He will return tomorrow for ... all of the things we will need."

She lifted a hand, and the tall, silent man driving the indigo wagon stepped down, causing a flutter of alarm. With his black clothing and long limbs, he moved through the parted knot of townsfolk like an unmoored shadow. He cast a smoldering glare over the crowd, and his regard fell on Sylvia, resting there long enough for her to see herself reflected on the dark mirror of his eye. His gaze slid away like a caress, leaving her pulse racing; and he strode to the rail of the porch. He held out a slip of paper to Mr. McCreary, who accepted it with a nervous dip of his head.

"Nathan." The woman's storm-edged voice cracked out over the silence. The tall man turned his gaunt, fierce face toward her. "Nathan, take this. Post it for the people to see."

She drew a scroll of fine paper from her pocket and held it out. Nathan plucked it from her fingers. In two gliding strides, he ascended the steps of the general store. His long fingers dipped into his breast pocket and fished out a stout black nail with a flat head the size of a penny. The uneasy crowd drew back. It was a coffin nail. Nathan unrolled the scroll carefully without looking at it, and Angus McCreary stepped forward as though pulled by a rope to offer the tall man a hammer. With one blow, the paper was affixed to the wall, and Nathan returned to his wagon. The townsfolk stood stunned and speechless. The copper-haired woman looked out over them, at the winter-dulled women clutching their children to their aprons, at the men gnawed to their bones by the harsh season, and at Sylvia who simmered with an unnamed yearning.

"Winter is over," she said. "Let it go."

She nodded toward the scroll fluttering from its dire nail against the wall of the store, then turned her face into the damp breeze and spoke a word to her horses. Their heads came up, eyes flashing, and they drew the wagon on down the High Street in a tinkle of bells. The indigo wagon followed. As it passed Sylvia, the eyes of the enigmatic driver found hers, and he touched the brim of his hat. The sound of the bells was like a sharp knife against the air, slicing a path through the chill of the village and on into the hungry gloom of the Johns Woods.

Sylvia pushed her way through the dispersing villagers and onto the porch of the store. Already, the news was running like a block fire up and down the High Street, and licking its way down the narrow alleys as folks hurried home, their tongues a-wag. She stepped up to the paper, and found Lucy by her side.

"What does it say, Syl?" The younger girl stood on tiptoe to peer at the notice.

"It says those people are here to take possession of something called Azimuth House." The girls exchanged a goggle-eyed look. "Where could ... oh! Do you think it means that old house out in the woods?"

"Mr. Johns told my Pa that place is the nest of demons. It's all boarded up and grown over. Why would anyone want to live out there?"

Sylvia shrugged and read on. "They want housekeeping help, Lucy. Says here they'll pay money, too, not just room and board." Her brow knit as she ran her finger over the lines of firm, black calligraphy. "I don't understand this," she whispered. "It says they've come to prepare the dead."

Lucy caught her breath. "Like for funerals? Ooh, won't Mr. Moss be mad! He's been doing our burying for as long as I can remember."

Sylvia stared at the paper, the name Fiona Dark slashed across the bottom with a flourish. She shook her head. "I don't think that's what it means, but you're right. Moss isn't going to be happy about it."

"Are you going to go out there, Syl? If you had a paid position, your Ma maybe wouldn't make you marry Jasper. And that young man in the coachman's hat looked like he'd taken a shine to you, too."

The girls giggled until Lucy fell into a fit of hoarse coughing, the kind that rattled and whooped in her narrow chest. Sylvia looked away in embarrassment. When Lucy regained her breath, she put a hand on Sylvia's sleeve and whispered, "Why were the townsfolk afraid? Nobody even asked where those people came from."

Sylvia pulled her arm away and rubbed it against her side. She wished Lucy would remember not to touch her. "I don't know. I guess the winter's made them fretful. I'm freezing. I'm going over to Doc's."

She ran down the steps to the street and picked her way across the mud and ice. When she reached the other side she looked back, but Lucy was gone.

2.

"Junie, give me some more hairpins." Mrs. Peach snapped her fingers at her younger daughter with her free hand, and wrenched Sylvia's hair into a tight twist with the other.

"Ow! Mama! You're gonna rip it out."

"Be still, girl, and stop fidgeting with that lace. You'll smudge it."

Sylvia stilled her ink-stained fingers. The pristine froth of lace at her cuffs was delicately crisp and itched like poison oak. She sat upright and unbending as a lodgepole, her mother's bridal corset cinched tight about her, pressing her small breasts upward like offerings. Her mother was peeved about the ink. Dr. Finchwhistle had shown Sylvia how to make it from walnut hulls, and it had settled into the fine creases of her fingers and dyed her cuticles a rich sepia that the vigorous application of a brush and coal tar soap had failed to eradicate.

"Honestly, I would think you'd have a care over your appearance tonight, Sylvia." Mrs. Peach thrust pins into the knot of her daughter's hair. "You couldn't do better than marrying into the Coltsfoot family. Jasper has taken over the farm, and it's a prosperous one. Promise me you'll make an effort to be pleasant tonight."

Sylvia flinched as a hairpin scratched a hot groove along her scalp. Her tongue felt inert as a lead bell clapper. She shrugged against the rough, unfamiliar caress of the silk gown.

"Sylvia? Will you mind me?"

"I don't see what I'm getting all gussied up for, Mama. It's wasted on the likes of Jasper Coltsfoot."

Mrs. Peach sighed. "It's more for his mother, to tell truth. Sylvia, you know this is important. I'd see you well settled. It's all I can do for you, and there are your sisters to think about."

63

Sylvia settled into stony silence, and the tenderness left her mother's face. "Stand up. Let's see how it fits."

She stood. The gown whispered around her. It was blue and simply cut, with lace at the cuffs and ruffling the bodice. In the dressing table mirror, Sylvia thought she looked severe as a schoolteacher and surprisingly grown up with her hair in a neat chignon.

"Well, it's decent and ladylike," Mrs. Peach said. "It's a pity you don't have more of a figure." She turned to Junie, hovering in the doorway with her finger in her mouth. "Tell Edward to go bring the wagon up."

Junie leaned into the hallway and yelled, "Eddie, Ma's ready to go. Get the wagon."

A door slammed and boots clobbered the bare wood of the stairs as Edward ran for the mule shed. Mrs. Peach put a hand over her eyes.

"June Alice, you are becoming an utter savage," she said, but it lacked bite and Junie only smirked at Sylvia in the mirror.

The spring wind had arrived at last, still bracing, but carrying a ribbon of warmer air at its heart that made Sylvia's blood race. It smelled green, a spark to set the whole forest alight with awakening buds. She could almost believe it had followed the strangers. Thinking of them, the ghost of honey filled her mouth and ran warm down her throat. She swallowed longing and looked up at the night sky. For the first time in months, a blue-black field of stars met her gaze. The wind had chased away the sullen cloud cover and revealed a polished vault blazing with cold drifts and crisp points of light.

"Mama, look. You can see the stars again."

Mrs. Peach glanced up. "It's about time. Thought spring wouldn't ever come this year. Come now, Sylvia, get in the wagon and mind your skirt."

Edward lent his clumsy assistance to the women as they climbed onto the hard plank seat. He handed up two scratchy wool blankets for their laps, and Mrs. Peach's glazed gingerbread in a cheese box.

"Sure you don't want me to drive you, Ma? I don't mind waiting in the Coltsfoots' barn. Jasper's got a couple of new horses I'd like to see."

"You stay with your sisters, Edward," Mrs. Peach said. "You can see Jasper's horses another day." She settled herself and draped a blanket over her knees, then turned to Sylvia. "Here, put this shawl over your head. You don't want your hair ruined by the wind."

Sylvia draped the lace shawl over her hair, and wished she could set it free in the frisking wind. The wagon lurched forward at her mother's imperious, "Walk on, Agatha."

The rhythmic clop of the mule's hooves was like a heartbeat in the dark. The road was wet and running with little rivulets of melt. The lingering snow in the woods had visibly slumped, revealing patches of rich, saturated earth. A fog breathed up from it and hovered over the ground, creeping across the stony road in shifting veils. The scant light of the village fell away behind them, and the trees stepped forward and dripped on them. Sylvia looked up, watching the stars flicker in the thick branches, there and then gone as though swallowed. Nearby, the Wicke River raced over its stones with a quarrelsome sound. Despite the night's hateful errand, she was happy to be out, riding along with the wind through the black trees, smelling the immense fertile body of the forest turning in its sleep and surfacing toward bloom.

At the crest of a hill, she was able to look for an instant over the woods falling away from them. A thick, silvery plume of smoke rose against the sky. It bulged and knotted in a fleecy column, and was torn asunder by the wind before rising again. The trees hid its source from view, but Sylvia knew where it originated. In sudden excitement, she pointed at it.

"Look there! It's coming from Azimuth House, Mama. That's where the strangers went today."

Mrs. Peach squinted at the smoke, and then the wagon dipped down below the crown of the trees and it was lost from sight.

"Is that what they call the place? What kind of word is 'azimuth'?"

"I don't know, Mama. I'll ask Dr. Finchwhistle."

"You stay away from that drunkard, Sylvia." Mrs. Peach turned her gaze on her daughter, who half stood to catch a last glimpse of the smoke. "And you stay away from those people back there in the woods. They have strange ways. That house isn't even theirs, most likely. They're squatters and traveling show folk, and maybe worse."

"Mama, you don't know any of that. They want housekeepers, and they'll pay money. Does that sound like squatters?"

Mrs. Peach fixed her eyes on the road again. "Housekeepers. I suppose you've formed an idea of going to them."

Sylvia held her tongue. She had formed precisely such an idea, but she had not planned to broach the subject to her mother this evening.

"Girl, you mind me. I'll not have you skivvying for strangers, not if I can arrange a good marriage for you."

They drove the rest of the way to the Coltsfoot farm in silence, their opposing wills skirmishing between them. At the turn onto the Coltsfoot's lane, Mrs. Peach pulled the mule to a stop. In the soft dip of the hills, the lighted windows of the farmhouse glimmered in the growing fog as though under water.

"Come, take off that shawl. Let me see your hair." Mrs. Peach fussed at it, wetting her fingers with spit and brushing down the stubborn tendrils that sprang loose. "You've got hair like a wild creature," she muttered.

The women sat in the chilly stillness and looked at each other. Sylvia pressed her lips together to hold back yet another protest. Mrs. Peach heard it anyway. She sighed.

"Look out there, Sylvia," she said. She gestured at the wide meadows, the big barn, and sprawling house. The scene, alternately etched in starlight and blurred by mists, spoke of prosperity. "All of that could be yours. Edna says Jasper's had his eye on you. He wants a wife. You could be well settled and comfortable, mistress of your own farm. Will you make an effort for it?"

Anger flamed up in Sylvia's cheeks. "I said I'd come, Mama, and I'm here. I'm doing it for Junie and Rabbit, not because I care anything about Jasper Coltsfoot's riches. Can we just go and get it over with?"

Mrs. Peach clucked to the mule, and Agatha drew them along the muddy lane to the dooryard. A man came out from the barn and helped them down, before leading Agatha away. The farmhouse door opened, and Edna Coltsfoot stepped out to embrace Cora Peach.

"Sylvia, your mother tells me that you help her with her bakery business." Mrs. Coltsfoot spoke over a forkful of glazed gingerbread. Her smile was warm, but her eyes were appraising. Sylvia felt as though she were being pinched and patted to determine her readiness for butchering.

"Yes, ma'am." She pushed the moist crumbs of gingerbread around her plate with her fork until she felt a gentle pressure on her foot. Her mother raised her eyebrows as she pressed Sylvia's boot with her own. She cleared her throat. "I bake bread every day, and some sweets when Mama doesn't have time."

"She's such a help, I don't know how I'd manage without her," Mrs. Peach said, then hastened to add, "I know she must set up her own household one day, of course."

Mrs. Coltsfoot's eyes did not stray from Sylvia, who put down her fork and sat staring into the candle glow. She felt her every flaw in a way that mortified her. Her long, angular body suddenly felt like that of a scarecrow, and she was sure her hair was unwinding from its pins. She knew she was plain, but she had never before felt so scattered and clumsy. In the lull of the conversation, the ticking of the case clock was loud and mocking. At the head of the table, Jasper shoved away his plate and slurped coffee from his saucer. The vulgar sucking noise seemed to be the cue Mrs. Coltsfoot awaited.

"Shall we sit by the fire a bit and talk?" She stood and held out a hand to Sylvia. "Come, I understand this is an awkward time for a young girl. Let us talk it over together."

The women moved to chairs before the fire, and Jasper stood at the mantle packing a long-stemmed pipe with tobacco from a leather pouch.

"You don't mind if I smoke," he said, and struck a match. It had not been a question.

Sylvia looked at him, at the gangly assemblage of him and the breadth of his shoulders that was starting to fill in with muscle. She looked at the firelight wavering over the long flat planes of his face, at his broad mouth and his big, hooked nose. She looked at his lank hair that was a duller brown than mouse skin, already receding from the widow's peak above his stern eyebrows. When he clamped his teeth on the pipe stem, she saw that they were brown, too, stained from tobacco and neglect, and big as a horse's teeth. She could smell him: pipe smoke and wood smoke, horse sweat and wool, and underneath a different smell - like salt, cinders, and stagnant water. Sylvia knew what marriage meant, and she imagined that appalling smell imprinted on her own skin. Something trembled in her chest, and she feared she might scream.

"Jasper is twenty years old now," Mrs. Coltsfoot was saying from somewhere far away. "He has taken the farm in hand, and he has great plans for it. He needs a wife and a helpmate. My dear, what do you think of joining our family?"

Sylvia was incapable of speech. Mrs. Peach leaned forward and took one of her cold hands. When she saw that Sylvia would not speak, she turned to Mrs. Coltsfoot with an exasperated smile.

"She's shy, that's all. She's young, and feels the weight of the honor of being considered." She looked up at Jasper. "Could you not tell her your feelings on the subject?"

Jasper puffed at his pipe and turned his watery, colorless gaze on Sylvia. *He's got eyes like boiled grapes*, she thought. Another bubble of hysteria rose in her chest.

"I need a wife," he said. His voice was iron and gravel, and Sylvia wondered when it turned so hard. Doc's ridiculous warning floated to the surface of her mind and shimmered there. "This farm is done with sheep. I'm going to breed horses here, fine horses. I got to have a woman to take care of the house. A man shouldn't be alone."

He stopped and smoked. He looked at the ceiling, and seemed to have no more to say. His mother touched his sleeve.

"Go on, dear. Tell Sylvia how you've thought of her."

Jasper blew a plume of smoke and pointed the stem of his pipe at Sylvia. "You're young and strong. Good stock, and I'm a fair judge. I ain't looking for beauty. I want a girl like a honey hive, sweet and productive. You'll suit me fine."

Mrs. Coltsfoot and Mrs. Peach looked embarrassed, but Mrs. Coltsfoot forged on.

"You see, Sylvia, my son is a practical man. A hard-working man with good prospects. This would be a fine match for you."

Sylvia looked up at Jasper, and found him staring at her. Smoke curled from his mouth, making him squint, but there was something more than practicality glinting in his eyes. Again, she caught the odd under-smell of him. She saw that his hands were hard and restless, ready to grasp what they wanted. A seething heat steamed from him, heavier than the warmth of the fire, as though the real, unseen Jasper paced close around her, hungry and impatient. A tickle of fear touched her, and her gaze fell to the braided, black-and-red hearth rug. A faint blot marred the neat job. She knew it was all that was left of the late Mr. Coltsfoot's blood. He had been killed in front of this very fireplace, savaged by a forest beast bold enough to enter his house. She looked back to Jasper. His homely face was in shadow as the fire burned lower, but his eyes were wickedly merry, watching her mind turn.

She bolted to her feet, startling a little cry from Mrs. Coltsfoot. "We must go home, Mama. We thank you for your hospitality, and for your kind offer, I'm honored I'm sure." She babbled, backing out of the firelight and taking up their cloaks from the fancy settee. "Mama, it's late. The girls ... and Edward ... wondering about us."

Her mother stood and gaped at her. She thrust forward her mother's cloak. Mrs. Peach took it, but turned to Mrs. Coltsfoot in consternation.

"Edna, I apologize. I can't think what's come over her. She must have more nerves than I'd thought."

Mrs. Coltsfoot did not stand. She had lapsed into an attitude of exhaustion and only made slight fluttering movements with her hands.

"Not to worry, Cora. I'll talk to you at the bakery tomorrow. Not to worry."

Jasper knocked his pipe against his boot heel. "I'll tell Jed to bring your wagon round."

He went out into the wind and fog. As he passed Sylvia, his pale eyes sparked at her, as expressive as a shout of laughter.

"Sylvia Peach, I have never been so humiliated." Mrs. Peach's lips were white, her eyes narrowed to angry slits. "I thought we understood one another. I thought you understood how much this means to us all."

Sylvia, relieved to be free in the night air, could not bring herself to apologize.

"Mama, did you notice nothing amiss?" she asked. "Jasper is so - "

"So what?" snapped Mrs. Peach.

Sylvia gave a cry of frustration and disgust. "I can't imagine letting him touch me, ever. I can't imagine living with him. Mama, he's not like he pretends, and he stinks!"

"Girl, I am tired in my bones. Since your father died, I've worked like a dray horse to keep food on the table, and sold near everything I can." Mrs. Peach's voice rose and trembled on the edge of hysteria. "I hope you haven't ruined this opportunity."

Sylvia rounded on her mother. "Jasper Coltsfoot isn't the only answer, Mama! You can't make me marry him. I won't do it." She crossed her arms over her chest and lowered her chin.

Around them, the Johns Woods reached its gaunt arms into a cotton bale of fog that had crept up the trees and squatted in the branches. The wind gusted and tore at the underbrush. Sylvia's hair had cast aside its pins and unwound in streaming banners.

With a shrill cry, Mrs. Peach grabbed a handful of the dark tresses and shook her daughter back and forth. Her strong, big-knuckled hand pulled at the girl's scalp, and Sylvia wailed in surprise and pain.

"You will do as you're told, Sylvia! You are a selfish child." Mrs. Peach spat each word on a harsh, explosive little breath, and punctuated it with a vicious tug on the hair wound about her fist. She released her and drew in a shuddering breath. "You're too young to know what's best for you. The subject is closed. I'll fix things with Edna."

The forest was silent. Tears rolled down Sylvia's face, and she rubbed at her head with a shaking hand, but she made no sound. An owl dropped from the invisible attic of the trees and glided ahead of them on soft grey wings. Where it passed, the fog swirled and parted. It dipped into the woods, revealing a rough lane and the tumbled remains of a stacked stone gatepost.

Sylvia sniffed and cast a sidelong glance at her mother's stony profile. She whispered, "I could go to Azimuth House, Mama. I could earn the money to help with Junie and Rabbit."

Mrs. Peach ground her teeth together. She pulled hard on the reins. Agatha stopped and shook her long ears.

"That's the road to those people." She pointed to where the owl had vanished.

Sylvia stared at her mother. She had never heard her voice so harsh. "I guess it is, Mama."

"I'm telling you to get down, girl. Get down and go back that road. Go back and be a skivvy, I'm done with worrying after you." She turned her face forward.

Sylvia crept down from the wagon and stood at the side of the road. Her breath hung in front of her, and the fog came to kiss her eyelashes with tiny beads of wet.

"Mama?"

Mrs. Peach made an impatient shrug and clucked to the mule. The wagon rolled on, with Mrs. Peach sitting tall and rigid. She did not look back.

Sylvia clenched her fists, and her blood thundered in her ears. "Fine!" she shouted. "Go on and leave me."

This elicited no answer, and the wagon started up the hill. Sylvia stepped into the road, her skirt bunched in her fists and her hair hanging around her.

"You're the selfish one," she yelled after her mother.

The wagon creaked and jangled over the crest of the hill at a stately pace, and Mrs. Peach made no sign that she heard. Sylvia watched until the wagon was out of sight. The forest seemed to grow taller and thicker around her. She gave a little hiccough and tried out a sob, but anger burned away her pain.

A soft snapping of twigs in the woods dowsed her fury. She stared into the fluid shadows, and, in holding her own breath to listen, thought she heard the soft panting of another. Shade upon shade of satiny black and shifting grey made monsters of the trees. Wild faces looked back at her, while she stood frozen under the certainty that something stalked her. Out of the charged silence, a doe burst from the brush and bounded across the path, crashing into the darkness. Sylvia gave a shaky laugh. Down that path lay

Azimuth House. There was no sense in standing there, freezing to a stone in the Johns Woods, when she could walk toward a warm hearth. She stepped forward, and moonlight spilled through the tattered fog to silver the way.

The lane ran in a straight line through the woods, which crowded close to it and formed over it a roof of creaking boughs. Sylvia had walked nearly a mile along it, feeling under her boots the saturated sponginess of moss interspersed with slippery shards of shale, when she heard the measured thud of hooves. A jingle of tack, and a horse's soft whicker reached her before she saw the rider. She was too tired and numb to feel alarm, and besides, there was only Azimuth House and its inhabitants ahead. She waited in a shifting wash of moonlight for the horseman to draw near. The long, lean rider was unmistakable as Nathan Love. He drew in his reins at the sight of her, and she saw that his horse was not one of the dappled prancers that had pulled the painted wagons through town. This was a massive black brute with rolling blue eyes, and she shied back from it. Nathan's white face glared down on her like a mask of bone. His hair hung long over his collar, straight and black as his mount's wild mane.

"I ... I'm on my way to Azimuth House. To take up work, like the paper in town said," she stammered. The man's unblinking gaze made her feel like one of Dr. Finchwhistle's insect specimens, waiting to be affixed with a pin in his collection. "You posted it there yourself, remember?"

As soon as the question passed her lips, she felt foolish and the blood rushed to her cheeks. Nathan blinked, dark lashes shuttering fathomless eyes. Without a word, he dismounted and held out his hand to her. The slender fingers were as white as his face, and attenuated as those of a shadow. Sylvia cringed away. Nathan's black gaze followed her, but he made neither move nor comment. His hand dropped to his side, then reached up to stroke the nervous horse. Sylvia felt foolish all over again.

"My mother let me off on our way home." She saw no reason to trouble the man with the details of her circumstance. "We were coming back from the Coltsfoot's farm. Your neighbors." She made a vague gesture in the direction of the farm.

Nathan's eyes narrowed as he followed the sweep of her hand. His cool expression turned grim. He fixed her with a severe stare before turning away and bending down to lace his long fingers together. He was making a stirrup, Sylvia realized. He wanted her to get on that gigantic horse.

"Will you take me the rest of the way to Azimuth House? Why don't you say something?"

He turned his face to her and cocked an eyebrow at his clasped hands. She thought she might have caught the most fleeting of smiles about his lips, there and gone. She looked from him to the wild-eyed horse, and back again. He looked as though he could crouch there all night waiting for her, and he showed no inclination to speak, so she stepped forward, putting her foot in his hands. She steadied herself with a hand on his shoulder and felt it thin, but sinewy with muscle. He lifted her to the saddle as though she were weightless, and she swung a leg over. Her skirt bunched and crumpled around her, and her black winter stockings were on display. She tugged hopelessly at the recalcitrant skirt.

Nathan watched her struggle for a moment before shrugging out of his greatcoat. He whirled it up and around her in one graceful motion. The heavy coat hung to her ankles, and was warm in itself, but it seemed to retain no heat from its owner's body. She had no time to wonder at it. The horse danced under her and pirouetted to face home, and she clutched at its mane and at the saddle horn. Nathan walked along in silence, leading it with loose reins, his long legs making quick work of the remaining mile. They reached a clearing in the woods, and Azimuth House rose up before them, shabby and grand.

A bonfire still burned low on the sparse, mossy lawn in front of the house. It sent up a luxuriant cloud of black and pewter smoke spangled with tiny red embers. The huge, undisciplined smell of it, both sweet and acrid, wedded to the chill night air in a wild perfume that made Sylvia aware of her own pulses. Her skin thrummed like a beehive with sudden excitement. Even in the April damp, she thought she could taste summer like heavy syrup, could feel it in the press of heat against her bones. It whispered over her and spun through her as though she had plunged into a different atmosphere.

The house bulked out of the dark beyond the fire, its flat stone face made ruddy by the afterglow. The boards had been pulled from its windows to feed the fire, and Sylvia gasped at the expanse of glass revealed. Rows of tall many-paned windows looked out on the night, reflecting the undulant flames. The central block of the house soared three stories into the trees. To the east and the west of it sprawled wings of lesser stature under skins of ivy and Virginia creeper. The columns and broken roof of the portico hosted a tangle of naked wisteria vines thicker than a man's wrist. As neglected as it was, Sylvia had never seen any house so fine.

Nathan walked the great horse around the bonfire on the weedy remnant of a circular carriage drive. At the portico, he stopped and reached up for her. Entranced, she slid from the saddle into his arms and down the cold length of him to the ground. She stepped quickly away, confused and embarrassed. His body was unyielding as a locust post. She had never been clasped so close, and the feel of him seemed somehow part of the rough music of the fire and the windy night. If Nathan noticed the strange magic in the air, he made no sign. The thick oak slab of the door stood dark and silent under its shadowy mantle of vines, and he turned and thumped with his fist on it until it opened.

"Why, Nathan, what have you brought us? Surely not a traveler so soon." Sylvia looked into a lovely, elfin face dominated by dark eyes. Its owner peered out at her from the wedge of darkness behind the door, her milk-and-roses complexion glowing like a lamp.

"Well, don't just stand there, my dear. Come in." The woman reached out a child-like hand and pulled Sylvia by the lace cuff of her gown through the door, before turning her pert little face to Nathan. "The coach has arrived. We had it driven around to the stables."

Without waiting for a response, the woman closed the door with a decisive bang. She whirled over to a simple pine table and, snatching up the candlestick that burned there, whirled back again to thrust it near Sylvia's face.

"She's pretty, Maura. And so tall!" The woman's voice was like the little bells that had announced their arrival in the village, laughing but sharp.

From the shadows came a second voice, this one hoarse and whispery enough to make Sylvia think of spider's feet.

"She's not one of them, Maeve. Pinch her and see."

"Here now!" Sylvia started back from the tiny white fingers. "I've come about the housekeeping position, but I can go just as quickly. My name is Sylvia."

Sylvia, Sylvia. Her name seemed snatched from her lips and flung to the rafters where it hung with the skulking candle smoke. She heard the scratch of a match, and a dim figure touched the long matchstick to the kindling in the entry hall fireplace. The fire bit at the dry wood, leaping up the chimney with a crackle and a whoosh. Sylvia blinked and looked around at the cavernous hall. The floor was stone, littered with dry leaves and bits of twig and pinecone. More woodsy debris adorned the table, along with several blackened silver candlesticks that held the gnawed stubs of beeswax candles. Across from the fireplace, a broad staircase curved upward into darkness garlanded with cobwebs.

The figure by the fireplace glided closer, and Sylvia caught her breath. Maura looked enough like Maeve to be her twin, but where Maeve's face was sweet and smooth, her sister's was bitter and etched with lines of pain.

"Why do you come here, girl?" she asked with her voice like a rasp.

"She said she comes to do the housekeeping - "

"Let her speak, sister. There is more to this one. I smell it."

Maura leaned forward and sniffed delicately. The lines on her face deepened, and her eyes glimmered as though from the bottoms of two wells.

Sylvia's throat felt parched, her tongue a toasted coal. "There isn't any more, I swear. I came for work. The paper in town said you would pay for housekeeping."

A tiny crease appeared between Maeve's perfect brows. Her gaze was riveted on her twin's suspicious face.

"We should tell Fiona. Shall I fetch her?"

"No, she's busy enough just now."

With an effort, Maura ratcheted her thin lips into a ghastly smile. She plucked a tarnished candlestick from the table behind her, lit the melted knob of candle from the flame of her sister's taper, and thrust it at Sylvia.

"You are welcome here," she said, her tone sepulchral. "Maeve will give you a room, and tomorrow we'll see what's to be done with you."

Sylvia took the candlestick with its ancient freight of drippings, and hurried to follow Maeve who had flitted toward the staircase almost before the words had fallen from her sister's lips. The stairs were bare and black. The sound of Sylvia's boots against them echoed around them as they ascended. She trailed her fingers over the dark paneled wainscoting, snatching her hand back to rub against her skirt as she encountered a shroud of dusty web. She looked over the curved backbone of the banister to the hall below, and saw Maura crouched before the fire, stirring it into a swirl of sparks with an iron poker. In that brief instant, Maeve disappeared from view, and Sylvia climbed hastily to the upper hallway and looked about for her.

A carpet ran down the center of a corridor that branched away to the left and the right. It was laden with dust, and Sylvia left her footprints as though in snow. There was no sign of Maeve's passage. The night filled the old house with a throng of shadows too deep to fear a simple candle flame. A warm, fragrant whisper of wind tickled her cheeks, pulling at the flame as at a loose thread in a tapestry. The light leaned away in a dimming tendril, and she cupped her hand around it in sudden panic. She could almost imagine she was in the summer forest, with the sound of crickets and the shimmer of fireflies around her; and a moment of vertigo seized her.

"Maeve?" Her voice thinned and cracked. "Where did you go?"

Above her, an iron chandelier gonged in the wisp of breeze. The sound flew away down the corridor and became a laugh. A tiny point of light flared in the dark.

"I'm over here, my dear. We must climb again. Your room is in the attic."

Up they went, Maeve silently and Sylvia clattering on another bare staircase, this one narrow and twisting. At each turn, niches in the white plaster held fat slumps of candles whose wax had pooled and dripped over the ledges long ago. The stairwell felt warm and stuffy, and the spectral bouquet of honey haunted the air. At the top, a spacious landing presented two white plank doors.

"Which shall it be, hmm? That one, I think."

Maeve pointed at the first door to the right of the landing. Sylvia lifted the latch. The door swung inward on a cozy, firelit room under the eaves. A narrow bed with a plump feather mattress dressed in clean, white linens stood near the little fireplace, enclosed in lace bed curtains. There was a washstand and armoire. A stout burgundy chair, somewhat threadbare but free of dust, sat before the single window that looked out over the carriage drive. Sylvia gasped.

"Did you know I was coming?" Nothing seemed impossible to her this night.

"Not I," said Maeve. "But someone in the house must have known. They often know things before we do."

With that enigmatic statement, she slipped through the door and stood looking in at Sylvia. "You'll find night clothes in there." She pointed at the armoire. "Good night."

Maeve pulled the door closed, and the light of her candle vanished from beneath it.

Nighttime in Azimuth House was an interval of soft whisperings, rustlings, and sighs. The wind scratched at the window and scrabbled in the chimney. Loose shutters clattered against the stone, and the sound traveled through the thick walls to arrive diminished to mere bumps. The fire hissed and grumbled as it settled to sleep on its bed of ash. Every sound was muted, but

Sylvia heard them all. Once, the attic stairs creaked as though trodden, and she bolted up in her narrow bed and clutched the quilt to her breast. The footsteps continued their climb, and soon there was a whispering shuffle over the slate tiles of the roof above her.

Nor were its varied voices all the house had to display of its strangeness. The phantom of summer seemed to rise from its foundations and to wend its way through the seams of the floorboards. It floated from beneath baseboards and smoked through keyholes. It slid up the staircases like fog. Aromas of green leaf and honeysuckle, warm rain, and wild rose caressed the air. A balmy breath of a breeze, too light to lift the lace bed curtain, walked over the fine hairs of Sylvia's arms and kissed her lips. Like a golden thread through it all drifted the sweet scent of honey. She fell into an uneasy sleep, teased by tenuous dreams of summer, and passed the darkest hours of the night suspended in a bewildering haze of sensation.

Just before dawn, the sounds of a team and wagon drifted up to her from the carriage drive. She slipped from her bed and crept to the window. A long black wagon, stacks of canvas folded in its bed, stood in the dark behind a pair of dappled horses. Nathan sat on the driver's box, his battered coachman's hat on his head, and looked down at a woman in a crimson cloak. The cloak had a deep hood, and Sylvia could not see the woman's face, but she felt sure this was neither Maura nor Maeve. The woman spoke for several minutes to the lanky driver before returning to the house. Nathan shook the reins, and the horses drew the wagon away into the woods. Sylvia wondered if, when he returned, he would bring companions for her from among the village girls.

Sleep was flown, the dawn arriving with its thin line of pink and gold behind the ink-dark trees, and she was eager to see more of Azimuth House. Rose-scented water beckoned from the pitcher on the washstand. She made a hasty toilette, and dressed again in her good blue gown, leaving behind the despised corset on the rumpled bed. In the skinny, crooked stairwell she breathed in the sweet scent of beeswax, skipping down it in high spirits. In the second floor hallway, she took note of the size of the place and of the prodigious amount of dust, web, and dirt that covered everything. She opened a few of the many doors and found bedrooms, salons, and a smoking room, all grey with dust. The furniture was ghostly in voluminous coverings of muslin, once crisp and white but now yellowed, draped with spider windings, and fragile to the touch. She drew back a corner of sheeting from a claw-footed desk, and the fabric tore like paper. Far from being discouraged, Sylvia hummed as she made her way to the main staircase. The Darks needed her, and her wages would help keep Junie and Rabbit. She spared Jasper Coltsfoot one shuddering thought, dismissing him from her mind.

A voice climbed the air from the gloom below her, even and amiable, amplified in the deep throat of the stairwell. "Come into the library, Sylvia."

A fleeting glow in the dusty pallor of the walnut wainscoting accompanied it. The broad iron wheel of the entry hall chandelier caught and echoed it with a solid metallic purr, and the candles flared into haloed splendor. For one breathtaking instant, Sylvia saw the house as it had been, and then the chill, dirty darkness crept back like a stain. She hurried down to the entry hall and peered about.

"This way."

The voice slipped over the heavy slate of the floor and under a door tucked behind the staircase. Sylvia approached it and saw a razor slash of candlelight gild the narrow gap beneath it before it swung inward. The woman from the fabulous painted wagon stood in the nimbus of buttery light that sprang out into the corridor. Her copper hair, hanging loose to her waist, snatched at the light and shattered it in a shower like live sparks. Sylvia felt her jaw unhinge and knew she was staring like a simpleton.

"Come and have some breakfast, Sylvia. We have much to talk about." The woman smiled, and turned back into the room. "I am Fiona Dark, and this is my family's house. We are glad to have you with us."

She set her candelabra on a table near the fire. A tea service arched its graceful arms atop a tray laden with good things. Sylvia noted that all of the silver in this room was as bright and gleaming as ice from the Wicke. She gazed wide-eyed at the walls of books, more books than she had seen in her whole life, all marching in neat rows along shelves that soared to the coffered ceiling. Not a speck of dust marred their gorgeous bindings. The paneled walls glowed with polishing. Layers of exotic rugs rioted underfoot in a kaleidoscope of pattern and color. She tiptoed across them and sat in the chair Fiona drew out for her.

"Will you have some coffee?" Fiona did not wait for an answer, but poured the strong, steaming brew into a cup and set it before the girl. "My sisters drink tea, but I prefer something richer. This life is brief and hard, and we must feed our senses, eh?"

"Thank you," Sylvia mumbled.

She sipped the hot coffee without cream or sugar, and the knot of anxiety that had been growing tighter in her stomach unfurled in a lovely, dark blossom of awareness. The firelight washed out over the hearth and joined with the surging shadows - light, dark, light, dark – blending into faces and transitory figures. She saw a girl her own age, a weathered man of fifty, a shaggy dog that bounded over the wall, and a young woman with a baby in her arms who slipped down through the floorboards with a knowing smile. She clutched the edge of the table, her lungs become too small for the measureless atmosphere that tried to rush into them. She was drowning in the peopled air.

"First meetings are the hardest," Fiona said. "Here, try a little honey in your cup. It is soothing."

Sylvia sipped the thick sweetness, like a river of sunlight under the dark earthiness of the coffee, and the dizzy writhing of the shadows fell still. She heard a faint laugh, but the ghosts were gone. She set the cup down with trembling fingers.

"You saw them, too!" She turned an astonished face to Fiona. "Do you know what they want?"

Fiona sipped from her cup. "They dwell here. They do not choose to travel, at least not yet, though they have been here a long time. We do not compel them." She leaned forward, and her dark eyes grew wide and owlish. "Everything depends on a delicate balance, Sylvia. Life, death, and the many places in between. Azimuth House sits at the fulcrum of that balance. In a larger sense, this entire area sits at that fulcrum. It is a special place." She sat back again. "Things are not well here. The Old Road has become difficult to pass. The dead cannot travel and they attract unwholesome creatures that would prey on them. Even the dead may suffer violence, which spills over onto the living. It creeps into the bones of the forest, into the blood of the river. We have come home to reopen the way."

Sylvia sat paralyzed like a bird before a snake. "The way to what?" she whispered.

Fiona stared into the fire for long minutes before answering the girl with another question. "The winter has been a hard one for your people, hasn't it?"

"Yes. It was the third bad one in a row. A lot of folks died this time."

"Where are they?"

A shiver ran down Sylvia's back. "What do you mean?"

Fiona put her cup on her saucer and smiled. "Where have your people put the bodies of those who died? Surely they could not have buried them, with the earth frozen."

"Oh. No, we couldn't dig for them. They're in the root cellars. Moss's boys wrapped them up nice, first. As soon as it thaws, they'll bury them right."

"Moss. That is your funeral man?"

Sylvia nodded.

Fiona tapped her spoon against the shell of a soft-boiled egg. "And the townsfolk have been burying their dead all along? Putting them into the earth?"

"Well, sure. The cemetery is about a mile out of town. It's a pretty place, with the woods all around it."

Fiona sighed. "One should never invite a hungry wolf to supper, Sylvia. It will learn to enter the houses by night and take what it wants."

Sylvia thought of her father's last visit, and his sad pronouncement. She thought of Simon Coltsfoot, snatched from the false safety of his own hearth. Fiona touched her napkin to her lips, and stood.

"There is work to do," she said. "Balance to restore. Would you like to see the agents of that restoration?"

Sylvia nodded, happy to abandon her dark thoughts.

Outside, the air was chilly, but it no longer captured the plumes of their breath. Sylvia looked about in wonder at the faint green fuzz of opening buds. Spring had arrived full-blown in the night, and the Johns Woods was alive with birdsong and anticipation. They trudged around to the stables, a long, low building of heavy beams and ironwork. Horses blinked out at them, some dappled grey and others black as moonless night, and Fiona spoke softly to each as they passed. A handsome coach, sinister in its obsidian perfection, sat on the cobbles of the carriage bay. Sylvia stopped to stare at its sleek lines, the opulence of its sable draperies and its urn-shaped lanterns, and then sprinted to catch Fiona as the red cloak whisked around the corner of the stables.

A long arbor stood at the end of the building, so grown over with ancient grapes that its pillared structure was only a faint suggestion. Inside, the arbor was dim and paved with stones. The muscular vines made gnarled walls studded all over with round vessels affixed in clusters. A lantern hung near the entrance, and Fiona took it from its nail and lit it. As Sylvia's eyes adjusted to the sudden flare of light, the vessels resolved into skulls. More than two hundred empty eye sockets gazed blindly at her. The bones were dark, burnished, and strangely waxy. The air thickened with the smell of honey and the memory of frost-sugared grapes.

Sylvia recoiled with a cry and would have fled, but Fiona dropped a steadying hand on her shoulder as she raised the lantern high. The light washed over each skeletal face. The skulls, though ancient and long since robbed of any power of expression, were not blank masks. Each thrummed with energy so potent that Sylvia feared it would speak. She turned a pale face to Fiona.

"What is this?"

Fiona hung the lamp from an iron hook above her head. Shadows undulated over the living walls as it swayed there.

"They are my ancestors. On the road, they ride in willow baskets in my wagon. Here, they are at home, and their magic is most powerful. Watch, and I will show you."

Fiona stepped close to the wall of skulls and began to whisper to them, touching them reverently. The air became flat and taut, as though before a thunderstorm. The hairs rose on Sylvia's arms. An eddy of wind blew through the arbor, and its origin could only be the skulls. She felt a sweat of fear crawl out on her skin. *Something's coming*, she thought, and then a sound erupted from the slack jaws of the skulls. At first, it was like a soft purring, but it soon rose to a deep drone like the sound of a thousand rough voices chanting in unison. When Sylvia thought she could bear no more of the swelling din, the bees burst into the arbor. They poured from the mouths and eye sockets of the skulls in a feverish tide, their plush bodies dark as soot, their wings like flakes of night. Fiona grasped her arm and pulled her into a crouch as the bees shot over their heads and through the archway to rise in black ribbons against the weak sunlight.

Fiona stood, brushed her skirt, and leaned down to help Sylvia stand. The girl cast a worried glance at the skulls, but they were quiet now. It was impossible that so many bees had slept in such small quarters.

Fiona anticipated her question. "The skulls are doorways. Soon they will run with honey, and we will sell it in the village. These are singular bees, Sylvia. They have traveled a great distance to arrive at our little outpost. The elixir they make will help us to reopen the Old Road, and Azimuth House will once again be a busy inn."

Sylvia tossed her head in frightened impatience. "Nothing you tell me makes sense. People don't build inns in the middle of the wilderness."

Fiona chuckled. "My dear, Wickeford Mills is not the first village to plant its roots here. Long ago, there was another, and fire took it. With no travelers to look after, my family left this place."

"Well, I don't see how honey is going to help open an inn. Those bees will starve. No flowers are blooming yet."

"Indeed? Look there."

Fiona drew her to the end of the arbor, and together they bent to peek through a gap in the vines. As far as their eyes could see, tiny blue and white flowers carpeted the forest. The bees foraged among them. Sylvia looked at Fiona in amazement.

"They will not starve, Sylvia. They seek more than pollen, and we will feed them." Fiona straightened and dusted her palms together in a business-like manner. "Enough questions for now. It is time to take up your duties and make the house ready for guests, for we shall have a parlor full before nightfall."

Sylvia followed her out of the arbor. Her mind waltzed with each of Fiona's revelations and exhausted itself without arriving at any meaning. As they approached the house, she glanced over her shoulder at the winter-stunned arbor. It was alight with tender green leaves and curling shoots.

3.

"How lovely everything is," Maeve exclaimed as she performed a solo twirling dance over the scrubbed stones of the entry hall. "It is as if we had never left."

From her knees in front of the massive hearth, Sylvia watched the tiny woman dip and flutter about the hall. Maeve's white, gossamer skirts riffled over the stones as though she were floating, and she swooped so near the polished table and its gleaming silver candlesticks that Sylvia feared a collision. She returned her attention to the wood she was laying in the fireplace, and completed the construction with precision. She stood and wiped her hands on her skirt in satisfaction. A well-laid fire was an economical one.

Maeve skipped over to her. "Dear Sylvia! How tired you must be. How many rooms have you done?"

"Only the hall, the parlor, and the dining room."

"Only! Oh, your poor hands." Maeve snatched them up in her diminutive ones. She raked the hall with a stern gaze. "Has no one helped you?"

A sigh, a giggle, and a swirl of warm air answered her. Sylvia watched the shadow of a young girl flit across the clean wainscoting. It vanished down the corridor to the kitchen. All day, the shades of Azimuth House had brushed past her with shy looks, sweeping away the dust and cobwebs with their vaporous hands, or blowing the leafy debris along the floors and out the open door in happy gusts. They were not strong enough to be of much help with the heavy scrubbing and polishing, although the older man among them had popped up the chimneys and cleaned them with brief, vigorous force.

Sylvia pulled her hands back under her apron. There was something in Maeve's touch, however kindly, that disturbed her.

"I've had a great deal of help, but I don't know how you'll ever get anyone else from the village to work here."

Maeve laughed and whirled away, her arms curved gracefully around empty air. "Sylvia, you do tease. I know very well that you have the sight, and cannot be shocked or frightened by what you find here. Why else would Fiona have invited you?"

"But she didn't - "

"Oh, I hear the wagon! Nathan has come back."

Maeve flew to the great door and wrenched it open. Sylvia followed, and they stood together in the doorway, watching as the black wagon bumped along the forest road and onto the weedy carriage drive. Nathan saw them and lifted his hat in salute. Beside him on the plank seat sat a small, pale figure, cloaked and curled into itself as though cold. A harsh cough shook it, and its hood slipped back to reveal long, white-blonde hair. Sylvia caught her breath. Lucy! Maeve stepped out, waving back at Nathan.

"Drive around to the west wing entrance," she called. She turned to Sylvia and said, "I must go. There will be guests at supper tonight, and much to do before then."

Maeve lifted her skirts and dashed after the empty wagon. From somewhere in the house behind her, Sylvia heard a door slam and the rush of feet along the kitchen corridor. She closed the door and turned toward the hall. The late afternoon light tumbled through the half-moon transom and cast an immense spider's web of shadow on the floor. The ghostly residents stood together amid its dark strands. She read sadness in their bloodless, earnest faces.

"What guests are they expecting?" she asked. She did not expect a reply, but stout, aproned Cook glided away toward the kitchen with a meaningful backward glance. Sylvia followed.

Cook led the way past the library and down the wide, shallow steps to the draughty corridor leading to the pantries and kitchen. The corridor ran perpendicular to the entry hall, lined with windows that looked out on the ruined kitchen gardens and a lawn reclaimed by the woods. A door led onto a stone-paved terrace, now furred with moss and spangled with violets. Cook passed through the unopened door and melted into the dusk. Sylvia struggled with the stiff bolt and latch, dragging the heavy door open on protesting hinges. From the terrace, she peered around the projecting wall of the west wing and saw the Dark sisters gathered around the wagon. Nathan had climbed down and begun rolling back the canvas covering the bed. The women crowded close, each reaching into the wagon to touch whatever lay there. Their voices carried clearly on the cool air.

"Which one? This? No. This?" Maeve rummaged in the wagon, her voice eager.

Maura glanced up at Lucy, shivering on the driver's seat. "Hurry. She suffers."

Fiona, patient in the background, pointed. "There, that is the one. Nathan, please bring this one first." She walked to the front of the wagon and reached up a hand to Lucy. "Come, child. Come with us. All is well."

Lucy climbed down from her seat, and Fiona enfolded the girl in her own red cloak. Together, they went into the house. Nathan pulled something from the bed of the wagon and hefted it in his arms. When he turned to follow Fiona, Sylvia saw that he carried a limp canvas bundle tied with waxed twine. She recognized it as Moss's work, and as the realization came to her that the bundle was a body, a hank of pale hair tumbled free from the wrapping. She put a hand to her mouth to stifle her gasp of horror. Maura paused, looking toward her, and Sylvia flattened herself against the cold stone. When they had all gone inside, she crept from the terrace and along the wall toward the wagon. She had to see what was in it.

The door to the west wing stood open, but she could hear no voices. She took a deep breath and pushed away from the wall, scurrying in a half-crouch to the side of the wagon. There, she knelt by the wheel until she was sure no one had seen her. She duck-walked to the open back of the bed and raised her head high enough to peek in. A cloudy eye stared back, and she gave a little shriek and dropped to her hands and knees. She glanced toward the door, but it seemed no one had heard her. She stood on shaky legs and forced herself to look into the wagon bed. A dozen wrapped bodies lay there, trussed in their canvas shrouds like India rugs. The eye she had seen belonged to Charlie Finchwhistle. His shroud had come undone, and his waxen face looked blue in the evening light. Sylvia could not remove her gaze from it. She stood as though rooted beside the wagon. When a long, cold hand clasped her shoulder, she started so violently that her teeth clacked together. Her knees turned to water and the ground rushed toward her, but strong arms caught her up. She was dimly aware of floating toward the house, her head pillowed on something that felt like granite sheathed in rough wool. She opened her eyes and saw above her the sturdy jut of Nathan's chin with its subtle cleft. She was caught, as surely as were the helpless dead, and she surrendered to oblivion.

The ticking of clocks and the muttering of a dwindling fire made a lullaby of homey comfort in the little parlor. Sylvia opened her eyes and looked into the red coals of the fire. She lay on a low green divan among a wealth of brightly patterned pillows. A velvet throw pressed her into the silky upholstery with its luxurious weight of plum fringe and dangling brass baubles. She rolled to her side and looked over the fat edge of the divan for her shoes. An immense wolf lay on the floor, its brindled hide stretched flat and its mouth frozen in a perpetual snarl. Its tawny glass eyes glared back at her. She moaned and flopped onto her back.

"You're awake! Oh, Syl, I'm so glad to see you." Lucy flew from her nest in the leather wing chair and knelt by the divan. Her hands crept near to Sylvia's, but she did not touch her friend. "Do you feel well? There's mulled wine in the jug on the table. I can get you some."

Sylvia struggled to a seated position among the pillows and swung her stocking feet to the floor. She was careful not to put her toes on the wolf skin rug.

"I don't want any wine. Lucy, what are you doing here? I saw -" She swallowed the lump in her throat. "I saw your body. I saw all of the bodies, in the wagon."

"I know, Syl. That tall man brought us all here. Oh, the town's in a state. You won't believe it."

"Tell me."

Lucy glanced about as though fearful of listeners. "I'm supposed to tell them when you wake up. I don't want to get in trouble."

Sylvia reached out and grasped the girl by her thin shoulders. "Lucy, you tell me right now. What happened in town?"

"Syl! You're touching me. Don't it make your bones ache?"

It did not. She let go of Lucy and studied her in the ruddy glow of the dying fire. Lucy seemed pinker. A healthy flush touched her cheeks and lips, and her eyes were bright. Most significantly, her cough was absent.

"What's happened to you?" Sylvia whispered.

Lucy grinned. "That's the best part. One of the ladies, her name was Maura, she took away my sickness. I was scared, and I don't remember how it happened, but I'm well now." Lucy's smile faded. "They talked about us traveling somewhere, all of us...from town. I don't want to go, Syl."

Sylvia stroked Lucy's pale hair. "Don't worry. I won't let anything happen to you. Now tell me about Nathan - the tall man."

Lucy climbed onto the divan beside her and curled up in the pillows.

"Well, he came this morning and went right on through town without a nod or a word to anyone. Old Moss saw him turn up toward the cemetery, and he followed him. Pretty soon, Moss came back hollering that the stranger was poking around the graves, and a bunch of men went up there to see. They was gone a long time, and when they came back they was all white as wax. The graves was all torn up, and some of the dead missing. Moss was furious. He tried to say the tall man done it, but there was no way he could have in just that little bit of time."

Lucy paused and tilted her head as though listening. Satisfied that she had heard nothing, she went on.

"That man, Nathan, he's scarier than my Gran's bogey stories. He came back into town and started going from door to door. He never spoke a word the whole time, just handed a black calling card to each person he met. I couldn't see the writing on the cards; I didn't get too close. Whatever was on them, it gave the people a turn. They'd take him on around to the root cellars, and he'd come out carrying the dead ones. He put them in his wagon and drove on, and no one tried to stop him. My own Ma handed me over, and I had to go." Lucy leaned close to her. "He can see me, like you can. He handed me up to the driver's seat, but he never said nothing to me the whole way here."

Sylvia bent forward and wriggled her feet into her boots, lacing them with quick fingers. She crossed the room to the tall, narrow window that looked out onto the carriage drive at the front of the house. A heavy drape hung across it, and she stepped behind it to wrestle with the latch. It was stiff, but rose with steady pressure, and she swung the window open. She turned to Lucy.

"We have to get out of here. I don't know what they want with all the dead folks, but it's not right. Come on, it's only a few feet to the ground from here." She dragged a chair over to the window and stepped from it to the wide stone sill.

"No, Syl! If you run away, I'll get in trouble."

Sylvia scraped her loose hair into a horsetail that she twisted into a knot. "Don't be a baby, Lucy. We'll go together." She held out her hand toward Lucy, who had cringed into the pillows until nearly hidden. "Hurry! It's only a few miles to town, and we can hide in the woods if they look for us."

Lucy shook her head, her eyes huge and welling with tears. "I can't, Syl. I can't leave here."

Sylvia crouched on the windowsill and looked down into the overgrown shrubbery. She grasped the hem of her gown and tore the fabric into two long flaps, freeing her legs for running.

"I'm going, Lucy. So help me, I'll leave without you if you don't get moving."

Lucy sobbed and clutched the pillows. "I told you, I can't leave. I - " She broke off, listening, then leaped from the divan. "Someone's coming. Run!"

Sylvia stood and let the drape fall across her, hiding her from view. The door opened and she heard Maura's hoarse voice. "Well, my dear, how is our patient?"

Lucy mumbled, "She woke and went to her room."

Maura's feet scuffed across the floor, slow and limping. "Why didn't you come to tell me she awoke, Lucy? Fiona wanted her." The halting tread grew closer to the window. "I feel a draught. This old house is cold."

A tinkle of breaking glass cracked the tense quiet in the room. Lucy cried out.

"Oh, I'm sorry. I'm not used to being able to move things."

"It's quite alright, my child. It's only a goblet." Maura moved toward Lucy. "Come. They need us in the preparation chamber."

A single inhuman shriek rent the air and strangled to silence. Maura gasped.

"Hurry, girl. They have begun, and she wakes."

The woman's dragging step accelerated, and soon the room was quiet. Sylvia peeked around the drape at the empty parlor. Behind her, the open window beckoned, and she glanced out at the waiting woods. Curiosity tugged her toward the door to the corridor. She wavered on the windowsill, but another hellish screech decided her. She hopped down to the floor and sprinted to the door. As she passed the wolf skin rug, she thought she heard it growl, but the escalating sounds of agony from somewhere down the corridor claimed all her attention.

The room was a sub-chamber at the end of the wing, shut away behind ironbound doors. One of those doors stood ajar, and the terrible howls erupted from the gap and clawed their way up the raw granite slabs of a short staircase hewn from the earth on which it stood. Sylvia crept on trembling legs down the stair and stood transfixed at the open door. Inside, the whitewashed walls and ceiling gave back the waves of light from the fire roaring in the hearth. They echoed, too, with the screams and moans of the thing writhing on the bare plank table in the center of the room.

Sylvia recognized the corpse as the blackened and twisted remains of Ava Smith. It lay on its back on the smooth pine planks, its jaw wide, its arms and hands shriveled to its breast, as cold and dead a thing as could be. Out of that wreckage, Fiona Dark dragged something by a shining thread, and it thrashed and shrieked as it came. It glistened wetly and tore free of the charred body with painful, rending sounds. It smoked in the warm room like a block of river ice. Fluid in form, it grew more solid as Fiona wrestled it from the horrific shell of the cadaver, and Sylvia's stomach clenched as she watched Ava's delicate features emerge. Ava's eyes were wide and wild, and her mouth opened in a long despairing wail as the pale substance of her arms and torso pulled away from the fragile, crumbling corpse on the table. A long, grey caul tethered her head to the bald, scorched skull. As Fiona tugged her forward, it sloughed away to release her golden hair with a series of electric snaps. Ava screamed as though flayed.

"Help me, sister," Fiona panted, and Maeve rushed to the table bearing a heavy wooden mallet.

With a mighty swing, she brought down the mallet on the corpse's head, crushing it. She gave a lady-like grunt of effort and swung again, smashing the ribs. The shining, naked thing that was Ava turned on Maeve with a snarl and sprang free from the corpse. Like a cat, it landed in a crouch. The firelight flickered over its damp, smoking skin, and it howled, scuttling to a shadowed corner where it curled against the wall and pulled its hair over its face.

Maura shuffled toward it. Without hesitation, she flung herself down and embraced the creature, and the two of them twisted and wailed in unison. Soon the cries were only Maura's, and those grew quieter until they were soft moans. Maeve hastened to her twin's side, and Fiona, bearing a crisp sheet, approached the nude, white form that lay exhausted in the corner.

Sylvia had seen enough. She stumbled up the stone stair and ran back along the corridor to the little parlor with the wolf rug. It took her only a minute to scramble onto the windowsill and leap. She cleared the shrubs, but the trailing flaps of her skirt caught on the twiggy branches and she fell, rolling and cursing, onto the hard ground. She tore her stockings and scraped her knees; and her elbow struck the stony ground, sending numbing tingles shooting to her fingertips. She rolled to her knees, cradling the injured arm, and staggered upright. Her hair had tumbled down around her in a dark torrent. Tears streaked her face, but she was unaware of them. She looked toward the woods where the night was rising from the roots. It would soon be too dark to make her way. With a groan for her burning injuries, she limped toward the forest track the Darks called the Old Road.

4.

It was dark under the trees, and cold. Fog slithered about their feet, still tender in the twilight, but Sylvia knew it would expand into a smothering cloud as the night drew on. The Old Road was wet and soft under her boots, and the damp breeze chilled her legs where her skirt hung in tatters. She walked briskly with her head down, rubbing at her aching elbow. Once she gained the High Road, she hoped to be able to flag a passing wagon. At any rate, she would be no more than five miles from town. Her mind raced over what she had seen at Azimuth House. Was it witchery? She felt a stab of guilt about leaving Lucy behind. When she got back to town, she would tell the people what she had seen. They would come for their dead, and she could free Lucy.

Lost in her thoughts, she approached the High Road and almost stumbled upon Nathan. He bent toward the earth like a questing hound, his great black horse nuzzling his shoulder. She stepped into the trees, her heart pounding, and watched. In her panic, she had assumed he was searching for her, but she now saw that he was tracking something else. He reached forward and pressed his slender fingers into the soft soil, tracing some shape there. A long rifle rested across his knee and gleamed dully in the fading light. Sylvia saw that he was outfitted for hunting in black breeches and tall, soft boots. He had exchanged his greatcoat for a close-fitting vest over a wool shirt. The coachman's hat was gone, and his dark hair hung loose. He looked sleek and quick, and Sylvia held her breath as he stood and scanned the woods. His gaze swept over her hiding place and paused for one heart-stopping second before he turned and swung himself into the saddle. The big horse danced, and then they were leaping for the High Road in a clatter of iron on stone.

She pushed away from the sheltering oaks and crept to the mouth of the Old Road. She crouched behind one of the slumped gateposts there, peering through the laurel and winter-flattened fern. Nathan had ridden toward town, and she saw his lanky silhouette against the indigo and lemon sky at the crest of the hill. He sat there, unmoving, and she could not tell if he looked ahead or back toward where she hid. A cold star flared above him, and night arrived. The last ember of sunset guttered out. Nathan vanished, black on black, and Sylvia strained her ears to hear if he rode on. For an eternal minute, there was only the sound of the wind walking through the pines, creaking across the greening boughs of the oaks, and then she heard the hushed thud of hooves. He was coming back, and keeping to the thick mat of moss and pine needles along the verge of the road. She stifled an exclamation of frustration and alarm. She could not get past him. If she took to the road, he would run her down in an instant. She looked into the woods. The spare thread of a deer path glimmered where the ground mist slipped along it.

Biting her lip against the ache in her stiff, bruised joints, Sylvia stood and ran. Across the Old Road, lit by a brief haze of moonlight, and through the nearly invisible gap in the undergrowth, she darted with all the speed she could muster. Branches whipped at her, and she stumbled over the roots and rocks, but kept her feet and ran along the little trail as though the Devil himself were after her. Behind her, she heard Nathan's horse thunder onto the road, and imagined sparks flying from its massive shoes as it stretched into a gallop. She turned off the deer path and battered her way deeper into the woods, where the trees grew close enough to clasp one another's roots, and slabs of stone slept under blankets of lichen and slippery moss. The moonlight fell in narrow beams through the thick web of branches and ignited the fog that swirled over the forest floor into a glowing pool of witchlight.

Sylvia pelted over the treacherous ground with no regard for the danger, her breath whistling, until her foot twisted under her in a slick of wet leaves and loose stone. She sprawled her length onto a gnarled lap of roots, bruising her ribs and opening the scrapes on her knees and palms. The air burst from her lungs, and she rolled into a ball and rocked against the rough trunk of the oak, whimpering and clutching her wounded knees. Blood smeared her fingers with hot stickiness.

"Oh, Mama, I should have listened to you," she moaned.

A guttural chuckle that slid deeper into a growl answered her. Her pain shrank to a minor inconvenience, and she sat up and pressed her back to the tree, listening. The growl seemed to come from everywhere, an almost inaudible rumble that resonated in her chest. She heard breathing, too, a measured panting. It circled her, coming close then dancing away. She forced herself to her feet and stared into the dark woods. The grey, slouching shadow of a wolf flickered through the trees. Terror blossomed inside of her as it moved close enough for her to take its measure. It was no natural creature. Big and rangy, it gazed back at her for the space of a heartbeat, its eyes winking with malevolent, un-wolfish mirth before it vanished in the foggy dazzle. It was toying with her.

Somewhere behind her, she could hear the low roar of the Wicke. It was near, and if she could reach it, she might be able to hide in the willow caves, deep under the root-laced banks. She hobbled a few steps away from the tree, her knees and ankles protesting. The sound of snapping branches spurred her into a graceless lope, and she careened through the woods, colliding with the trees and staggering over the rough ground. Always close behind her she heard the harsh panting, and a few times, the low, growling laugh. Hugging her aching ribs, she burst through a thicket of hazels onto the grassy ribbon of a forgotten fishermen's trail, and saw the Wicke speeding away under the smoky moon like a highway of mercury. Momentum propelled her down its bank and onto a short spit of silt and stone, where she fell to her knees. She looked out over the frigid swirl of the river. In summer, this would be a beach of smooth stones, but the snowmelt had swollen the shallows into a swift flood that scoured the banks and plunged angrily around her rocky little peninsula. She could run no further, and she stood and turned to face her pursuer.

"Sylvia." The voice percolated out of the undergrowth, thick and clotted with an animal snarl, pushed from a throat unfit for human speech.

The hazels rustled, and a shape pressed forward, hunched and long-limbed. It growled and shook itself, and slowly stood upright. It panted and snuffed the air. When it stepped into the moonlight, Sylvia screamed. Jasper Coltsfoot stood naked on the riverbank, his eyes shining like silver dollars. He stooped with his head thrust forward, his big shoulders drawn up and back into a muscular hump, and his mousy hair bristled into a shaggy mane across it. His bony face was a mask of long-jawed savagery, and the teeth crowding his mouth were sharp. He pointed at her with a misshapen finger, the nail grown into a black, curved claw.

"I smell your blood, Sylvia," he said, his words distinct but gruff. "I've come to claim my bride."

"Stay away from me!" She bent and picked up a rounded stone the size of a duck's egg.

Jasper laughed. "Sweet Sylvia. I don't want to hurt you." He sniffed again, and the growl rose in the back of his throat. He licked his lips. "I only want a husband's due."

He took a step forward. Sylvia drew back her arm and threw the stone. It struck him on the chest, but he merely grunted and kicked it away. In a single bound, he landed in front of her and reached out his horrible hand to clutch the front of her gown. He yanked her to him and buried his nose in her hair.

"Mine," he snarled against her scalp.

He pressed his nakedness against her, and Sylvia's flesh cringed away from his heat. He smelled wild and dirty, his breath fetid. He ran his long, hot tongue along her neck and tore at the remains of her skirt with his free hand.

"Let me go," she whimpered. She struggled in his grasp, gagging at his stench.

"Fight all you like, little morsel," he said into her ear. He clutched her bodice in both hands and lowered his leering face to hers. "You're good and caught."

"No!"

She shoved at him with all her failing strength, and the blue fabric of her dress tore away. Freed, she staggered backward into the biting cold of the river. Jasper looked down uncomprehendingly at the rag in his claws, then slung it aside and voiced a howl of lust and rage. He gathered himself to leap at Sylvia, who splashed away from him, thigh deep in the sweeping current.

A shot rang out, and Jasper howled again, this time in agony as the lead ball smashed into his hip. He fell on his side in the churning water, his skin rippling and changing. Sylvia cried out and lost her footing as Nathan leaped lightly onto the sandbar. The tall man unsheathed a shining blade from his own hip and waded into the river after the injured wolf. Sylvia flailed against the icy current, swallowing a mouthful of it.

"Nathan," she sputtered. Her heavy hair dragged her under, and her cold limbs refused to push her upward. The moon floated above her, fixed on the racing surface of the water like a beacon, but she could only watch it recede as she sank to the pebbled riverbed.

A strong hand grasped her arm and hauled her into the night air. She coughed and retched, her lungs burning, as she clung to Nathan's arms. The moon on her bare shoulders felt like frost. She looked wildly around for Jasper.

"Where is he?"

Nathan nodded toward the forest. Jasper was gone, and only his blood on the stones of the riverbank told Sylvia that she had not dreamed the encounter. She bent forward, shuddering, and coughed until her knees buckled. Her thin chemise was like a glaze of ice on her skin. Nathan swung her up into his arms and waded to shore. He held her limp body against him while he unbuckled a rolled cloak from behind his saddle, then swaddled her in it and eased her to the ground. From a saddlebag, he produced a silver flask. He knelt and held it to her lips, and Sylvia made an effort to open them and swallow some of the liquid. It felt like hellfire flowing through her veins. Nathan tipped another swallow down her throat, and she felt her voice return.

"I'm sorry," she said. Her teeth chattered, and her voice was a hoarse whisper. "It's my fault he got away."

Nathan shrugged and stood to replace the flask in his saddlebag. His rifle lay in the grass, and he bent to retrieve it. He took a powder horn from his saddle, a ball from his vest pocket, and reloaded, ramming the shot home with practiced efficiency. When he turned back to Sylvia, she had composed herself enough to ask the question she most needed answered.

"Nathan, did you see - " She paused to find the words. Nathan leaned the rifle against a tree and squatted in front of her, his eyes cool and serious. "Did you see Jasper change? Did you see him become a beast?"

Nathan nodded.

Sylvia swallowed the raw fire in her throat. "Something's been killing folks and livestock all winter. Not in town, but out on the farms. At first, when it only took sheep, people said it was a wolf. Later, they said it was a spirit from the woods. It was Jasper, wasn't it?"

Her lip trembled. The warmth of the whiskey in her blood dimmed. Suddenly, she felt very young and fragile.

Nathan watched her from behind the wet tangle of his hair. He held up one long hand as though to show her it was empty, reached out, and touched her face. He caught a tear on his fingertips and brought it to his heart where it wicked into the black wool of his shirt. Sylvia stared at the tiny damp spot, and her own heart slowed and fluttered. She lifted her eyes to his, wondering how she had not noticed before that he was handsome.

A ragged howl from the woods shattered the moment. Nathan uncoiled like a snake and took one long stride toward his rifle before the wolf erupted from the underbrush. It leaped onto the back of Nathan's horse, slashing at it with claws and teeth. The horse reared screaming, the wolf slid from its back, and Nathan fell under the platter-sized hooves. Sylvia shrieked, but he rolled smoothly away as the mighty iron shoes came down with a sound like cannon fire, and the horse fled snorting and kicking along the trail. The wolf bounded toward the fallen man, stretching in mid-leap into a shaggy man-shape. It crashed into Nathan as he tried to regain his feet, and the two went down wrestling, Jasper snarling and laughing as he rolled atop his thrashing prey.

"I'll crack your bones, dead man," Jasper panted, snapping his long sharp teeth in Nathan's face. He twisted Nathan's arm under him, attempting to tear it from him. He threw back his head and howled as the change took him over.

Nathan struggled in silence. Sylvia could read no sign of pain in his face, but she wailed when she heard the rending of his shoulder. She watched the wolf burst from Jasper's flesh and shake its fur, and found herself darting toward Nathan's rifle before she had even fully formed the intent. The beast saw the movement and swung its huge head toward her, its lips writhing back from yellow fangs. Nathan's undamaged arm wriggled free and came up in a flashing arc, the hunting blade in his hand. The wolf tumbled backward with a surprised yelp. Nathan rolled to his feet and crouched in a fighting stance, his dislocated arm hanging useless at his side. He turned the injured shoulder away from the circling wolf and held the knife with a light, sure grip in his good hand. Sylvia grappled with the heavy long rifle, using both thumbs to cock it, and raised it trembling to her shoulder.

"Get away from him," she rasped in her cracked voice.

The wolf glanced at her, calculating. She saw Jasper's cruel humor in its eyes as she let out her breath to steady her aim. With a snarl, the beast sprang at Nathan. The rifle roared, rising in the air as if jerked away by an unseen hand. The recoil deadened Sylvia's shoulder and knocked her into the hazels. Frantic, she slapped aside the budding twigs, clambering out to see Nathan standing over the body of the wolf. The creature's side heaved and its huge paws twitched once, before Nathan bent over it and drew the blade across its throat.

Sylvia ran to him. "You're hurt. We've got to bind up that arm."

Her hands fluttered around his crooked shoulder without touching him, unsure how to help. Nathan caught both of her hands in his good one and held them until she was still.

"What can I do?" she asked. "Your shoulder, it's torn out of place. If we don't find a way to fix it - " She thought about Nathan without the use of his arm, crippled while trying to save her, and an icy fist formed in the pit of her stomach.

He released her and swept the hair back from his face. He set his jaw, wrapped his long fingers around the injured shoulder, and gave it a tremendous wrench. There was a sickening, popping sound as it grated back into the socket. Nathan drew in a hissing breath. He rotated the shoulder and raised his hand, flexing it into a fist. For the first time, Sylvia saw him smile, but she could take no pleasure in the dimples that formed in his lean face. Exhaustion mixed with weary horror overcame her.

"Nathan, what are you?" she asked. "Am I surrounded by monsters?"

The smile vanished as though she'd slapped it from his face. He made an oddly formal little bow and stepped away from her to gather up the fallen rifle and the cloak. Sylvia's heart broke a little.

"I'm sorry. I didn't mean what I said." She followed him, speaking to his long, straight back. "I'm so tired, I don't know what I'm saying."

He turned to her, his eyes unreadable. He handed her the cloak and watched her wrap it around herself. He slipped his fingers under the collar of his shirt and tugged out a slender, silver whistle strung on waxed twine. Raising it to his lips, he blew a high, thin skirl of music. An answering trumpet sounded from further down the trail, the shrill whinny of a horse, and then hoof beats shivered the air. The big horse had not run far. It trotted to Nathan and laid its head on his shoulder, and he stroked the thick neck before running his hands over its body and legs. When he was satisfied that the animal had sustained no grievous harm, he rummaged in his saddlebags and found a flint and a small glass jar. He turned to Sylvia and held up the flint, then pointed to the hazel thicket.

"Fire?" she asked. "Can't we just go, please?"

For answer, Nathan only held up the flint again. Sighing, she began to gather deadwood and dry leaves and to heap them in the narrow clearing by the trail. The damp cloak dragged after her like a shadow, and while it preserved her modesty, it did little to warm her. She threw down a second armful of kindling and blew into her numb hands as she watched Nathan. He had unsaddled the horse and was applying some salve from the little jar to its scratches. The black, glossy hide shivered under his gentle touch, and the horse puffed a soft whicker at him. Even with her senses half deadened by her dunking in the river, Sylvia could smell the summery, floral scent of honey and a pungency of aromatic herbs. Somehow, it made her feel homesick and hollow, and she dropped to the grass beside the tumble of firewood and sobbed.

Through the wet drape of her hair, she saw first Nathan's boots and then his knees as he crouched beside her, and she flung herself into his arms, rocking him back on his heels. He was as cold and wet as she was, and there was no softness in him, but his long fingers cradled her head and stroked her back. She wept on his shoulder, crying out all the horror of Jasper's attack, the humiliation of having his hands on her, and the longing of a young girl for the familiar, if mundane, surroundings of home.

When the storm of emotion passed, she felt an unaccustomed shyness creep over her. She had clasped Nathan to her, encircling his thin ribs in such a fervent embrace that she had forced him into a seated position. Now she found herself half-reclining across his lap, her head thrust under his chin, her cloak crumpled around her hips. She sat up and dragged the cloak over her white shoulders, unable to look Nathan in the eye.

"I'm very sorry. I didn't mean to be such a crybaby, or to ... to grab you like that. You must think I'm shameless." Her cheeks burned, and she was distantly amazed that she could still blush after everything that had happened to her.

Nathan plucked a tendril of hair from in front of her face and tucked it behind her ear. He knelt in front of the pile of kindling and struck fire from the flint. Sweet-smelling smoke curled up from the dry leaves and a flame licked out with a crackle. Soon, the fire filled the quiet with its whispery roar. Sylvia held the cloak out from her body like wings so the delicious heat could bake her. Nathan fetched his saddle and laid it on the ground beside her. Kneeling by it, he began to unbutton his quilted vest. She stiffened and swept the cloak tight about her so quickly that sparks flew upward into the darkness in a red plume.

"What are you doing?" Her tone was curt.

Nathan's fingers grew still, and he looked at her with mild reproach. He patted the smooth, oiled leather of the saddle, then his vest. When Sylvia only stared at him in fearful outrage, he shook his head and freed the final button. He shrugged out of the vest and folded it into a cushion that he placed on the saddle. He pointed to it, then to Sylvia, and drew two fingers down over his eyes, closing them.

She felt her face flush again as tears prickled her swollen eyes. He had made her a pillow. She was so tired she thought she might fall onto it as though it were the finest goose down.

"Oh. Thank you. Will we camp here all night?"

Nathan shook his head. He pulled the knife from its sheath on his hip and pointed to the body of the wolf that lay outside the comfort of the firelight.

Sylvia did not think she could bear to watch him skin the beast.

"I'll just lie down for a little while," she said.

Nathan nodded and stood over her until she had settled and closed her eyes. When she heard him leave the fireside, she turned her face to the woods so she would not see what he did in the flickering moon haze.

The fattening moon illuminated the slate roof tiles of Azimuth House with silver streaks and washes. Observing it from beneath heavy eyelids as they drew nearer, Sylvia thought the house, in this fickle light, looked like the ones in the etchings that hung on the walls of Dr. Finchwhistle's office. Her head nodded gently with the rhythm of the horse's gait, her cheek brushing against the rough fabric of Nathan's shirt. His arms were snug around her and she sat across his hard thighs, one of her legs hooked over the saddle horn. She could not remember mounting the horse, or the ride back along the river. She had woken sometime after they turned onto the Old Road, and had allowed herself to rock in a pleasant daze for the rest of the journey. The woods threw a mesmerizing patina of shadow over them. She turned her nose into Nathan's shoulder, inhaling the smoky, herbal smell of him. It was good to drift this way, sheltered in the midst of the wild night, and yet part of it.

The door of Azimuth House flew open and lanterns appeared to bob by themselves in the interior darkness before their bearers stepped into the moonlight. The Dark sisters gathered on the carriage drive, and Nathan turned the horse toward them.

"Oh, thank goodness, you've found her! We've been a flock of worried old hens." Maeve darted forward and gazed up at Nathan and Sylvia.

Maura limped to Nathan's stirrup and appraised Sylvia. "She looks a fright. Had a lovely stroll in the woods, I expect. We'd best get her to bed." Maura's eyes fell on the rolled pelt tied behind the saddle, and she stiffened. "Fiona! Nathan got the bastard!"

Nathan yanked at the leather ties so that the pelt sprang loose and tumbled to the ground. The women gathered around it, muttering.

"A big one. Some farm lad this time, I think?"

"There will be no more missing corpses."

"I am relieved it has been dispatched so speedily." Fiona nudged the wolf's head with her toe. "Maura, please ask George to take care of this. I want to see to Sylvia."

Nathan dismounted and helped her down. After the rhythmic swaying of the saddle, she found the solid earth dizzying. Maeve reached to steady her, and the cloak slipped from her shoulders. Her ruined gown hung in rags about her, and a colorful collection of bruises and scratches tattooed her skin. Maeve gasped.

"Sister! What's happened to her?"

Fiona's face was grim. "I suspect *that* happened to her." She pointed at the wolf pelt, then turned her attention to Nathan. "Did he rape her?"

Nathan's fist tightened on the saddle horn until the leather groaned. Sylvia put a hand on his arm.

"I can speak for myself. Jasper didn't get a chance to hurt me. Nathan shot him."

The forbidding look went out of Fiona's eyes, and she stroked Sylvia's hair. "Of course, child, forgive me. Come inside and have a hot bath, and some supper, too. Then it's bedtime for you. We'll have a long talk in the morning, hmm?"

Sylvia nodded. Bath, supper, bed. The words were like elixir to her, and her body yearned toward their promise. Fiona led her to the door, but Sylvia stopped under the leafing wisteria and looked over her shoulder at Nathan. He had turned away, leading the tired horse toward the stables.

"Wait. Nathan was hurt. We have to see to his wounds."

Fiona smiled and gave Sylvia's hand a squeeze. "Don't worry about Nathan. It isn't easy to harm him, you know. Come now. There is a cauldron of water heating on the kitchen fire, and Lucy can help you to scrub off some of the forest."

Whether because of the madness of the day, or despite it, Sylvia found that entering Azimuth House now felt like a homecoming. Her very bones were weary, her flesh a tender map of pain. The sweet-smelling candles and the warm sizzle of the fire in the entry hall hearth welcomed her, and Cook hovered in the soothing dimness, waiting to take charge of her.

A soft murmur of voices came from the parlor. The doors were open just wide enough for Sylvia to see figures moving about the room. Someone struck up a bawdy tune on the piano, and there was a brief spate of laughter before Maura's thin face appeared at the partially open door. She glanced at Sylvia and pushed the heavy, paneled door shut with a soft thud.

"Are those the guests you were expecting?" Sylvia asked.

Fiona paused before answering. "Yes. They will be with us until tomorrow night, and then they will travel on. If you feel well in the morning, I will introduce you. There is much you must learn if you stay here, Sylvia, but tonight rest is all that is required of you."

She beckoned Cook closer and pushed Sylvia gently toward the big woman.

"Go with Cook. When you've bathed and eaten, Maeve will give you a chamber in the east wing for tonight. Sleep well, my dear." Fiona gave her a distracted smile and glided away into the library, closing the door behind her.

Cook looked her up and down, clucking in dismay.

"My lands, Miss, you look like you've been through a mangle. Come with me, and we'll set you to rights."

Sylvia gaped at the change in the woman. Cook's voice was firm, and she looked solid and rosy. The generous slab of her arm had real weight and strength as she put it about Sylvia's waist and steered her toward the kitchen. She smelled of cinnamon and cloves.

"You can speak," Sylvia blurted. "And I can touch you. You weren't like this earlier today."

Cook chuckled. "Oh, well, it's been a long time since we here have had aught to do with the living. A body grows frail on shadows and cobwebs. It's good to have the family home again, I can tell you." She gave Sylvia a friendly squeeze. "Good to have your young self here, too."

Sylvia thought the gleam in Cook's eyes was a bit too avid for her light tone, but she had no time to ponder it. Lucy straightened from poking the kitchen fire and flew to meet her, the iron poker clattering to the stone floor. Cook clucked again, and hurried to put it in its place and polish away the soot from where it had fallen.

"Syl! They said you come back! I thought you left me here forever." Lucy danced around her. "Oh, look at you. Are you hurt bad? Look, I got a big pot of hot water for you, and there's a real bathtub."

She pointed to the bath pulled up near the fire. It looked like a hammered copper slipper, Sylvia thought, and she could not wait to get into it.

"Here you, Lucy," Cook barked. "Lend a hand."

Cook swung a huge kettle out of the fire and positioned it at the lip of the bath. Lucy skipped to help her tip it. Steaming water hissed into the cold copper vessel.

"All right, Miss. Off with them rags now, and climb in while it's good and hot."

Cook bustled about, finding soap and a brush on a long cane, and tossing herbs tied up in cheesecloth into the bath. A powerful scent of sage and lavender rose on the steam. She took down from a pantry shelf a squat crock that she handled with care. While Lucy helped Sylvia to strip off her ruined gown and chemise, Cook swirled a honey dipper in the crock and dripped a thick, sunny ribbon of it into the water. She closed the crock, swished the dipper in the bath, and licked her fingers. A blissful expression crossed her face.

"Delicious. Now, Miss, in you go, like a lamb in a stew."

Sylvia eased into the bath, hissing as the heat seized and kneaded her aching body. The aromatic water was a balm, and she moaned with pleasure as her shoulders sank beneath it.

Lucy laughed. "Dunk under, and I'll soap your hair."

The girls giggled and splashed. Everywhere the honey-laden water touched her, Sylvia felt soothed.

"Don't flood the whole kitchen," Cook scolded as the water dashed on the stones. "I've got your supper ready for you, Miss. Come out of there before you shrivel. Miss Maeve's left you a lovely dressing gown to wear."

If the west wing was a haunt of shadows, the east wing was a realm of light. The white paneled walls, the floor of pickled parquet in white and grey, and the lofty ceiling gleamed like polished bone. Hexagonal lanterns of wrought iron lace and blue glass hung from chains along the length of the wide central corridor. Racks of fluttering candles cast pools of pale golden radiance. The moon added its cool glow through the many windows that looked out on the carriage drive. Sylvia stepped into the placid luminosity, but Lucy hung back.

"Come on," Sylvia whispered. The quality of the light was that of clear water, and she felt reluctant to cause ripples in it.

Lucy shook her head. "This place isn't for me, Syl. I can't come in." The younger girl peered around the doorframe, her eyes wide and curious. "Gosh, ain't it beautiful, though? I wish I could have come here before ... you know. Before I died."

A chill walked over Sylvia. She could accept that Lucy was a spirit, but it was hateful to think of her as dead.

"Well, I have to find Maeve." She raised her arms and flapped the wide silk sleeves of the dressing gown she wore. "How do you like my finery?"

Lucy reached out and rubbed the jade silk between her fingers. "It's so pretty." Her face lit with a mischievous grin. "Give it a twirl, Syl."

Sylvia looked down at the gown. It cinched in her waist in a broad, laced band of chocolate damask encrusted with gold embroidery. Above this, her small breasts perched in a snug nest of heavy, green silk with wide lapels like those on a man's coat. The open V caused her some embarrassment, and she tugged at the fabric to no avail. The long, belled sleeves and the flowing skirt of the dressing gown were bejeweled with little bees picked out in gold. She whirled about, and the skirt flew out like the opening petals of a flower. Lucy laughed and clapped her hands, then gave a little cry of alarm and vanished. Sylvia was stopped mid-whirl by strong hands that caught her waist. She looked up, flushed and breathless, into Nathan's dark eyes.

"Oh! What are you doing here?" she stammered. She felt the heat mount in her cheeks, and wondered if she was doomed to blush whenever they met.

"Nathan was just leaving, Sylvia." Maeve glided toward them from a room at the end of the corridor. "I have a room all ready for you, my dear. You will sleep deeply tonight, I'm sure."

Maeve took her by the hand and made fluttering, shooing motions at Nathan. He stepped away from Sylvia, but his eyes followed her. When Maeve turned to lead her away, Nathan touched the tiny woman on the shoulder.

"Don't worry," Maeve said, patting his arm. "We'll wait until morning. I'll send for you."

Nathan gave a curt nod, swung on his heel, and stalked from the wing. Sylvia watched him over her shoulder as Maeve led her to an empty room.

"What was that about? He seemed worried."

"He's sweet on you, Sylvia. We thought he'd never fall in love, poor boy, and now that it's happened he finds he's not prepared." Maeve laughed. "Do you like your room?"

Maeve's casual declaration had rendered Sylvia insensible to her surroundings. Nathan loved her! A warm giddiness hummed along her nerves, as though she had drunk too much of Dr. Finchwhistle's hard cider. She wanted to question Maeve, to speak of Nathan until sleep took her, and she wanted to go quietly to bed and nurture the coal glowing in her heart. Maeve flitted about the room, drawing the gauzy white bed curtains and taking an equally gauzy nightdress from a drawer that released a scent of roses on the air.

"Shall I help you undress? No? Well, then I'll say goodnight, dear Sylvia."

Maeve laid the nightdress on the bed, where it floated on the white quilt like sea foam. She drifted from the room, and as the door closed behind her, Sylvia lifted the filmy garment to her nose, inhaling a bouquet of sunlight and roses. She thought of how she had fussed at having to dress in her Mama's good blue gown. She thought of how Jasper had torn the gown from her, and of the hot press of his naked body. She thought of how the cold moon had felt on her bare shoulders, and of the feel of Nathan's arms around her, and all these things seemed to form a kind of key that compelled an expectant lock inside her to open.

A long mirror stood in the corner of the room. Sylvia crossed to it and examined her face. It was a pale oval. Her skin was clear, her eyes grey and fringed with dark lashes. She bared her teeth. They were good teeth, strong and even. Her hair was a thick, walnut-glossy rope tied at the end with a green ribbon. She undid the bow and shook it free. Did Nathan like it? She thought of his hand cradling her head against his chest and caught her breath.

Her fingers hesitated, then began to undo the hooks of the dressing gown. In the luxurious light of the beeswax candles, she let it fall from her to pool on the floor in a hoarse, silken whisper. She knew she was thin and straight, but the tall young woman in the mirror shyly cupped small, perfect breasts. She laid a hand over her flat stomach, and touched a fingertip to each tender hipbone. She turned and appraised her reflection from all angles. Her legs were long and strong. Her back was a lean slide of smooth, white skin. Sylvia did not know or care if what she saw was beauty. She felt her body speaking in a new and intoxicating language. She raised the sheer nightdress over her head and let it tickle down over her. It was lovely, with its ribbons and little cap sleeves. Her hair was a sable river flowing over it. She climbed into the big white bed and blew out the candles. A new thought came to her in the warm dark. Spring was blossoming, and so would she.

5.

Dawn slipped through Sylvia's window like a satisfied cat, and stretched itself across the snowy field of her quilt. She lay against the plump pillows, letting the quiet clarity of it tease the curtain of her eyelashes for a moment, savoring the deep hush of the house. Outside, the woods seemed to hold its breath as it welcomed the first touch of rosy sunlight, and the song of an early wren unraveled the silence. She stretched and rolled from her bed, splashed her face at the washbasin, and took her brush with her to the window. The morning was glorious. Already, she could see the strange bees winging from the arbor to the violets that carpeted the forest floor.

She saw something else, too, a curious thing that she had not noticed before. Under the leafing eaves of the woods, flat in the loam and crosshatched with trembling sun-dapples, lay seven long, stone tablets. They looked like native granite, but they were of uniform size and width, each like a tabletop. Or a gravestone, Sylvia thought with a sudden chill, the kind that lay over a crypt. The brush stilled in its descent through her hair, and she stared at the stones with a mounting feeling of dread. They were scattered randomly across the violet-covered ground, and the delicate little flowers brushed their edges. The bees that were not foraging in the blossoms crawled across the grey faces of the stones as though seeking something.

A grinding sound drew her attention toward the kitchen terrace. Nathan walked along the garden path pushing a mounded barrow, its heavy load covered with a clean canvas tarp. The barrow's wooden wheel squeaked and scraped on its axle. Behind him strolled Fiona and Maura, deep in conversation. As the little parade passed through the shaggy ruin of the garden, Sylvia heard Fiona laugh. On they went, through the dilapidated garden gate and into the blue-and-white shimmer of the flowers, Nathan pushing the wobbly barrow with ease. When they reached the first stone they stopped, and Maura flapped her handkerchief at the bees on its surface, chasing them into lazy flight. Fiona drew back the canvas. Sylvia moaned low in her throat and bit her knuckle. The hairbrush fell from her hand with a clatter. The barrow was heaped with naked bodies as white as tallow, their limbs dangling over its sides.

She watched with a dispassionate sort of horror as the three of them worked together to wrangle a body from the cart, Nathan grasping it under the arms and each of the women taking a leg. With remarkable economy of effort, they swung the dead man over the stone and lowered him almost lovingly onto it. The women took some pains to arrange him so he lay on his back with his limbs straight. They smoothed his hair from his brow, then they stood and repeated the process with the bodies remaining in the barrow. Sylvia counted two women and a child. The trio then made their way back through the garden and disappeared into the west wing. Sylvia looked out on the dreadful tenants of the stones. Her joy at seeing Nathan had turned to ash. How could he be part of such frightful doings? As she gazed on the reclining dead, the bees began to settle on their bodies. Soon, the dark, seething insects had blanketed each one, and she could watch no more.

She turned from the window and returned to her bed, where she sat with her back against the tall pine headboard, her knees drawn up to her chin. Outside her window, she could hear the squeak of the barrow wheel as it again trundled through the garden. She thought about what she had seen, and about what she knew of Azimuth House. She was aware of a disharmony between her ability to accept the dead in the form of spirits, and her loathing of their abandoned shells. She did not yet understand the purpose of Azimuth House, but that it had everything to do with the dead was certain. She plucked at the neat white knots on the quilt. Never had she known such people as the Darks. They were steeped in some old magic, wound and wound about with fairy tale wonders and terrors. In this place, her strange ability was as commonplace as a woolen pot-grabber. It was good to fit somewhere, and that acceptance had changed her.

She would not run back to her life in the village like a frightened child, but she would find answers to her many questions. She hopped from the bed with renewed verve and ransacked the drawers of the tall dresser. She found undergarments and a plain workday dress of claret-colored cotton. They must have belonged to Fiona, for they fit her tolerably well. Her boots sat outside her door, cleaned and dried. She slipped them on and laced them, and set off for the kitchen.

"Well, Miss, I didn't expect to see you up and about so early. You look a sight better this morning, so you do."

Cook's hearty voice boomed in the depth of the copper pots and rang from the stones. She swept the floor vigorously with a birch broom, humming with tuneless aggression as she worked. Sylvia noted that this morning the aproned figure floated several inches above the offending floor, and that Cook's legs ended at the hem of her dress.

"What's happened to your feet?" she asked.

"Oh, it's faster this way, dearie. Have a seat at the table. I've got fried pies keeping warm for you, and good buttermilk."

Sylvia joined Lucy at the rough plank table.

Lucy grinned over the rim of her mug, and licked dark foam from her upper lip. She leaned across the table and whispered, "Miss Fiona's gonna show you the travelers today, Syl, and will you ever be surprised!"

"Here now, Nimble Lips, you're not to tell tales." Cook thumped a pewter plate to the board in front of Sylvia and followed it with a frothy cup of buttermilk.

Lucy set her mug aside and stuck out her tongue at Cook's turned back. Sylvia lifted the abandoned mug and looked into the dark, viscous contents. She sniffed it and pushed it away in disgust.

"Is that *blood*?"

Lucy looked sheepish. She thrust her small hands under her apron and looked at Sylvia from under pale brows.

"Well, it sort of is, but then it isn't. It ain't nothing bad, Syl, honest." She cast a beseeching gaze at Cook.

Back on her feet, Cook stumped to the end of the table and fixed both girls with a stern look.

"It's the special honey. Oh, all that those bees turn out is special, all right. But this is just for us, the resident spirits, as you might say. A peculiar vintage. It gives us substance, as you mentioned last night, Miss. Look here, we've our own hive."

She pulled Sylvia to the kitchen door, and through into the scraggly garden. There, on a tall post topped with an old birdhouse, hung five ancient skulls like the ones in the arbor. Bees prowled over them, vanishing into the eye sockets or strutting on their cracked domes, and the strange, red honey dripped from their jaws. The honey smelled sweet and wild, but there was a thread of salt and copper in its scent that made Sylvia gag.

Cook patted her shoulder with a callused hand. "It'll run all year, long as there's travelers. Oh, it's good to have me strength again, and be able to work as I should." Cook's face grew somber. "Don't you go tastin' it now, Miss. It's not for you lively ones. I'm sure I don't know what would happen to you."

She nodded gravely and whisked back into the kitchen. Sylvia wandered onto the sunny terrace and breathed in the vibrant smell of spring. A tender warmth rose from the garden and from the stones of the terrace, and the biting chill that had battened on the woods for so long was gone like a bad dream. The birds were busy with their nest building, and she listened to their trills and their rustling in the dry stalks of the old herb beds. Another sound droned on under the bird chatter - the mumbling growl of thousands of bees hard at their mysterious work.

A dull, thumping sound like a mallet striking wooden pegs started up near the stables and drew her attention. She could see George hammering away at something on the ground, but her interest in his doings was fleeting, for Nathan and Fiona emerged from the carriage house. At the sight of the tall coachman, Sylvia's heart began to beat with a heavy, measured shudder. He was so handsome in the morning sunlight, his hair tumbling over his collar and sparking blue like a raven's wing. He listened as Fiona spoke, his head cocked to the side as though considering something of great importance, and then he strode toward the house. His gaze flickered over Sylvia, but he made no sign of greeting nor slowed his pace. Her heart lurched almost to a stop, and a doomy feeling swept over her. She turned to go in, thinking she might catch him in one of the hallways.

Fiona called to her. "Sylvia! Wait, I'd like to talk with you."

She watched Fiona make her way through the garden, and felt a stir of impatience. The copper-haired woman stepped onto the terrace, plucking briars from her skirt.

"What a disaster the garden has become! I think we will soon have help in putting it right, though. Oh, Sylvia, you can't imagine how magical it was long ago, before we left. Everything, this entire place, was bright and beautiful. It will be again." Fiona smiled. "I have much to show you today."

Sylvia nodded. "I guess I'd best get a start on clearing away the dust and dirt."

"Oh, never mind about all that today." Fiona waved away her words. "I want to show you the soul of Azimuth House." She gripped Sylvia by her wrist, her expression earnest. "We need much more than a maid of all work here. We need a housekeeper who can oversee our unorthodox staff. A person who can manage the daily needs of this house, and who can keep secrets older than its stones. You are perfectly suited for such a position, I knew it the moment I saw you in the village. But you must understand what we do here and why. You must be able to accept it."

Fiona's eyes burned with an eldritch fire, and Sylvia felt a prickling of fear.

"I saw what you did in the woods this morning," she blurted. She thrust out her chin and pulled her wrist from Fiona's grasp. "Explain that, if you can. And tell me what you were doing yesterday in that little room, you and your sisters. I won't be party to devilry."

"Devilry? Oh, my dear, what do you think you saw?" Fiona looked amused.

"I saw you do something to poor Ava Smith. You snatched her soul. I saw, I saw..." Sylvia trailed off in confusion. She was not sure what she had seen. Angrily, she pointed toward the woods. "Why did you put those bodies in the forest? Why did you take them from the townsfolk in the first place? They should be decently buried."

"Do they frighten you, those bodies?" Fiona gave her a searching look. "You seem so at ease with the spirits, it never occurred to me that their empty flesh would repulse you."

"Nobody likes the idea of a corpse," Sylvia muttered, her gaze turned toward her shoes.

Fiona snorted laughter. "I suppose that might be true, in general. But here at Azimuth House, corpses are treated with the respect due to valued garments that have served their span. And sometimes, the spirits need help in doffing them, and more help in accepting that they exist still without their bodies. That is part of what we do here. Would you like to see Ava?"

Sylvia raised her eyes to Fiona's in astonishment. "You mean she's still here?"

"Indeed. She and others you will know. Come. It is time you met our guests."

A hum of voices filtered from the dining room. As they walked briskly past the open doors, Sylvia saw Charlie Finchwhistle, old Mrs. Greenbriar who had died of the fever, and Lawrence Ridenour who had fallen through the ice of the Wicke and drowned. They gathered around a punchbowl on the long, gleaming table. Lawrence ladled the red, syrupy "special" honey into cups for the others. Charlie looked up as they passed and waved at Sylvia. Numbly, she waggled her fingers at him.

Fiona pushed open the door of the parlor. The room faced north and held a faultless light softened by a layer of pale shadow that hung on the air like smoke. A low fire rustled on the hearth. A woman sat on the cranberry striped settee and gazed into the glow of the coals. Her hair was a cascade of clear golden waves that Sylvia recognized. She did not turn her head as they entered, but spoke as though she had risen to welcome them.

"I'm so happy to see you again, Syl. Come and talk with me, I have so much to tell you."

A shiver ran through Sylvia's frame, and she looked at Fiona.

"Go on," Fiona whispered. "Talk with your friend. I'll wait for you in the hall."

Sylvia shuffled forward, afraid of what she might see in Ava's face. The blacksmith's wife had not moved. Her back was very straight, and her bright hair hung like a shroud around her shoulders. Sylvia edged around the settee and sank down on an ottoman beside the fire. She lifted her gaze to Ava's and gasped. She had seen the terrible thing that had been Ava's burnt corpse, and she had seen the mad, frothing creature the Dark sisters had pulled from it. The woman sitting before her was composed and lovely, her flawless, golden skin a reminder of sunny summer days. Ava smiled, and there was real warmth in it, but her eyes were distant, as though she dreamed or looked beyond Sylvia and the opulent parlor to some far vista.

"Hello, Syl. Are you well?"

Sylvia cleared her throat, but before she could speak, Ava went on.

"I am well. I was very ill before, trapped in a dark place. It was so dark, Syl, and everything smelled of char. I think it might have been a burnt house, but I couldn't see anything, or move to escape." The dreamy blue gaze roamed the room, then came back to fasten on Sylvia. "I know I am changed. They told me why, but it's hard to remember, and it doesn't matter anyway since I feel so well. Do I frighten you?"

"No," Sylvia whispered hoarsely. She cleared her throat again. "No, Ava, I'm not afraid. Do you remember anything before you were ... trapped?"

Ava smiled. "Oh, yes! I remember how we went to the meadow in the summer to lay out the new-washed quilts in the sun. And how they smelled of the sweet grass when we folded them into the trunks at home. I remember the lovely summer nights, and how Henry laughed when I brought the fireflies home in a jar and let them go in our bedroom. All night, they winked and glittered above us, like stars." She laughed at the memory. "Syl, have you seen the others? They are traveling tonight. It's very exciting."

"Aren't you going with them?" Sylvia asked.

"No." Ava shook her blonde hair until it covered her face, then reached up and smoothed it back. "I'm staying. I'm going to wait for Henry, and then we'll go together."

Sylvia swallowed the lump in her throat. "But that might be a long time from now, Ava."

"I know it." Ava looked momentarily pensive, but soon smiled again. "I will have to find an occupation to while away the time. Fiona said I could have command of the kitchen gardens. Charlie is staying, too. He'll help me." She clapped her hands in glee. "Oh, it will be such fun, and I'll make them beautiful, Syl, I promise."

"I'm sure you will. You've always been a wonderful gardener." Sylvia stood, all of her yearning to be away from Ava's disturbing, childlike calm. "I have to go now, but we'll talk again soon."

She walked to the door. As she put her hand on the knob, the sound of restless movement behind her froze her. Her heart knocked against her ribs, and she looked back at Ava, suddenly sure she would see the golden-haired spirit rising like a vengeful witch on the warm currents from the hearth. Ava sat upright and unmoving, just as Sylvia had left her, but an eerie awareness radiated from her.

"I remember the fire, you know," Ava said. Her voice was soft and hollow. "I remember burning. Maybe someday, I'll tell you what it was like."

Sylvia slipped from the room, her skin prickled into gooseflesh and her heart galloping.

"She is still healing."

Fiona, waiting in the hallway, took Sylvia's hand and squeezed it reassuringly. She led her away from the parlor. "Those who die so traumatically are often fragile at first, and some...well, we won't speak of that today. You mustn't fear her, Sylvia. Every day, she will improve."

They passed the library, and Sylvia was dumbfounded to see old lady Greenbriar shinnying nimbly up and down the great rolling ladder, plucking titles from the shelves. The old woman's once crooked back was now straight and strong, her once milky eyes now bright as she surveyed the leather spines of the books.

"Here's one for you, Larry. *An Angler's Journal.* Too bad there isn't one about ice fishing," Mrs. Greenbriar cackled, delighted with her morbid joke.

Below her, sprawled in a huge armchair with an atlas, Lawrence Ridenour gave a deep bark of laughter.

Fiona paced on, and Sylvia skipped to keep up.

"Where are they going?" she asked. "Everyone talks about traveling, but where do the dead go?"

They had reached the door to the kitchen terrace, and Fiona burst through it into the sunshine and threw her arms wide as she whirled in circles across the stones to the two wide steps leading down into the garden.

"That is a big question, Sylvia," she laughed. "It doesn't have just one answer." She stopped and looked at the girl. "Do you remember when I told you that everything depends on balance, and that there are many places between life and true death?"

Sylvia nodded. She remembered, but she was no closer to understanding.

"Those who have left their bodies travel to those in-between places. There are many, many stops on that long, dark road." Fiona gazed toward the stables where Nathan was rubbing down the big, black coach horses until their hides gleamed. "I do not know more than a few of those stops, but I do know that what separates our world from those other realms is thin here. And so, my family built this house, and the inn was born. We have been stewards of the dead for more generations than you would believe."

A fragrant breeze waltzed through the garden, and Sylvia heard the hollow knocking of the skulls as they stirred sluggishly on their post beneath the birdhouse. She felt as though she stood on a precipice, with understanding as close as the last fatal step.

"And Nathan drives them?" she asked.

Fiona nodded. Her eyes filled with the green light of the burgeoning spring. Sylvia imagined she could see within them the perfumed snow of dropping blossoms and the color burst of ripening summer.

"What about the honey?" She glanced sidelong at the skulls on the post, slobbering their sticky red bounty.

"You saw the bees descend on the bodies we laid on the stones. They sup on them as on the native flowers, and the honey binds the people, the forest, and the far lands of the traveling dead. It opens the road, Sylvia, and none need be lost."

Sylvia was uncertain. It sounded noble and good, and she liked the Dark sisters. At least, she liked Fiona and Maeve. Maura frightened her. She chewed her lip and asked the question that burned in her heart.

"Is Nathan from that other land, where the dead travel?"

Fiona sighed. "Nathan is a special case. He belongs to neither the living nor the dead. He is a dreamer. Would you like to see what I mean?"

"Yes," Sylvia said.

The east wing breathed with living light. The unblemished, lemony wash of morning sunlight glowed from the white shell of the hallway, brilliant yet lusciously mellow. Curtains like diaphanous sails stirred in the breeze of partially open windows, and fluttered their cloud-colored fingers along the pale parquet. The scent of the forest wafted along the corridor, green and anticipatory. The wing lay under the spell of a restorative hush, and Sylvia felt some of her anxiety ebbing despite the gravity of their visit.

Fiona drew her into a tiny parlor. The room was simplicity and grace in colors of Queen Anne's lace and chicory. The fireplace was that of a woodsman king, built of pallid, grey fieldstone and mantled by a stout oaken slab. The chimney hulked against the brocade-covered wall like a cliff face and wore the head of a great snowy stag on its rough breast. Maeve sat at a dainty ladies' desk, pen in hand.

"Good morning, sister," she said, shutting up the silver-capped inkwell. "And Sylvia, how does this morning find you?"

Before Sylvia could reply, Fiona stepped forward and kissed Maeve on each cheek.

"I've brought her to see Nathan, sister. Will you attend us?"

Maeve turned her impish smile on Sylvia. "Of course. My dear, you are about to witness a great mystery, but you mustn't be afraid." To Fiona, she said, "I'll send for Nathan."

Maeve pulled a tapestried bell-cord, and a pretty young woman bustled in, a shaggy dog slouching at her heels. She wore a black woolen shawl slung about her torso and tied at the shoulder, and a baby slept in the snug hammock it made. Sylvia remembered the trio from the previous morning in the library, and she saw they had changed as much as Cook and Lucy. The girl's black eyes snapped at her.

"Did you need something, Miss Maeve," she asked in a husky voice.

"Liana, will you go to the stables, please, and ask Nathan to come here? Tell him it is time."

Liana nodded and turned to go with an insolent flip of her skirt, but in the doorway she faced Sylvia and spat, "You won't hold him. You're not like us."

She was gone before any of them could draw breath to speak.

"Well, how do you like that? Whatever possessed her to speak so sharply to poor Sylvia?" Maeve seemed caught between indignation and amusement.

Fiona frowned at the empty doorway. "It is as I feared. Sylvia, it seems you have a rival, if not for Nathan's affection, then for the privilege of loving him."

Sylvia bristled. "Who said I loved anybody?"

"Do you not? Come, the time for childish pretense is gone. It is a time for blooming, and I know you feel it."

Sylvia kept her silence, chagrined to hear her own late-night thoughts from Fiona's lips. She did love Nathan, in a fierce, shy, unexpected way that wrung her heart. Liana's words had been like a dagger of ice, not because of their venom, but because she feared they had the ring of truth. Maeve rose and went to the door, patting Sylvia's arm as she passed.

"Let's go and see our dreamer. There will be time enough to fret over Liana's silly infatuation."

The introduction that followed branded itself on Sylvia's brain in a series of dreamlike scenes and sensations. Another white bedchamber, its sun-dappled walls seething with the shadows of the wind-tossed forest. Maeve drawing aside the filmy bed curtains with an expectant smile. The sudden, blood-and-sugar smell rising from the porcelain cup on the nightstand in the cool current of air from the open window. The drowsy purr of the bees browsing the crocuses in the derelict garden. Each formed a distinct impression, yet they seemed unconnected to one another. Fiona was calling her name, but Sylvia stood frozen at the foot of the narrow bed.

"That can't be Nathan," she said tonelessly. "I saw him at the stables. Liana went to fetch him."

Maeve took Sylvia's hands and chafed them between her own.

"Sylvia, this is Nathan as he was. He suffered a terrible accident, and he has slept ever since, unable to return fully to life and unwilling to accept death. He is a dreamer, able to travel in both worlds. It's a matter of intense desire, to escape the damaged body and to project the living spirit. Nathan is the strongest we have ever encountered. It is rare, but we care for those who have the ability until ... "

Sylvia could not take her eyes from the familiar, bloodless face on the pillow. The man's eyes were closed, but they rolled and twitched beneath the purpled lids. Were they to open and animate the face, it would be handsome, but it was not young. It was lined with years of outdoor life and laughter. His black hair, shot through with silver, was combed neatly back from his forehead, exposing a scar and an ugly dent in the perfection of the skull. His long body was rail thin under the wool blanket.

"Until, what?"

"Until they choose, dear. Life or death."

The sound of boot heels on the oak floor broke the spell, and Sylvia turned. Nathan stood in the doorway, his hair pulled into a sleek tail at the nape of his neck, his sleeves rolled up exposing his sinewy forearms. Though he was as pale as the failing body in the bed, the resemblance was superficial. He was young, and strong, and whole. He smelled of the spring morning, of horses and leather. He gazed at her with steady, sorrowful appeal, and her heart cramped with sudden yearning. She had seen all manner of wonders since arriving at Azimuth House, she had been astounded or terrified almost hourly, and she had reached a point of perfect, buoyant acceptance. She stepped forward and held out her hand to Nathan.

"None of this matters," she whispered. "Tell me that's true."

He grasped her hand and carried to his lips, then turned a despairing look on the Dark sisters. Maeve dabbed delicately at her eyes with a wisp of lace. Fiona moved to put her hand on Sylvia's shoulder.

"He cannot speak. His voice is chained to his dreaming body. He could not, in honesty, tell you that this existence of his makes no difference. It is finite, and he must make his choice very soon. Indeed, it is nearly made for him, for he is closer now to death than to life."

Nathan dropped his gaze to Sylvia's hand in his. He pressed it fiercely to his chest, and stood, head bowed, while she sorted out what Fiona had said. She drew in a hitching breath.

"If death is his only real choice, then he can stay here. Like Cook and Lucy and the others. It ... it wouldn't be so bad, would it?"

Fiona shook her head. "It's not that simple, Sylvia. Nathan is a Coachman, and that carries a heavy contract. It is a powerful position, not suitable for just anyone. Dreamers who have served cannot remain after death unless they retain the post."

Sylvia interrupted. "But then, he can just keep driving the coach -"

Fiona held up a hand to silence her. "It is no easy matter. There are ... wards to pass. If Nathan attempts it, he risks utter destruction. If he does not attempt it, he must remain in the far lands, and we will see him no more in this life."

Sylvia was stunned. She splayed her fingers under Nathan's hand, pressing her warmth over the silent house of his heart. He looked up, his eyes full of resigned doom, and she felt all of her hopes fall away into a black sea of grief. Swallowing her tears, she reached up and pulled him closer. She stood on her toes and put her lips against his cold ones, then tore herself away and ran from the room. Behind her, she heard Maeve wail, 'Oh, sister!" as she gave in to sobs.

She ran from the east wing and out into the wild garden. She fled along the paths, her tears welling in a scalding torrent that blinded her. Dashing around a tall grove of elderberries, she collided with a hard, wiry figure, and both fell to the ground. The scent of burning tobacco gusted past her face, and a tiny pipe with a long stem bounced across the moss beside her.

"What's this?" croaked a hoarse voice in outrage. "Girl! You great, clumsy thing, help me up."

Sylvia scrambled to her feet and bent to help Maura Dark stand. She brushed at the crow-like little woman's skirt.

"I'm very sorry. Are you hurt? I didn't see you."

"That is apparent," Maura snapped. She shook her skirt free of Sylvia's hands. "Help me over to that bench. You've rattled every bone in me."

She sank onto the weather-worn bench with a groan and fixed her gimlet gaze on Sylvia. "Tears, eh? Well, I can guess their cause. Fetch my pipe before it sets the garden afire."

Sylvia plucked the smoldering pipe from the garden path and brought it to Maura, who sat with her hands pressed to the small of her back.

She held out the pipe. "I really am sorry. Shall I fetch someone?"

Maura's face was white, the lines of weary pain stamped on it like heavy ink on paper.

"No, no. I will be fine in a moment." Maura looked up at with her piercing bird's eyes. "It's the work that does this."

She waved a thin claw before her to indicate her appearance.

"The dead aren't always easy, girl. Someone has to manage their pain. It's a gift." She gave a sharp cackle of bitter laughter. "I haven't recovered yet from that poor burned creature, Ava."

Sylvia perched on the end of the bench. She knew she was staring rudely at Maura's drawn face, but the ruined mirror image of Maeve fascinated and horrified her. Maura puffed at her pipe and favored her with a glittering sidelong look.

"Twins occur every few generations in our family," she said. "When it happens, one is always marked for the light, for helping the dreamers and preparing the bodies. The other is for the shadows, for eating the pain of the dead. How would you fare on a diet of nightmares? Plays hell with a woman's beauty, I'll tell you."

"Why do you do it, then?" Sylvia asked.

Maura drew on her pipe and blew a series of smoke rings onto the air. A little color had crept back into her complexion, and she seemed content to rest in the sunlight.

"You have the sight, girl. Have you ever seen a mad ghost? Or an angry one? Just try loading one of them in the coach!" She gave a cough of humorless laughter. "You surely wouldn't want one to stay. I've no great love for my work, but it's what I was born for, and none of us escapes her fate."

The barking of a dog and a metallic clatter erupted from the direction of the stables. George's voice boomed in reproof, and Maura chuckled.

"Rags is making mischief, and where that dog goes, Liana is bound to be nearby." She tipped a slow wink at Sylvia. "Sometimes, girl, it is fate that must be pursued and seized."

Sylvia stood and ran along the path toward the stables.

The cobbled coach yard was slick and wet, and she lifted the hem of her dress as she entered it. George muttered under his breath as he stacked pails against the wall. He waved his hands at Rags. The big dog bounced around him and followed when George went into the gloomy depths of the carriage house. Sylvia stood in the empty coach yard and looked about.

"Nathan isn't here."

She whirled to face Liana. The dark-haired girl stepped from the lilacs at the edge of the yard, her baby in her arms.

"I've been waiting for him. He's finally made his decision, and I'm going to go with him tonight, when the rest travel." Her mouth twisted into a parody of sympathy at the sight of Sylvia's stricken face. "I know how you feel. You love him, too. But you can't follow where we're going."

Liana's expression turned sly, and she drew close and hissed in Sylvia's ear. "Unless you cut the thread that ties you here. Would you die for love, Sylvia? Take this." She thrust the hilt of a small knife into Sylvia's hand and, laughing, flitted to the tack room door.

"Here is one who had no fear of death." She swung open the broad door. "He gambled all for love."

A gigantic steely wolf hide stretched the height and width of the door, pegged tight with its tongue lolling. Jasper. Sylvia staggered back from the awful sight, and the knife fell to the cobbles with the ringing alarm of a bell. Liana rubbed her cheek against the wolf's thick fur and fixed Sylvia with a glare of simmering hatred. Rags came bristling from the coach house as though called, his lips lifted in a snarl. George was nowhere in sight. Faced with such hostility, Sylvia turned and fled to the house.

On the kitchen terrace, she stopped and bent forward to ease the stitch in her side. Her heart ached, and for one wild moment she wished she had not dropped the knife Liana had given her. *Would you die for love, Sylvia?* The words spun in her mind, wheeling like crows against a bleak horizon. If what Liana had said were true, then Nathan would not come back from tonight's coach run. Sylvia thought she could, indeed, die for love, but death might not be the only answer. From the corner of her eye, she saw the five skulls swaying gently on their post in the garden. The soft, hollow knocking as they jostled one another was like a voice. It soothed and invited her. It whispered of another way.

A battered tin cup, its lip pinched into a rough spout, hung from a rusty chain beside the skulls. She straightened and looked at the cup, and it swung toward her on an unfelt current of air. The world slowed. A mockingbird lifted from the honeysuckle tangle at the base of the post, and she heard each pulse of its wings as it climbed toward the cloudless sky. The smell of the red honey crept about her, warm and gratifying. Without seeming to move, she found she stood before the macabre hive, and the bees stepped courteously aside as she stroked her fingertips through the sticky sweetness. She brought her fingers to her lips and hesitated. The smell was very strong now, floral and peppery, with a spice of corruption that was not unpleasant. She put her fingers in her mouth, and rolled her tongue over the viscous delight of the honey.

Flame and velvet darkness. Soaring desire. The gorgeous drum of her own blood beating through her veins. An instant of piercing clarity, so bright and brief she could not cling to the revelation, burst in her mind; then it was gone - all the delicious sensation - and in its absence the world seemed made of dust. Sylvia snatched the swinging cup and thrust it beneath the bony chins of the skulls. For a desperate instant, nothing happened, and then the honey began to flow in a fat, silken stream. It filled the little cup and ran over her hand, and she snatched it back so quickly the rusty chain snapped. She didn't care. She raised the cup and drained it, her head thumping and burning, and licked the honey from her hand. She used her fingers to scoop the cup clean. The amber fire rushed through her like a river, and the air sliding through her lungs became an almost unbearable pleasure. She felt light as swans' down and realized with a start that she had risen from the weedy path so that only the tips of her toes skimmed the ground.

Her notice broke the spell. She fell back and sat down among the primroses, the cup bouncing away into the honeysuckle. The bees, so accommodating a minute before, now swarmed over the surface of the skulls. The honey flow had stopped, and five pairs of empty eye sockets regarded her with sinister curiosity. She tried to recapture the sumptuous cascade of sensation, but it had passed. She felt heavily normal and dull. She stood and brushed herself off and plodded into the kitchen, slamming the door behind her. The noise brought Cook from the cold gloom of the stone pantry. Her eyebrows rose and her jaw dropped when she saw Sylvia.

"I want to go home," Sylvia said. Her voice sounded rough and unnatural to her ears. "I want to see my people."

6.

Wickeford Mills was still and silent. Black ribbons adorned the houses, tied around porch posts and knotted on front gates. Sylvia rode slowly up High Street, the dappled horse beneath her picking up its feet and arching its neck as though on parade. Accustomed as she was to Agatha's stolid plod, the ride into town on the Dark's fine horse had been like floating. She was glad not to have her heavy, pounding head jostled. Despite the warm day, she shivered and pulled her cloak around her. She felt feverish and chilled at the same time.

The windows of Founder's House were draped with black crepe. Dr. Finchwhistle's bay mare stood by the gate, and one of Moss's coffin boys rubbed her nose. Sylvia pulled up and squinted at him. In the bright sunlight, his face looked featureless, hammered flat by the glare. She recognized him by his jug handle ears.

"Jubal Watts, what's going on here?" she said in her new rusty voice.

"Hey, Syl. I heard you went out to that big old house in the woods." He cast a covetous gaze on her horse. "Good job, is it? Think they might be needing a boy?"

"Never mind that now, Jube. What's happened?" She waved at the black-ribboned houses.

115

"Well, heck, Syl. Old Abram Johns died yesterday." Jubal drew close to her knee and lowered his voice to a whisper. "Doc said he took on something terrible at the end, yellin and ravin that the woods was a locust, or something, and the whole town was doomed. It sure gave folks the jimjams. Doc's in there now, seeing to Ella Berrybright. She's got to sit up with the corpse at night, and she's near crazed from it. Says she thinks he moves when she ain't lookin at him."

Sylvia half tumbled from the saddle and tossed the reins at Jubal. The earth rolled under her feet, and she clutched briefly at the stirrup before squaring her shoulders and wiping the glaze of perspiration from her forehead with her sleeve.

"Here, hold my horse. I want to see Doc."

"I'd say you'd better, Syl. You don't look so good."

She ignored the boy's look of concern and climbed the steps to the deep porch of Founder's House. She raised the heavy iron knocker and let it fall against the door with a reverberating boom. Nothing stirred inside. She banged with her fist on the black-painted wood. She could hear no footsteps, no raised voices bidding her enter. She pushed open the door and stepped into the musty vestibule. It was dim and smelled of wool coats and boot polish. Ahead of her, a faint glow of candlelight fell across the hallway runner from the open door of the parlor. She walked toward it, pausing at the foot of the dark stairway to listen for the housekeeper or Dr. Finchwistle. She did hear a sound, a soft sighing sound, not from upstairs but from the parlor. She turned and peered through the doorway.

The furniture had been pushed to the sides of the room. In the center, surrounded by candles, lay Abram Johns in the plain pine coffin he had commissioned of Moss. Sylvia could smell the resinous sweetness of the wood. Mr. Johns was austere in his best suit, his grey beard combed out on his immaculate, white shirtfront. His hands were quiet and prayerful, folded across his stomach, a good linen handkerchief bound his jaw, and two copper pennies glinted on his closed eyelids. He was terrifying. The breathy sound came again, and she staggered forward, her gaze pinned to the dead man, but a faint scuffle in the shadows by the fireplace drew her attention. Ella Berrybright's younger sister, Janet, sat napping in the big chair. She shifted in her sleep and exhaled a dainty warble. Sylvia retreated to the stairs and sank down upon them in relief. Wherever Abram Johns's spirit may have gone, it did not seem to be lurking in the parlor.

She heard a soft tread on the stairs above her and turned to see Doc hurrying toward her, wearing a nearsighted squint. His spectacles swung from a loop of red yarn around his neck.

"Doc, how's Ella?" she asked.

The doctor's thin face brightened at the sound of her voice.

"Oh! Sylvia, I couldn't see who you were, there in the shadows. Damned black stuff over all the windows makes a tomb of the whole house. Glad to see you, my girl. I heard you'd gone out to the newcomers to keep house for them." He sat on the step beside her, and fumbled in his pockets for his rolling papers and tobacco. "I've missed you."

"Who told you? My mother?"

"Well, yes, as it happened, she came by for a tin of throat lozenges for Rabbit. Your sister has a delicate throat, you know. And I asked after you, although I know your mother doesn't approve of your helping in the surgery. She was a bit short with me. Daresay I deserved it."

Doc had found his fixings, but his fingers trembled so that the tobacco shook free of the paper and sprinkled the step between his small, neat shoes. Sylvia took the makings from him and rolled a cigarette with practiced flair.

"Thank you, my friend. I guess Ella's nerves are catching." He stuck the slim smoke in the corner of his mouth, but did not light it. Instead, he put back his head and peered down his nose at her.

She recognized the look. It was Doc's medical bloodhound look, and she tried to turn away from it. He reached out two fingers and caught her under the chin, tilting her face back toward his appraisal.

"Now, now. What goes on here? Sylvia, you are ill. Tell me your symptoms."

"I'm okay, Doc. Just a little tired. I want to know about Mr. Johns. Jubal Watts said he was raving about locusts when he died."

Doc looked annoyed and bemused at the same time. "Locusts? Where on earth did he get that idea? It's true, Abram was delirious at the end. Not that young master Watts need be spreading that about."

"Jubal said Mr. Johns was yelling that the woods were full of locusts, something like that."

"Good heavens!" Doc chuckled, then began to laugh until tears squeezed from his eyes. "No, no, no. Abram said the woods were a *locus*, a center of activity, for unnatural beings. You have to understand, Sylvia, the poor man was not himself. He thought his own soul was being stolen, bite by bite, by a wolf demon. He'd had too much of delving in dark books, if you ask me, and it all came back to haunt him in his final moments." He took out an ink-stained handkerchief and blotted his eyes. "You and I know better, Sylvia. We understand scientific principle."

She nodded, but her throat felt tight. Her voice, when she could muster it, sounded strangled.

"So Ella was just nervous, being alone at night with Mr. Johns? He never really moved like she thought, did he?"

"Jubal Watts is a fount of gossip, isn't he?" Doc muttered. He stood and strode toward the parlor door, pausing to motion for Sylvia to follow. "Look at this, the earthly remains of Abram Johns." He pointed a quivering finger at the corpse. "Dead as dust and about as useful. He won't be dancing any jigs, or even turning in his sleep. Watch."

He snatched a burning candle from a nearby candlestick and tipped it over the dead man's hand. A drop of hot wax fell onto the white flesh and congealed there, as though Mr. Johns were a cryptic letter awaiting the author's seal.

"See. Not a twitch. No, Sylvia, the dead are inert, abandoned clay." Doc lifted the candle flame to the tip of his cigarette and inhaled. He jammed the taper crookedly into the candlestick, and emitted two plumes of pungently sweet smoke from his nostrils. "I'm concerned with the living. Why don't you come over to the office with me and let me have a look at you."

She shook her head. She had been taken aback by Doc's callous treatment of the dead man, but she was relieved that the demonstration had elicited no response from Mr. Johns.

"I have to go see my family."

Doc stared at the body of Abram Johns with a faintly hostile regard. He was silent for a moment, then looked at Sylvia from under his shaggy chestnut brows.

"Of course. But stop in and see me afterward." He reached out and gripped her wrist with his fingertips, assessing her pulse. His hands were steady and sure now. "You aren't well, young lady, and I want to see that reversed."

She nodded and fled back to the white dazzle of the street. Jubal was gone, but he had looped her horse's reins over the fence. Still, she felt an instant of black rage at him for leaving his post. Doc was right; she was not well. The houses across the street tilted toward her, leaving their afterimages on the blue sky. The whicker of her horse in her ear sounded distant and echoing, and for a dizzy moment she felt as though she were receding from the world around her at incredible speed. She did not trust her ability to mount, so she walked along the High Street. She did not notice when she dropped the reins, but the horse trailed along behind her as she turned down Market Street toward her mother's house.

"Well, Sylvia, I am surprised to see you. I thought your new position would keep you too busy for calling in town." Mrs. Peach was prim and frosty, blocking her door as though defending her home from a rude peddler. "Or have you been dismissed?"

Sylvia stood on the doorstep, her head hung low. She could not remember why she had thought it so important to come here, or what she had meant to say. The woman in the doorway, her mother, was a stranger to her. Her voice was a meaningless cawing. With a great effort, she raised her head and looked at Mrs. Peach's haughty indignation. A cloudy smoke seemed to lift from the older woman, and Sylvia saw her as though through a powerful lens, the air around her swarming with symbols of dark flame.

"Your remaining children will come to Azimuth House, two to serve, and one to travel the Old Road," she said in the hollow tone of prophecy. "The honey will come to you, and through you, to the town. By this, the people will be saved, for the Old Road is opened."

Mrs. Peach started back, her hand to her heart, and then a scowl replaced the fear on her face.

"Sylvia Temperance Peach -", she began, her voice beginning to rise.

Sylvia cut her off. "No longer. That girl is gone."

She turned and walked back toward High Street, the dappled horse following like a dog.

"Sylvia! Sylvia, come back," Mrs. Peach called.

She did not look back. A fire raced through her blood, burning away everything familiar, rewriting the story that was Sylvia Peach. Her body was a numb puppet, her vision narrowed to a keyhole view of her surroundings, but the eye in her mind was wide open and staring. It saw beyond the village, beyond the trees of the Johns Woods, far up the shady length of the Old Road, and where it looked she felt compelled to follow. She stumbled and reached out to catch herself. Her hand caught at a gatepost, and she saw that she had wound her way to Dr. Finchwhistle's office. His door opened. He was before her, speaking from a great distance a language she used to know. She fell forward. He caught her, and she spoke the only words she could remember.

"Azimuth House."

The setting sun had become a fiery clock. Sylvia, reclining in the back of Doc's buggy, watched its slow descent into the pool of its own simmering melt. As it spread itself across the horizon, she felt closer to the surface of her skin, as though she were rising toward her pores like vapor. With the coming of night, she thought she might pull free of her body entirely. The trees entwined their arms above them, a black filigree against the red-gold sky, and the buggy bounced and swayed through the dim tunnel at a dangerous pace. Sylvia feared it would not be fast enough.

"Hurry," she said, the word slurred and slippery in her mouth. It was difficult to make her lips and tongue work together.

Doc hunched forward, the reins wrapped around his fists as he fought to slow the bay mare.

"We're here, Sylvia, we made it."

The buggy lurched to a stop, and Doc leaped from his seat. She heard him batter the door of Azimuth House with a frantic fist.

"Open up, in there," he bellowed. "Where is everyone? Open this door!"

The door creaked open.

"What's the ruckus about?" a gruff voice asked. "Who are you?"

Sylvia recognized George's surly growl. She struggled to sit up, but her limbs seemed to have nothing to do with her. She could not command them.

"I'm Dr. August Finchwhistle, and I must see Miss Dark immediately," Doc snapped. "I've brought Sylvia Peach. It's an urgent matter."

She heard a crunch of gravel, and then George was staring down at her. He gave a low whistle.

"They said they feared you'd had a nip o' the special honey, Missy. I see ye have." He looked fascinated by her pitiful appearance. "Never saw a lively one what had drunk it."

Doc was at George's elbow in a rage. "Get the ladies of the house before I thrash you," he shouted. "Can't you see we've no time to waste?"

George emitted another low whistle and trudged away. A bell began to ring. The sun flattened under the indigo press of night, its golden blaze no more than the glimmer of light under a heavy door. Sylvia breathed in the twilight. She clung to consciousness the way fog clings to the liquid hide of the river, awaiting the breeze that would separate them.

More voices poured over her, quick and feminine, vibrating with concern and purpose. She saw the forms of the Dark sisters like shadows on a wall. She was lifted. She floated from the buggy into the cool night. They were taking her to the house, and Doc was lamenting the time he had spent in his surgery trying to revive her. She wanted to tell him not to blame himself. She wanted to tell Fiona she understood ... everything, all that she had been told and shown, all that she had felt and feared. She wanted to kiss Nathan again. But something was coming, the wind that would snatch her away from them, and it was too late. Doc cradled her against his chest. Over his shoulder, she saw the black horses plunge from the night beyond the west wing of the house, the black coach behind them. Its lanterns burned like enormous eyes. Nathan, in his greatcoat and top hat, cracked his whip over the heads of the horses as the coach flew onto the Old Road, the iron-shod hooves and the iron-rimmed wheels striking sparks from the cold stones. The thunder of it filled the world, and Doc turned in alarm. Sylvia was caught in the maelstrom of its passing. It wrenched her from Doc's arms, and with a wail, she whirled away behind it into the dark.

When she was once more aware of her surroundings, Sylvia found herself crumpled by the side of the road. She lay on her stomach, half in a ditch, marshy water seeping into her stockings and skirt. She wore only one boot, and, lifting her head from the dirt, she saw the other lying in the road some distance from her. She crawled from the reeds, disturbing several frogs. Their deep booming and the shrill scraping of crickets were the only sounds. She did not seem to be hurt, and she stood and looked up and down the road. Under the stark regard of the moon, it was white as chalk. The tracks of the coach were written clearly upon it, rushing away to the west. On either side stretched low, uneven fields with here and there a glint of water in the moonlight. A clammy mist slithered over them, ragged and faintly blue, and the forest was a thin, dark line in the distance.

She limped over to her boot and put it on. She needed no map to tell her she was no longer in the Johns Woods. The stars here were strange and the smell of the air altered in some subtle way. She fought down a paralyzing fear that she would be lost here forever and decided to follow the coach. She started along the road at a brisk walk, keeping close to the ditch. The frogs croaked and grumbled, and a breeze rattled the reeds. The long marsh grass whispered and waved, and more than once she stopped to listen, certain that under its cover something kept pace with her.

"You've just got the willies, that's all," she muttered to herself.

She tried singing, but her voice got smaller and smaller until it died away. The sound of it against the immense quiet had been more disturbing than cheerful. The eyes of the frogs glared out at her from the roadside weeds, along with the flat, shining stares of other small animals she could not identify in the darkness. She felt the marsh teemed with hidden beasts, and that she was on display on the bright stage of the road, yet it was worse when clouds hid the moon. Then, the inky black swarmed up out of the marsh like a presence and walked along behind her, impishly placing its inhuman feet in her footsteps, breathing in her ear.

Finally, she stopped, unable to endure it any longer. Her heart raced and her breathing was shallow, for this time she was sure she had heard something creeping through the marsh. For a long moment, she heard nothing but the sighing of the wind. Then came a faint splash and the squelching creak of a tussock pressed by some great weight. Sylvia's nerves sang of flight, but she forced herself to be still.

"Who's there?" she called.

"Who's there?" repeated a voice that made her hair stand on end.

It was thick and bestial, trailing away in a husky growl. She heard another mucky splash, closer this time, and the light breeze brought her a smell woven of equal parts marsh mud, decay, and butcher's offal. She gagged and put her hand to her nose. She looked about for somewhere to hide, but there was only the marsh. She did not want to leave the road, but if she were forced to it, she could not afford to flounder in the bog. She bent and tied up her skirt in a knot at mid-thigh. She did not take her eyes from the tall reeds at the roadside.

"What do you want?" she asked.

Only the sound of panting breath answered her. The frogs and crickets were silent, and even the breeze had died. The reed tops quivered like rattles, and the heavy breathing hitched and snarled in a strange way. She realized the thing was laughing, a low, evil chuckle that rumbled like stones in a sluice. Panic and anger flared together, and she shouted at it.

"What do you want of me?"

The reeds parted, and the creature reared out of them in a sudden flood of moonlight. It was tall, even in its crouched stance, and massive about the neck and shoulders. Its jaws were long and toothy, but its eyes were human. Ragged patches of fur mottled its pale skin, and its limbs were twisted and muscular, ending in long-toed paws. It dropped onto all fours and fixed her with a maniacal glare.

"I want you to run, Sylvia," it said.

Horrified, she recognized Jasper. She turned and fled into the marsh, leaping from tussock to tussock. Behind her, Jasper let out a murderous howl and splashed in pursuit. She moved across the shifting skin of mud and grass while he bulled his way through the pools and root tangles, and for a time she managed to outpace him. Then her foot came down in cold, oily water that surged to her knee, and she pitched forward with a strangled cry. Biting her lip against the pain in her twisted ankle, she scrabbled her way into the heart of a stand of cattails and curled up in the water at their feet. The moon covered its face in clouds. In the deep blackness, she could hear splashing and snarling. The smell of torn grass and mashed earth mixed with the slaughterhouse reek of the monster. He was very close.

"Did you hurt yourself, Sylvia?" Jasper growled. "Come out and let me kiss it better."

He moved away, and she began to ease herself out of the cattails. She moved slowly so as not to disturb the water, but the catkins swayed just a bit above her head. She froze at the edge of the cattail bed and held her breath, listening. She could not hear him, and had nearly made up her mind to move when he loomed over her.

"Caught you," he crowed, and pounced.

Sylvia screamed and kicked backward, and Jasper captured only a piece of her skirt. The water churned around them. The thick mud bubbled and burped. Globes of phosphorescence rose from the mire and drifted free on the air. She struggled to her feet beside a submerged log with cold, blue flame rippling along its length. As Jasper shook the muddy water from his hair and reached for her, the flame contracted into a ball of foxfire that shot from the log and caught him full in the face. He roared in shock and staggered away with the eerie light ablaze about his head. Sylvia fell back into the depths of the pool. When she surfaced, he was gone, and the frogs had taken up their dirge once again. She raked her wet hair from her face and looked around, but the Old Road was nowhere in sight.

The marsh rolled away from her like a sea. Its long, rank grasses rippled over a terrain pocked with bottomless bog holes and peaty pools, and a rich smell of vegetable decay rose from it in a thick fume. She labored through it with only the distant smudge of the forest as a compass, giving wide berth to the pits of greasy water where unseen creatures carved long, sinuous curves just beneath their dark surfaces. The foxfire orbs floated over them, and she learned to use them to navigate around the treacherous pools. Green jaws topped some of the grasses, and these snatched at her hair with their spiny teeth. Others bristled in low-growing mats and clawed her ankles.

At first, she feared that Jasper would return to stalk her, but after a long hour of wandering, the susurrus voice of the marsh lulled her. The flare and fade of fireflies in the deep black hypnotized her, and she trudged through a blank passage of time in which she seemed to float in a bowl of night disturbed only by their arbitrary glimmers. When her foot struck hard earth it jarred her senses, and she stumbled to her hands and knees in cool, sweet grass. A cloud of soft, white insects rose around her, their wings trembling and transparent. She knelt in the meadow, looking toward the line of the forest, which was suddenly close. Amid the blinks of the fireflies, some remained steady, and she realized she was looking at the lights of a small village.

Sylvia crossed the meadow and approached the village from the rear. Its houses huddled in a ramshackle tumble. Steep roofs with crooked peaks like the points of witches' hats staggered against the skyline. Some had rubble chimneys that squatted on them like toads. Others puffed thin trickles of smoke from bent snouts of tin. The village grew mushroom-like from a circle of bare earth, and the forest crowded around it.

She crept between tall, leaning buildings, their dark unpainted walls warped and splintered, and out into the square where the heaped stone cylinder of a well jutted from the hard-packed dirt. Its crumbled, mossy lip spoke of neglect, as did everything she saw in this place. The faint, wheezing hilarity of a concertina floated across the square. It came from a swaybacked hulk of a house with sagging shutters that might once have been red. The remains of flower boxes rotted on its peeling windowsills, parts of them dangling over the street and supported by the grace of a few rust-bitten nails. Smoky lanterns hung in its shadowed porch, and a battered sign swung from the broken harpoon of a weathervane jammed into a porch post. The crudely lettered sign introduced the house as the Black Coach Inn.

Sylvia wandered along the street, keeping to the jagged shadow of the houses. Light flooded from some of the windows, but no people stirred. Except for the breathless squall of the concertina, and the intermittent, angry neighing of horses from somewhere in the dark behind the inn, the village was silent. The wide square narrowed at each end into what she hoped was the Old Road. The village had no streets, only black-throated alleys between the buildings. She crossed the square and stole back toward the inn. As she reached it, a thunder of hooves shattered the stillness, and she ducked into the foul smelling damp of an alley as a rider rushed past like a gale. He disappeared down a wider lane at the opposite end of the inn, and shouting arose. Sylvia sprinted along the alley and peeked around the corner of the inn, her cheek against rough planking that smelled dank and mousey.

A broad-shouldered man in tall, black riding boots, his white shirt open at the throat, sat atop a snorting chestnut stallion and bellowed into the night.

"Jim, you whoreson, where are you? Get out here and see to my horse."

A bucktoothed boy, skinny but tough as a pine knot, appeared from the stables and ran to snatch at the stallion's bridle. The rider sprang to the ground and slapped the horse's neck affectionately, before turning to Jim.

"Coach is coming fast. I passed it back by the crooked oak, going like a house afire. Rub the sleep from your eyes, boy-o, and get those black devils ready." He raised his crop and pointed toward the dark stables. A shrill scream of equine rage erupted from inside. "We've a new coachman, appointed this night by the Prince, and he'll have none of your damned sloth."

Jim bobbed his head and turned away, leading the stallion. The burly rider put a boot to the boy's backside and hurried him along. "Nor will I," he laughed, then swung on his heel and strode into the inn.

Sylvia leaned against the wall and closed her eyes. A new coachman. Nathan was gone, vanished in this strange land where only the dead traveled, and she would never see him again. She forced down a sob.

A hard hand gripped her arm and her eyes flew open. The scrawny stable boy thrust his face near hers.

"Who're you, then?" he asked in a reedy voice.

The moon bobbed out of the clouds and cast a harsh glare over them, and Jim started back with a strangled caw.

"You ain't supposed to be here. You ain't even fit!" He made a strange warding motion. "How'd you get here, girlie?"

She cringed at the hostility in his voice. "I was following the coach, but I ... got lost."

Jim snorted. "I'd say you got lost." He moved closer and peered at her. "You ain't a dreamer. Live ones don't never come here. I mean, never!"

"I didn't mean to come here," Sylvia said. "I just want to find a way home."

A sly look glittered in Jim's eyes. "Bet you'd be worth a pretty coin in the City. Got a Prince's man right here at the inn, too." He seized her arm again in his hard grip. "You come with me, girlie."

"Let go!"

She twisted and kicked, but Jim only chuckled and clouted her hard enough to make her ears ring. He dragged her dazed and stumbling across the coach yard toward the inn door. Once there, he grabbed her by her hair and gave her a little shake.

"Now behave yerself, or I'll cuff ye again," he said.

He opened the door and hauled her through behind him. The room was dim and smelled of grease and ashes. A few rough-looking men sat at a game of cards, and the innkeeper in his stained apron stooped at the hearth, dousing a roasting haunch with something that made the fire sputter and flare green. Everyone turned to stare at Jim and Sylvia.

"Where's Mr. Crowe?" Jim called. "I got somethin' for Gideon Crowe."

His fist, wound about with Sylvia's hair, was all that kept her from falling to her knees. She could feel the imprint of it burning on her face, and one eye had begun to swell shut.

In a dark corner behind the chimney, a chair scraped across the dirty floor. The rider in the white shirt leaned back into the firelight, balancing the chair on two legs. His hair was a dark, burnished chestnut, much the same color as his horse, and a cocky grin lent his handsome face a mischievous boyishness.

"What have you there, Jim? A doxy?" He lifted a tankard to his lips and drank deeply. "Well, take her up to my room and I'll be along shortly."

"No sir," Jim said, "somethin' a sight rarer. Somethin' I'm thinking's worth a gold coin."

The chair came down on all four legs with a bang.

"Gold is it you're wanting? Bring your prize over here, Jim, and let's see what you've found." The easy bravado had gone out of Gideon Crowe's voice, and now it was soft and dangerous as a silk noose.

"Remember what I tole you about behavin," Jim hissed in Sylvia's ear.

He swung her in front of him and marched her toward Crowe, her neck bent backward to accommodate his tight grip on her hair. They stopped in front of the man, and Jim thrust her forward at arm's length. She gave a little cry of pain.

The inn was quiet, the air thick with fearful tension. The card players sat as though frozen, and the innkeeper had crept to the furthest edge of the hearth, his ladle clutched before him like a staff of office. Gideon Crowe regarded Sylvia in silence, then stood and grasped her jaw, turning her face to the light.

"Well, well, Master Jim. You have found a thing of value, after all." His lips were close enough to hers to stir the air between them in the parody of a kiss. "Tell me, pretty one, how comes a living woman to the realm of the dead?"

Emboldened by Gideon's interest, Jim pulled Sylvia back and cleared his throat.

"What reward will you give me for her, Mr. Crowe?" he asked.

Gideon's fist shot out and broke Jim's nose. The boy squawked in pain and let go of Sylvia's hair as he fell back with his hands to his bloody face. She staggered forward, and Gideon caught her against him with easy strength.

"Why, Jim, you surprise me, you really do. Let's agree that I won't drag you back to the City behind my horse." He gazed down into Sylvia's terrified face and stroked her cheek with possessive fingers. "You, my dear, will be traveling with me. The Prince has never seen a living body, nor touched one." The cool fingers trailed down her throat.

A great clatter and roar, and the screaming of horses, shook the inn. Boots thudded across the porch. The door slammed open, cracking the dingy plaster from the wall.

"It's the coachman," squeaked the innkeeper, and he rushed behind the long plank laid across two cider barrels that served as his bar. He snatched up a filthy towel and began polishing a tankard.

Nathan filled the doorway, his clothes and hair blacker than the night behind him, his dark gaze scouring the room. It fastened on Sylvia, struggling feebly in Gideon's arms. He tossed aside his gloves and, for the first time, she heard him speak.

"Boy, get up and see to my horses." He addressed Jim in a deep, cold voice, but his eyes never wavered from Sylvia and Gideon.

Jim rose from his crouch and scuttled around Nathan and out the door to the waiting team. The card players rose as one and retreated to the back of the room. Nathan stepped forward, and his eyes held a darkness that was like the caress of death itself. Her joy at seeing him turned to fear. He was so different.

"You have my passenger," he said to Gideon. "Give her to me."

She felt a tremor run through Gideon's muscular frame, but he put on a brave face.

"Come, friend, why so surly? I've done her no harm. Surely, you can see I have a duty to take her before the Prince."

Nathan's expression did not change. "Give her to me. I won't tell you again."

Gideon drew himself up in anger. "You overstep your authority, Coachman. I am a sworn deputy of the Prince."

"I will take my passenger, Prince's man or no, and I care not if I take two."

"Is that a threat?"

Nathan stared at Gideon, and the dark in his eyes spun crazily. "Take it as you like. Give her to me now, or I promise I will tear you from this world." He drew a heavy gold watch from his pocket and glanced at it. "I've a schedule to keep, Deputy. Decide."

Outside, the heavy iron shoes of the coach horses pummeled the ground with impatient violence. Jim burst through the open door, his hair on end.

"They're harnessed, sir, and wild to be off," he blurted at Nathan's back.

Nathan dropped the watch into his pocket. "Time to go," he growled, and stepped toward Sylvia and Gideon.

"Take the bitch, then," the Deputy spat.

He shoved her from him, and she fell to the floor at Nathan's feet. "You and I will meet again, Coachman."

Nathan bent and, grasping Sylvia by her arm, pulled her to her feet. She leaned against him, her forehead resting on the black wool breast of his great coat.

He tipped his hat to Gideon Crowe. "It will be my pleasure."

He whirled and strode from the inn, and she struggled to keep her feet under her as he whisked her out to the coach. Jim had the door open, his eyes fixed on the ground. Nathan boosted her inside and slammed the door, knocking Jim backward.

"Never again make me wait, boy. Understood?"

Jim nodded and babbled, but Nathan had already vaulted to the driver's seat. The long whip unwound fluidly on the night air, and the crack started the horses forward with a mighty plunge. Sylvia tumbled back against the quilted leather bench, her heart in her mouth. The inn fell away in a cloud of dust, and then they were speeding along the Old Road, as swift as the wind.

She curled onto the hard seat and cried herself to sleep. The flapping of the sable curtains and the rough jouncing of the coach infiltrated her uneasy dreams, where she fought against a mob of laughing men, all wearing Gideon Crowe's face and the bat-like wings of gargoyles. She woke with a stifled shout, but the coach was still. On the seat across from her, Nathan sat with his hands on his long thighs, his coat and hat beside him, regarding her with his frightening eyes. She scrambled upright and pushed herself into the corner.

"Why are we stopped?" she asked. Her voice trembled, and she cleared her throat. "I thought you had a schedule to keep."

Nathan bowed his head. "Is that all you have to say to me, Sylvia? After everything ..."

His voice trailed away, and he heaved a deep sigh. A fragrant breeze slipped past the curtains, freighted with the scent of grass and night blooms. Nathan reached over and pushed the draperies away from the window. Moonlight streamed in.

"We are close to home," he said. "Another hour, maybe less, will see us at Azimuth House. You're safe, Sylvia." He turned his gaze to her. "I will never harm you."

She uncurled from her corner and put her feet on the floor. Smoothing her skirt, she tried to reconcile her fear with the sudden longing that rose inside her. Nathan did not move. He only sat and contemplated her, and his stillness filled the coach until she felt he was all around her. He was in the very air she breathed, his unspoken need pressing on her lungs.

"You're ... different. You scared me, back at the inn. You still scare me." She stared at her hands. "What's happened to you?"

"So much, Sylvia. So much, I can never tell you half of it." His deep voice was soft and sad. "I am not the same, and yet my heart has not changed. Has yours?"

"I don't know," she whispered.

He moved then, opening the coach door and slipping out into the firefly-dotted dark. She looked up in panic, not ready for him to leave her, and he stood at the door and held out his hand.

"Come. Come and see the night. Not all on this side is ugly or vicious."

She hesitated, then put her hand in his and let him draw her from the coach. They walked a little way from it, under the eaves of some dogwoods whose white blossoms glowed like stars. Before them, a meadow flowed away from the moon-silvered woods, and deer grazed there. The four does and their fawns stared at them for a moment, before dismissing them. Above the meadow, a star fell across the sky in a gorgeous, fiery arc. Nathan watched it, his head tilted back to follow its course, and Sylvia looked up at his strong jaw and his white throat where his shirt lay open. A pulse beat there, a sign of some strange life that was not life as she knew it, and she remembered Fiona telling her that there were many stops on the long road to true death.

Nathan lowered his eyes to hers, and her breath caught in her throat. The awful depths in his gaze that had so frightened her had grown warmer. Now she saw a perfect summer dark, an endless velvet night of shooting stars and caressing shadows.

"Do you see?" he murmured. "Not all here is monstrous."

He lifted her hand and pressed it against his heart as he had at Azimuth House, and she understood that he spoke not only of this place, but of himself. Something uncoiled inside her and bloomed.

She reached up and touched his face, her thumb tracing his lower lip. He drew in a sharp breath and gathered her against him. His mouth came down on hers, and any lingering doubts she might have had were swept away. Together, they sank to the sweet-smelling grass.

Wickeford Mills, Summer

Late-day summer sun baked the streets of the village, and the young couples found respite in the shady woods, or down by the ever-cold river. Mrs. Peach kneaded and punched her bread dough on the floured board. She took a perverse pleasure when a bead of sweat slid from the tip of her nose and splashed onto the dough, and she folded it in, wondering if anyone would taste her labor in his morning loaf. She knew what they were doing, out in the woods, and never mind the picnic baskets they took with them. All around her, the abundant summer had turned the townsfolk into lustful animals. In the simmering meadows, under the forest canopy, even in the icy currents of the Wicke itself, they indulged their desires. They had no shame, coming back to town with smug, satisfied expressions, the women with their hair unpinned and full of bits of twig and leaf. The men swaggered about smiling, and she could almost smell the sex on them. One had even winked at her!

In the evenings, instead of folks going decently to their homes to see to their families' meals, they gathered at the new pavilion off the town square. They all ate together, with the children running barefooted and dirty-faced through the crowd. They played music and danced until all hours, they built bonfires, and more couples sneaked off into the dark.

Mrs. Peach knew what had ruined the town, but she was powerless to act against it. She knew the honey from Azimuth House had changed everything, and she suspected the change had only just begun. She cast flour over the dough and pummeled it, and as she brooded, the red painted wagon rolled up outside the bakery. Already, folks had begun to gather, eager to buy honey. She understood their greed. The honey from Azimuth House had a wild, spicy sweetness that lingered on the tongue. It entered the blood and heated it. It tasted of summer, of the woods and fields, and something else. The honey embodied the essence of life in the Johns Woods, but a thread of death, like a delicious toxin, ran through and under the sweet.

Mrs. Peach knew that was what it was, that faint bitterness she detected, that hint of salt. Her palate was adept at identifying ingredients, and though she had never before thought of death as a flavor, she recognized it as surely as she knew her own name. She dusted her hands on a towel and went to the door to help the red-haired witch bring in the crates of amber poison. If the townsfolk were so eager to fall under its spell, she could not help them, but the local honey would never again pass her lips.

THE QUEEN OF EVER AFTER

1.

Sorrow fumed from Gran's casket the way night mist simmered up from the earth in the old family plot behind the apple orchard. The sorrow wasn't silvery like night mist, though. It was black, but just as fine, and the relatives breathed it in all unknowing. Cricket sat on the shadowy stairs, watching the black fog of sorrow leak from the satin-lined box. Soon, when the men decided to hoist the box on their shoulders and take it to the opened earth, that dark vapor would be sealed in with Gran. They would put the dead woman in the ground with her living sorrow and shovel dirt on top of it, but first they would all breathe some of it in. They would take it with them everywhere they went, and it would color all that they touched until they, too, shucked their flesh and flew. Sorrow was the dark thread in the family blood, stringing them all together.

Cricket shifted her skinny buttocks on the hard stair. She hadn't had to dress in a black skirt and shiny shoes for this funeral the way she had for Mama Gail's. In fact, no one had said anything to her about it at all. She guessed it seemed like a half-hearted event to many of the relatives, there being no pastor or hymns. Gran had made her provisions long in advance of her death, knowing the family's appetite for overblown funeral parlor nonsense. She had wanted to lie in her own parlor, and to sleep in the bosom of her own land with the bones of her ancient ones around her. Cricket thought the old woman had probably foreseen the milling great-aunts and -uncles, their hands full of heavily laden plates and plastic wine glasses, swaying and shifting on the purple floral field of the parlor rug, but she'd have bet even Gran would have been shocked that they hadn't allowed Rob in the house. A shout of laughter went up from the crush of relatives. They were getting drunk and forgetting the solemn nature of the gathering. Cricket squeezed her eyes tight closed and gritted her teeth. When she opened her eyes again, she saw Rob looking at her through the window, and she slipped down the stairs and out the open front door into the hot August evening.

"Hey, Bug," Rob said, and tugged her hair.

On one vast palm, he balanced a paper plate heaped with a mash of food. Cricket grimaced. At least they had fed him.

"Don't call me that," she growled, and swatted his fingers.

The nickname was Rob's idea of a joke. He didn't have much of a sense of humor. Gran had said he was simple, and that he couldn't help the way he was made. It made Cricket mad when he called her Bug, but he never remembered from one time to the next. She appraised him critically. He was sweaty and mud-streaked, his tee shirt clung wetly to his bull's chest and shoulders, and his hands were none too clean. His nails were grimed black, and the calluses and work creases looked as though they had been rubbed with ink. He smelled like wet earth and the forest, and a little bit like an old campfire – a good wild smell. Cricket could see why they hadn't let him into the parlor, but she didn't care how filthy or bedraggled he looked. He had come from digging Gran's grave, from battling the old, thick roots and the slippery clay. He had bent his strong back to the task and made a place for Gran beneath the feral grasses of the abandoned family plot, and so he was a hero.

"Sit down and eat your supper, Rob. They're gonna carry her out soon."

"Are you sad, Bug?" He sat at the edge of the porch, and his legs were long enough that he could put his feet flat on the grass.

Cricket stared at him, then sat beside him. "Of course I am. Gran's dead. Aren't you sad?"

Rob shrugged and stuffed a heaping spoonful of potato salad in his mouth.

"She was old." He chewed thoughtfully. "I'll miss her. What are you going to do with the farm?"

"I'm only nine, Rob. They won't let me run the farm." She hesitated, then rushed on. "My dad's coming. Someone called him, and he has to come because there isn't anyone else to take care of me."

Rob gave her a sideways look. "I'll take care of you."

Cricket's heart went bang. She loved Rob for his loyalty, but she would have to take care of him. Pop had said so, and Pop was never wrong. *There's a storm coming, my girl*, he had said. *Be ready to take your dog and head for high ground.* That was how he always referred to Rob, as her dog. She didn't think it was very nice, but Pop's face was so mild and his voice so gentle that Cricket supposed he meant it well. He hadn't put in an appearance at the funeral gathering, and she worried that he was upset about her real father being invited. Pop was kind, but he had a streak of hard bark that was scary when it showed.

"Here comes Dean the Machine."

Rob's deep rumble was as close to contemptuous as it ever got. Cricket looked across the lawn to where her mother's younger brother emerged from the tractor shed. He strolled toward them, his eyes squinting, his mouth mean. She could smell the pot smoke on him at twenty paces, but he didn't look mellow.

"Jesus, kid," he said. "Go in the house and get cleaned up. Your dad's going to be here soon, and you look like you've been sleeping rough."

His voice was a burned rasp, and though he addressed her, he stared hard at Rob. He pulled himself up a little straighter, stretching for his full six feet of height. The pectoral muscles under his tight tee shirt twitched and jumped.

Cricket wrinkled her nose. "I'm clean enough. Gran told you before not to smoke around here. You're lucky she can't see you."

Dean's red eyes focused on her. His hand shot out faster than she would have thought possible. He grabbed her by her arm and yanked her from the porch. Her sneakered feet thumped to the grass, and she staggered against him.

"You got a smart mouth, girlie. Now do what I tell you." He shoved her toward the porch steps hard enough that she fell to her hands and knees.

Rob set his plate aside and stood. From under the red curtain of her hair, Cricket watched Dean take an involuntary step back. It didn't matter how much iron he pumped, she thought, he was never going to be anything but dwarfed by Rob. It would serve him right if Rob squashed him, but she minded what Pop had told her. She climbed to her feet.

"Rob, it's okay. I'll see you later."

She rubbed her stinging palms on the front of her cutoffs and gave him a twisted smile that held back angry tears. Rob glanced at her, the only indication of his thoughts in the reflexive curling of his fingers. He reclaimed his seat on the porch.

"Yeah, you better sit back down, dummy." Dean shrugged his shoulders like a boxer loosening up. "This isn't the day to make a scene, but we'll talk again."

He swung away from Rob and propelled Cricket ahead of him into the house.

"Dean! Been wondering where you got to." Great-uncle Max had a buoyant paunch that bobbed before him and a voice like an earthquake. His shirt buttons strained at the seismic rumble of it. "We're ready to take Emma on home. Come get a shoulder under this box."

Dean gave Cricket a commanding, if bleary, glare and slunk off to help the men carry Gran's casket away.

"I want to go, too," she said.

Max looked down on her as though surprised to see her. "Well, now, young lady. I don't think it's fitting, you seeing such a heathen display. Your granny should be in the churchyard with decent folks, not out here in the godforsaken wilderness. A lot of old-time nonsense, if you ask me." He put on the spectacles that hung around his neck on a gold chain and considered her over the tops of them. "No, I think you'd best stay here. You can go up tomorrow and put some flowers on her grave, and say a prayer for her eternal soul."

The casket came swaying from the parlor on the straining shoulders of six red-faced men. Gran had been an ample woman. The great-aunts paced along behind, pinning their hats in place and whispering around their good, church hankies. As the small procession passed, Cricket got a noseful of their perfumes and powders, and the melting, cosmetic-counter smell of their newly re-applied lipsticks. She wondered how their nylons and sensible heels would fare in the orchard plot, where thistles grew unchecked and the bindweed lay in the thick grass like rabbit snares. She followed them onto the porch and watched as they struggled across the lawn and up the slight rise, Rob at the tail of the parade with his shovel over his shoulder. Behind her, the house was empty and silent.

"Farewell, sweet Emma. A pity you haven't better company to wish you bon voyage." Pop put a hand on her shoulder.

"Where were you? I looked for you in the library."

"Ah, these dark festivities hold no appeal for me, my girl. Entirely too much bullshit fouls the air."

That was vintage Pop, flowery-tart and sharp as a razor's sting. Despite the misery of the day, Cricket found herself snorting in laughter.

"I have a book I want to show you," Pop said. "I've kept it with care for just such a day as today, and we want to be quick about its perusal. There isn't much time left, I'm afraid."

Cricket leaned her head back to look up at him. His long, scholar's face no longer wore its customary dreamy expression. He looked stern as a revival preacher, and his grey eyes glinted like gunmetal behind his little wire-rimmed glasses.

"What do you mean, Pop? Time for what?"

His chilly hands cupped her upturned face. "Time for you to grow strong, Cricket. I know you are brave. I know you are bright. But, my dear, you are so very young." His smile was a little too grim to be comforting. "Well, needs must, eh? Come and let me show you one last, astounding story."

The library had once been the dining room, a large space dominated at one end by a massive fireplace. *A real ox-roaster*, Pop called it. It only held fire on Christmas and Halloween, Gran's favorite holidays. Gran had scorned the idea of a dining room, preferring to hold meals around the scarred kitchen table where apples rolled about loose and cats slunk between the dishes. She'd had Rob build shelves that soared to the ceiling where the china hutch and buffet had once stood. The mahogany dining table became a work space, piled with books, papers, and maps. Gran was mad for geography, and traveled the world seated at that table.

Cricket cruised past it, touching the heaps of books and breathing in the dry dust-and-leather smell. There was a dark space where Gran had been – it had been waiting to catch Cricket in its cold nothingness - and now it pounced. Tomorrow had become a strange country, empty and flat as an ink drawing of the moon. She sank into one of the sprung armchairs that flanked the fireplace and thought about crying, but no tears would come. She turned her face to the worn velvet and felt cautiously around the breakage of her heart.

"Now, now, child. It isn't as bad as all that, is it?" Pop hovered over her for an instant, looking pained and uncomfortable, before sinking into the other chair.

"Everybody's dead, Pop. First Mama Gail, and now Gran. Dean's in charge, and he's meaner'n a snake." She glanced at Pop to see if he was taking the full measure of the situation. "My dad's coming, and I don't even know him. What if he's mean, too?"

"Yes. Well. That's what I want to talk to you about. This father of yours, we can't know his plans, but I fear they won't include taking on this farm. He has a wife, you know. A city wife, and a baby on the way. You have a ... a ... stepmother."

Pop said the word as though it poisoned him a little just spitting it onto the air. Cricket felt an icy hand squeeze her insides. She hadn't considered the possibility that her father wouldn't want to live on the farm. She had certainly given no thought to his new family. She looked around at the walls and stacks of books, and wished she could disappear into them.

Pop smiled behind his steepled fingers and did his scary mind-reading trick. "I think you may be able to do just that, my dear. Climb up there and bring down the book at the end of the third shelf. Behind the others."

He pointed to the shelves in the far corner, the ones that held Gran's collection of fairy tales. They were beautiful books, some of them rare, and they came from all over the world. Cricket had read most of them, snuggled against Gran's pillowy bosom. The old woman had loved them, but had warned her to be careful of them, for they contained true magic mixed in with the fantasy. True magic was useful and unpredictable, like fire. If you weren't vigilant, it could destroy what it touched.

She climbed the ladder and stretched to reach behind the row of heavy books, her cheek resting against their cool bindings. Her fingers brushed against soft leather and rough-cut pages, a book curled like a cat's tongue in the dark. She pulled it out, and it flexed and stretched in her hand, rolling out flat. It was a large journal or album, with rawhide lacing for its binding, and though it was old, it was supple. She had never seen it before, but someone had paged through it often, oiling the leather covers with loving hands. It had no title, and she was about to look inside it when Pop rapped with his knuckles on the ladder.

"Bring it down where we can spread it out on the table. Quickly, before the mourning committee returns and begins robbing us blind. You'll have to hide it later - it won't be safe in here any longer."

2.

Once upon a time, there was a motherless girl named Cricket who lived on a little farm in the middle of the wilderness. She had come there by chance, for her poor dead mother, in her final illness, had wanted her daughter to be safe. The mother knew her girl was special, with the ways of true magic about her, and she brought her to the farm and placed her under the care and tutelage of a powerful, but kindly, witch.

Cricket looked up from the handwritten page in astonishment. "It's about me," she said. "Did you write this, Pop?"

"Not I. Your grandmother worked at this in the nights, after you went to bed, since your mother passed from this world. More than four years of labor."

"Why does it look so old?" Cricket passed a reverent hand over the heavy cream of the page, her fingers lingering on the fine handwriting and the fanciful drawings.

"The journal itself is quite old, though it had never been used. Emma picked it up at one of those musty book markets she loved." Pop made an ecstatic face and clapped his hands together. "*A peach of a find,*" he said in Gran's voice.

"Don't do that," Cricket scolded, but her attention had already fallen back into the beautiful, handmade book.

"Never mind all that storytelling right now. You'll have time to look at it later. Turn to the last entries. They are what matter."

She flipped through the pages, watching Gran's artwork speed by. In black and red ink, she saw the lanky old farmhouse with its frills of gingerbread and pelisse of roses. There was the forest, tall and shadowed, harboring wolves and giants. And here, the little girl who represented Cricket, always with her back to the viewer, always moving forward. Pop's pale finger came down, stopping the riffle of pages with uncanny precision.

"There."

She looked at the drawing of the Johns Woods – a spot she hadn't seen before, with a surge of water down a rocky bed, and trees vanishing like drifting smoke into the soft luminosity of the page. At the edge of the water stood a giant and the little girl with garnet-inked hair, both of them staring into the glow. She read the paragraph above the drawing.

They came to the unnamed creek. The water, on its way to join the Wicke River, sang against the stones with a voice like a thousand chimes and drums. Threaded through its song was the invitation: Cross me if you dare, and claim the crown. Moss grew on the stones in a curious pattern like footprints, and Cricket knew that, though it was the way, it was treacherous.

Pop turned the page. "And there," he said, pointing at the last entry in the book.

She took the first step, balancing on the slippery stone with the creek rushing around her. The fog that obscured the far bank parted a little, as though a curtain were being drawn back by a tentative hand. Another step, a further parting of the fog. Cricket stared through the opening in amazement. Instead of the dour ranks of oak, she saw the far, misty towers of a castle, banners flying against a bright blue sky. Her own crest shone in gold on the banners. It was true, then. She was the lost queen of Ever After.

Cricket gave Pop an angry glare. "Ever After isn't real," she said, slamming shut the book. "It's just a dumb old story Gran made up when I was sad."

"Is it? Look, there is even a map. Imaginary places don't have maps."

Pop tugged a folded sheet of paper from the book and opened it flat on the table. Cricket drew in a shuddering breath. The land of Ever After sprawled before her, drawn in meticulous detail by Gran's talented pen. She remembered the grey autumn evenings after Mama Gail had died, and Gran holding her in the golden lamplight of the library as the night smudged itself onto the windows, telling her the marvelous story. She remembered how it had comforted her to believe there was a place all her very own, where she was a beloved, magical queen. A place where she was special, and not a leftover little girl whose father didn't want her. Suddenly, the tears that hadn't come before crowded up in her eyes. She looked up at Pop through the shimmer.

He stepped back from the table and made a courtly little bow. "It is time to claim your crown, Your Majesty."

There was a fist in Cricket's throat, and she could hardly see Pop through the salty blur of tears. She would never believe he could mock her, but his words felt like a slap just the same. She snatched up the book and the map, crinkling the thick, soft paper, and ran from the room. The tears had overflowed, and with them came a flood of despair.

3.

Night had swarmed out of the Johns Woods, sparkling with fireflies, before Lee Carpenter arrived to take charge of his daughter. He rolled from the sedan and stretched his back, breathing in the clean, humid air. August was fading, its fierce heat cooling a little in the nights now, and he could feel the softer fingers of approaching September in its touch. He had always loved this time of year, the sensual swing from summer toward autumn. It had been a long time since he'd been this close to the wild source of such things.

"Lee? They did know we were coming today, didn't they?" Danica stood beside the car, peering into the dark at the unlit house.

"Yeah, they're probably in back, in the kitchen. We're later than I thought we'd be." He didn't mention their several stops at antique dealers along the way, but Dani bristled anyway.

"Well, it's not my fault. I had no idea Blackfern County was so remote. Give me a hand, please. It's an inkwell out here."

The porch light blinked on as he moved to help her, and she teetered toward it on her kitten heels, hanging her overnight bag on his proffered arm. She was surprisingly graceful, despite the precarious combination of her belly, the spiky heels, and the soft turf. Lee admired her sleekness. Not every woman could look so cool and put-together while eight-months pregnant in the August heat.

A man came out onto the porch to meet them, and his belly rivaled Dani's. "Well, well, there you are. We thought you got lost. Thought we'd have to send out a posse." The man had a booming politician's laugh, hearty and false as a gold tooth. "Don't know if you remember me, Lee. I'm Max Marchenwalder, Emma's youngest brother. We're sure glad to see you back, son. We've been that worried about what was to be done for your little girl."

"Max, of course, I remember. Where is she? Cricket?"

"Child's asleep, but I can wake her - "

Dani interrupted. "Mr. Marchenwalder, we've had a long drive. I'm exhausted." She turned her long-lashed eyes toward Lee. "Maybe we could meet Cricket tomorrow, when we're all rested."

"Well, sure, honey," Max said. "Why don't you come on in, and we'll get you settled." His smile was sweet, but his voice had a touch of vinegar in it. He stood aside, and held the door as Dani sailed through. When Lee passed him, he whispered, "We should talk."

The parlor had been put back together, the sagging sofa pushed against the wall under the family photos where Emma's casket had been. Lee and Dani sank into it, and Max squatted on the edge of an armchair, his bulk mashing the cushion so that he was nearly kneeling on the rug. The savory ghost of funeral food hung in the room, along with a fruitiness of wine that reminded Lee of communion. Max had put on a solemn, clergy-like expression to go with it.

"This must be hard for you, taking on a nine-year old girl at such a time." He gestured vaguely toward Dani's belly. When no one spoke, Max cleared his throat and rushed on. "Yes. Well, I wondered if you'd given any thought to what's to be done with the farm."

Lee's eyebrows rose in surprise. "This farm?"

"That's right, *this* farm." The new voice, slurry and whiskey-rough, rolled toward them from a darkened doorway at the opposite end of the room. Dean rested against the wood and plaster, his head swaying slowly back and forth. "You deadbeat bastard, you got some nerve comin' around here, putting your nose in where it don't belong."

"Dean Michael ..." Max struggled upright and raised a threatening voice.

"Never even came around when Gail died. Left your kid for us to raise. Well, why not? I see you got another one cookin. Hey, pretty lady, you don't want to be stuck with someone else's brat. Tell him."

Dani shrank against the sofa cushions, distaste written across her face. Lee stood up. "That's enough, Dean. You're drunk."

"Yeah, I'm drunk. And I'm sick. You make me wanna puke." Dean reeled from the doorway. "Think you're gonna come in here and take over. Take what's ours. I oughta bust you in half."

He staggered forward again, stopped and looked up at the ceiling with a bemused expression, and crashed to the rug where he let out a noise somewhere between a moan and a snore. Max stretched out a toe and rolled Dean gently onto his back.

"Out cold. My apologies. It's all come as a shock to him."

Lee stared down at his ex-brother-in-law, his hands curled into loose fists. He could feel the creeping red heat Dean's words had awakened on the back of his neck and on his ears, and he willed it to ebb. "What was he talking about? What came as a shock?"

"The family farm, son. Emma left it to Cricket, post and beam. You're her daddy, so it's up to you to ... manage her inheritance, if you take my meaning."

Dani gasped. "Oh, Lee -"

"We'll talk about it in the morning," Lee said, cutting her off. "We're all tired. It's been a long day, Max. Guest room still the first one at the top?"

Max's bright, piggy eyes had fastened on Dani in speculation, but he brought them up to meet Lee's. "Yes, yes, of course. Go on up, get a good night's rest. We'll talk tomorrow."

"What about him?" Dani nodded at Dean, stretched on the floor like a corpse.

Max chuckled. "I've half a mind to let him lay there, he's that heavy. I'll get that boy Emma hired to come in and put him to bed on the sofa. Lord knows that one's big enough to hoist Dean."

Lee put his hand on Dani's elbow and guided her to the staircase. A single bulb inside a cage of dusty crystals cast a sullen, fractured gleam on the bare wood of the stairs, illuminating

142

nothing. As they climbed into the creaking dark, he heard Max at the kitchen door bellowing for someone named Rob.

4.

Cricket lay in the close comfort of the night and listened to her father and stepmother getting ready for bed in the next room. To have them so close, not knowing she was there just the other side of the wall, made her feel nervous and exhilarated at the same time. The way a clever fox might feel, looking out at hunters from its hiding place in the brush. Rob, who knew about such things, had once told her that the fox could be invisible if it wanted. If it liked, it could charm its way in anywhere. It could travel for days without stopping, and never tire. Rob had said she was like a fox, with her red hair and small frame, and Gran had agreed.

She had been awakened by Dean's shouting. Thinking like a fox, she had slipped from her room and along the hallway, and had crouched unseen in the shadows at the top of the stairs. From there, she could see the grownups in the parlor below. Great-uncle Max looked puffed up and pale as a marshmallow, while Dean lurched around like a broken wind-up toy, yelling at her dad. She focused on the man in the blue polo shirt and khakis. He was blonde and stood very straight, tall enough to look Dean right in his bloodshot eyes. He looked mad, and the woman sitting on the sofa was holding a hand out to him, as though to pull him back down beside her.

The woman. Cricket took in the significant curve of her stomach, but she was more interested in the woman's beauty. She had glossy dark hair, swept into a smooth up-do, and a face made-up as perfectly as a magazine cover. Her skirt and white, sleeveless blouse were effortlessly chic and expensive-looking. She looked like a queen, and Cricket felt a stone roll onto her heart. She had sneaked back to her room, suddenly afraid that her fox-magic had worn thin.

"Pop?" Cricket whispered to the dark. "Can you hear me?"

"Indeed, I can. I also can hear those two in the next room, and it is a conversation worth the eavesdropping." What Cricket had taken for a long stripe of shadow falling on the wall straightened and turned its face toward her. When it came to being invisible, Pop was better than a fox. "You might want to come and have a listen, Your Majesty."

"Stop calling me that," she said, but she was already putting her bare feet on the floor. "What are they saying?"

Pop made a circle of his fingers and thumb, looked at her briefly through the tunnel it made, and then held it against the wall. "Listen through here."

She put her ear to Pop's hand, and the voices in the next room leaped at her, amplified.

"... couldn't have turned out better, Lee," the woman said. "There's still time to enroll her at Eastlake."

"Yes, I think that will be best for everyone." Her father's voice was soft and deep. The sound of it ran along her veins like the sound of her own heartbeat. "What a windfall. It'll make everything easier. I'm pretty sure we can come to an agreement with Max."

Pop closed his fist, and the voices were reduced to unintelligible murmurs. "Do you understand?"

Cricket shook her head, but one word circled her brain, freighted with dread. *Eastlake, Eastlake, Eastlake.*

"It's a boarding school," Pop said, plucking it easily from her mind. "Quite an exclusive academy for girls, in fact."

"Were they talking about sending me there?"

"Yes, Your ... Cricket. It's a lovely place, I hear, very civilized. Instead of a forest, it has a park. The wildlife is kept out, but the groundskeeper is permitted a dog. Everything is beautifully groomed and runs like a grand clockwork. The answers to life's great questions are all written down for you to memorize. You'll never have to wonder about anything again, or pretend - "

Pop's voiced cracked, and he looked away. With every word, Cricket had felt panic rising. The farm was home. Her friends were here. She thought of Rob, with his secret camps and his way with animals; and Pop, who knew more than all the books in the library. She thought of her classmates at the little school in Wickeford Mills, and the way they thrived together like saplings growing strong in sunlight. She put her hands over her face and wished for Gran. *Oh, Gran, Gran, where are you when I need you so?*

Pop knelt in front of her and pulled her hands away, forcing her to look at him. "She's in Ever After. You have the map. We could go there, Your Majesty."

"It's not real, Pop. None of that stuff is real. Is it?"

There was no answer. He had gone, as though hurt by her words, and she was alone in the dark.

Cricket awoke to the sound of Rob's axe, splitting logs and kindling for the winter. She padded to the window and looked down on him, concentrating hard. It took only a few seconds for

Rob to straighten and glance about, finally raising his eyes to her window. He waved, and she laughed and waved back. She never tired of seeing the trick. Rob had told her he'd learned it from the deer, and she had seen him, sitting still as a stone near them. They would take corn from his hand, their ears and tails fluttering, and would sometimes extend their whiskered muzzles to snuffle his face. It was a kind of magic, and he'd promised to teach her. She thought about the things Pop had said the night before, and the smile slipped from her lips. If he was right - and Pop was always right – she would have to leave the farm, and she'd never see Rob again.

A smell of coffee rose through the floorboards, and she heard the usual Saturday morning sounds of Dean banging cupboard doors and rattling crockery. Hunger pinched her. She hadn't been able to eat the funeral food, not with all the black sorrow smoking over it. If she got down to the kitchen before Dean finished his coffee, he would make her a bowl of oatmeal with maple syrup and cinnamon, and bits of dried apple. It was his one nice thing. Gran had said everyone had one, no matter how cantankerous they might be the rest of the time, and that it was smart to be receptive to what each person had to give. Dean liked to cook, and Cricket's growling stomach would be happy to receive. She dressed and hurried down the stairs, not even pausing to brush her hair.

As she neared the kitchen, she realized Dean was not alone. She heard great-uncle Max's rumble, and a feminine murmur. She tiptoed to the kitchen door and peered in. Her father and stepmother sat at the table across from Max, and Dean leaned against the counter, slurping his coffee.

"I think that's a fair offer," Max said. "It'll keep the place in the family, and give you enough money to see to Cricket's education." He leaned back in his chair, making the wood creak in protest. "You know, there's been a Marchenwalder on this land for seven generations."

Her father sighed and rubbed a hand over his face. "You've got a deal, Max. It's a load off my mind." The woman patted his arm and smiled at him, and he placed a hand on her belly. "I've got other things to think about."

Dean's gaze fell on Cricket in the doorway, and he spluttered coffee, wiping at his mouth with the back of his hand. "There's one of them right now," he said.

Everyone turned to look at her. Her father's eyes were blue. Gazing into them, she felt a peculiar sensation in her chest, as though a loose and troublesome stitch had been suddenly drawn snug. The woman was staring at her with interest, as though

Cricket were something she might like to eat. Her father stood up, then seemed to think better of it and came around the table, wheeled a chair to face her, and sat. He leaned forward, his face only inches from hers. He smelled good, and the snug little stitch in her chest tugged at her, urging her to throw her arms around his neck. She put her hands behind her back and clasped them hard.

"Hi, Cricket," he said. "I'm your dad. I've wanted to meet you for a long time."

Dean snorted, and Max flapped his hands at him, but her dad didn't pay any attention. He was quiet and still, holding her gaze with his, speaking to her the way Rob spoke to the deer.

"You must be pretty mad at me, for not being around," he said. "I want to make it up to you now, though. I ... we want you to come and live with us." He made a slight gesture toward the woman at the table. "Would you like that?"

A lie. It struck her like a bullet, and she felt the charismatic pull of the man fade. Rob had said you couldn't be false with wild things, because they'd always know, and shun you.

"That's not what you want," she said. "You want to put me in a school for girls. Eastlake."

Her dad looked as though she'd slapped him. She looked over his shoulder at her stepmother. The woman wore a tight, pursed-up kind of smile, and her eyes were now flat and bored.

"Where did you hear that?" her dad asked.

"Pop told me." It was out before she could think about what she was saying.

"Jeez-us," Dean spat, "not that again. Cricket, you're too old for that shit."

Her dad turned to Dean. "Who's Pop?"

"More like what. It's Cricket's imaginary friend. She's been talking to it ever since she came here."

"Pop is not an "it"," Cricket shouted. "He's real, and he's smarter than you! I'm not going to any stupid girls' school, either."

She turned and ran for the back door. Behind her, Max advised her dad to let her go.

"She's upset, poor child. She'll come around."

5.

I won't go. I won't go, and they can't make me. Cricket stalked around the woodshed, defiant thoughts crowding her mind and making her heart race. *I'll fight them. I'll run away.*

But, she didn't want to run away. She wanted to stay right there, on the farm, and go on like before. Something had shattered when Gran died. It struck Cricket that the things she loved were already gone - stripped from her without warning - and only she was left to dispose of, like Gran's body in the casket. She stood in the morning sun, and felt it erase her edges. Maybe, if she stood still long enough, she'd root there and moss would creep over her, and she could, like Gran, become part of the land. The wisp of sorrow that was her own connection to the place let itself drop from her navel toward the ground. She felt it pulling on the knot of despair at her center, and watched it vine around her shoes, seeking the soil. It slipped over the thin grass and the woodchips, but it wasn't strong enough to hold her or stop her aching heart. It wasn't strong enough to overcome her anger.

"What're you doing, Bug?"

The dark tangle of sorrow was nothing more than the swaying shadows of lilac branches. Cricket looked up at Rob, standing before her with a stout chunk of apple wood under his arm.

"You looked like you was dreaming," he said. His gaze fell on her like the sun, but instead of erasing her, it gave weight and strength to her limbs. *Rob's got the gift of sight*, Gran had said. *He can see what's real, and that's a rare thing.*

"I was looking for you," Cricket said, and knew it was true as the words passed her lips. "You still chopping wood?"

He gave her a long look that she endured with patience, then nodded and turned back to the pine stump he used as a block. He set the apple log on end. Cricket watched his deliberate movements, hoping they would soothe the anger that burned behind her eyes.

Rob was a brown man. His thick brown hair hung shaggily past his collar, his eyes were brown, and his skin was so darkened by his outdoor life that he seemed to vanish in the woodland shadows. Cricket believed Rob's thoughts were brown, too - calm and solid like creek stones, unperturbed by the sheet lightning of imagination. Sometimes, they were skulking and dangerous. Rob held danger within him, she was sure of it. Her rage scented his, though he cradled it deep. Rob's eyes were flat bogs that denied reflection. He lurked beneath them like a crocodile, powerful but dozing, content to watch and float. Only Cricket ever seemed to notice that this inner Rob had teeth.

She watched him swing the axe in a smooth, graceful arc. The old apple log split and fell open as though conjured into revealing its heart, and the blade halted a whisper from the surface of the block. Rob slid a shy glance at her. He was the only person she knew who could command the axe that way. It took enormous strength and a kind of intuition. You had to know the wood.

"Why don't you ever get mad, Rob? Why don't you ever fight?" If she had Rob's muscles, no one would ever push her around.

Rob straightened to his full height and let the axe dangle from his hand.

"Too big to get mad and fight. I could hurt someone."

The sunlight danced over the still bogs of his eyes. The crocodile watched her warily.

"They're going to make me leave here. I'll have to go to a girls' school." She waited, but Rob made no reply. "Don't you care?"

"I'm going to the woods," he said. "It'll be okay, I know my way."

She blinked back furious tears, and looked up at the great height of him, the flat, hard sheets of muscle and the big hands. All useless!

"You're a coward, Rob," she hissed and jabbed him in the gut with her tiny fist, as hard as she could. It was like punching a tree. She did it again, and again, the tears falling now in a shameful, hot cascade.

Rob absorbed the blows, and then reached out and grasped her by the upper arm. His strong fingers supported her shoulder, and he lifted her into the air without effort.

"Be still," he said, and she stopped flailing and hung from his hand like an obedient kitten. Her hair swung in her face and stuck to the tear tracks, but her heart slowed, and the red haze of her rage receded. She could hear again, the birds singing and the wind sighing in the treetops. Thunder rumbled far off.

She peeked at Rob, who studied her in his calm way.

"You okay now?" he asked.

She nodded and he lowered her to the ground. She massaged her shoulder in silent embarrassment, but it didn't hurt. With her anger departed, she felt hollow and tired. Rob went back to splitting logs as if nothing had happened. Cricket watched him for a few minutes, and then trudged away. She'd go to the orchard and talk to Gran. It would make her feel better, even if she was really only talking to a stone.

Twenty-two ancient apple trees stood on the rise to the north of the house. They were tall and muscular, and their heads had grown, unpruned for decades, into witchy twig-puzzles. Cricket dragged her feet through their shade, reaching out to run her fingers over their gnarled skin, and felt their compassion. It was slow and deep, and a little impersonal. Gran had told her that trees found it difficult to fix their attention on the fleeting lives of humans. They were, however, well suited to watching over the dead, and Cricket wandered past their patient guard until she came to the old family plot.

The headstones leaned in the embrace of the apple roots, lichen-spotted and washed blank of names and dates by a hundred years of rough weather. The sun came down upon some of them like a celestial spotlight, others languished in gloom. Coarse grass and wildflowers romped among them, and a fierce contentment rose from the subterranean beds of their owners. In the dappled light at the back of the plot, a bright, new stone stood. Seated on it, his long legs crossed at the ankles, Pop whittled at a bit of apple wood.

"They're signing papers down there," he said, the shifting sunlight winking off his glasses. "They've got a lawyer over from St. John's Port, the thieves, and they'll be ready to go back to the city tonight."

"Tonight? They're leaving tonight?"

Pop looked up from his whittling. He rarely left the house, and the sunbeams passed through him in vaporous clouds. "*You* will be leaving here tonight, my dear, for they surely won't go without you. And when you're gone, I suppose I'll come up here and lie down with the rest of them." He looked about him at the headstones as if confused.

"Oh, Pop! Won't you come with me? Rob says he's going to the woods." She felt her lips turn downward, trembling. "I'll be all alone."

"I can't leave here, my girl." Pop put his whittling piece in his breast pocket, took off his glasses, and polished them vigorously with his handkerchief. "You know that. I'm tied to the land as much as these trees."

He gazed off into the woods, and his face looked young and vulnerable without the wire-rim spectacles. Another rumble of thunder shook the air, still distant but growing in volume. The sunlight shivered and dimmed as the first storm-colored clouds glided overhead. In the greying light, Pop became more substantial, and Cricket ran to him and threw herself into his arms.

"Make some magic, Pop. Please, do something."

"I can't stop this. It's beyond my powers. But ..."

Cricket looked up at his thoughtful face. An expression of shrewd mischief had replaced his sadness. "What? Did you think of something?"

"There is one place we could go together. Do you still have the map of Ever After?"

"Pop ...." She couldn't tell him again that she didn't believe in fairy tales, not when the words cut him so deeply. "It's in my bedroom," she sighed.

He looked into her eyes, and his were like silver cloud alive with rainbows. "You don't have to believe, Your Majesty, not yet. But we'll need all of your bravery."

"Are we running away?" A prickle of excitement raced over her. She had been afraid before, but with Pop and Rob to help her, she could face anything.

"Not exactly running away, but running toward something wonderful, Your Majesty. We'll have to be quick and careful, can't let them catch us." He grinned a sharp and ferocious grin, and Cricket saw the scary part of him bare its teeth. "The storm's nearly here. Go and tell your dog that we are leaving today, before supper. He'll know what to do."

Rob had told her what to put in her backpack. It wasn't a real one for hiking and camping, but the one she used for school. Rob said it would work just fine, and she had been able to stuff some clothes and a cobbled-together first aid kit into it. It had not been difficult to avoid the adults. Great-uncle Max had gone back to his house in St. John's Port, following the lawyer's pearly-grey Mercedes. Dean went out to the tractor shed to "work on the old Farmall", but more likely to smoke and look at dirty magazines. Cricket was left with her father and his wife, who moved through the house like ghosts and spoke quietly to one another. Neither of them wanted a repeat of the morning's tantrum, and they regarded her with false smiles when their paths crossed hers. She heard bits of their conversation as she sneaked about the house, scavenging bandages, aspirin, and antibiotic ointment.

"... never thought she'd be so undisciplined and rude." That was the woman, Danica. Cricket bristled at the injustice of the words. "You'd think she'd be grateful. Eastlake is a good school, and expensive, too."

"I think she expected she'd live with us. I'm pretty sure Max thought she should." Her dad sounded distracted. Cricket peeked into the bedroom, her first aid supplies clutched to her chest, and saw him standing by the open window, watching the massing of black thunderheads.

"Oh, *him*! He doesn't like me, Lee." Danica's voice came from the tiny guest bath. "Can't he understand that you have a family to think about? A first child is a huge responsibility. I can't take on a half-grown girl at the same time."

"I'm sure he understands," her dad murmured. He leaned out into the cooling air, the long sheer curtains blowing around him like fog. "I think that storm's going to hit sooner than we thought. Maybe we should get an early start."

Cricket scuttled past the doorway and down the stairs. Her backpack leaned in the pantry, and she tumbled the bottles, tubes, and boxes into it and zipped it shut. Hurt and anger boiled in her stomach. She slung the pack over her shoulder and swiped the hair from her eyes. Why should she care what they thought of her? They weren't her family. If she could have cut the ribbon of blood that tied her to Lee Carpenter, she would have, in a heartbeat. She looked around her at the neat shelves of canned goods, and at the kitchen beyond where she'd taken all her meals since she was a baby. Without sunlight, or Gran's smiling presence, it was just a room. She turned her back on it and went out the pantry door to the woodshed.

Rob had a pack, too. It was as big as Cricket, with a waterproof bedroll strapped to it. She tugged at it, but it sat like a boulder beside Rob's cot.

"Can you really carry all this?" she asked.

For answer, Rob lifted the pack easily onto the old enamel-topped table by his cot and shrugged into the straps. "I could carry more, but we have to go fast. You got a raincoat?"

She shook her head. Rob rummaged on a shelf, and peeled a black trash bag off a roll. He poked some holes in the bag, enlarged them enough for her to wriggle her head and arms through, and fluffed it around her. It hung nearly to the ground, billowing and rustling. Rob grunted and rummaged on the shelf again. This time, he drew forth a bit of rope that he tied around her middle, cinching in the capering bag. He snatched Gran's old ball cap off the hook by the door, and dropped it onto her head. It was a little loose, but it felt comfortable, and Cricket looked up at him from under the bill.

"That'll do," he said, moving to the door. Thunder rolled overhead and the first rain spatters struck the building. "I'll go first. When I wave, you come running."

He slipped out of the woodshed and across the narrow back lawn to the edge of the woods. If Cricket hadn't been watching, she would not have seen where he faded into the trees. She stared hard at him, not wanting to miss his signal. His hand went up like the flicker of a bird's wing, and she sprinted toward him. The security light by the back door caught her movement and flashed on. Her impromptu rain slicker wrestled against her. She hitched it up and ran faster, her pack bouncing on her back. Rob had crouched in the undergrowth when the light glared out. He caught her and pulled her into the trees. They stumbled together along a slender deer trail as the sky opened, and the rain built a wall between her and the place she had called home.

6.

Lee floundered through the sodden woods. Around him, the men fanned out in the dark, calling for the girl and sweeping at the vegetation with walking sticks or with the barrels of their guns. A burly, old native called Poke commanded them. Their lanterns bobbed in the curling mist like ghost lights, illuminating bits of forest – boulder-strewn or root-strangled, moss-furred or festooned with vines – in nightmare snapshots of the worst kind of fairy tale. The rain had stopped, but the whole place dripped and trickled. Lee shivered as the leaves spilled their cold benediction down the collar of his borrowed flannel. The storm had snuffed the late-August heat like a candle flame. His feet, wet and pinched in a pair of Dean's boots, slipped on the treacherous ground, and he fell to one knee. It was like kneeling on a sopping sponge.

"Watch yourself, young feller. She's a bitch to get through in the day, but she'll bust you up good in the dark." Poke hauled Lee upright with a calloused paw. The old man peered at him in the light of the lantern. "You're white as wax, boy. Don't you fret, now. Those dogs'll find that child, and that's a fact."

Poke dealt him a tremendous clap on the shoulder, nearly forcing him to his knees again, and strode off, whistling for his hounds. Lee drooped against the cold bole of an enormous oak and rubbed the damp and weariness from his face. He didn't belong here. Back at the farmhouse, he had stood forgotten at the rear of the milling knot of men while they armed themselves and discussed their search strategy. The villagers from Wickeford Mills had looked at him from the sides of their eyes and nodded courteously, but they had addressed their concern and their questions to Dean. When Poke rolled up in a big, white truck with a motley pack of dogs in the bed, the men had raised a hearty cheer. The dogs, looking lean and business-like, had leaped silently to the ground and squatted on their haunches around the old man's feet.

"How long's she been gone?" Poke rumbled.

Nobody knew. The storm had brought an early night, and now full dark pressed down on them without a moon to aid them. The rain had no doubt washed thin the scent trail. The hired boy who'd taken Cricket was a consummate woodsman; everybody knew it. There were one or two remarks about the inevitability of Rob's turning on the folks who had sheltered him, as though the boy were a mad dog, and it was the consensus of the men that he had warranted more watching than had been dealt him. This was said without blame, in the laconic style of those who understand that regret is pointless.

Lee listened in alarm. The search for a lost little girl had turned into a potentially lethal manhunt. He shouldered his way through the crowd. "Listen," he said, and he had to repeat himself several times with increasing volume. "Listen! I think she's just run away. She was ... upset, naturally, and she did a foolish thing. She's lost out there somewhere, and if Rob is with her, at least she has someone to watch over her. Emma Marchenwalder was a shrewd judge of character. She wouldn't have hired a predator."

The final word left a bitter taste in his mouth. Was he sure? He'd been away for so long, he couldn't state anything with certainty.

"What do you know about it?" Dean hissed into his face. "That retard is dangerous. I tried to tell Mom, but she wouldn't listen."

Poke reached out and grasped Dean gently by the back of the neck, dragging him away and soothing him at the same time.

"Calm yourself, son. Nobody blames you." He squinted at Lee. "You're the girl's pappy. Well, you wouldn't know, not being from around here. That boy's a Dark."

Lee gaped at him, uncomprehending. Poke waved at the side of his truck, stenciled with the words Dark's Nursery and Landscaping.

"They're a fine family, but the boys ... well, sometimes they ain't right. The ladies don't keep 'em long. Send 'em off before their voices crack, to family from away." Poke's impassive gaze rested on Lee like the regard of God. "We got to find that child before the family trouble comes on Rob, and pray we ain't too late."

Lee tried to moisten his lips with a dry tongue. The nightmare was growing to monstrous proportions. "Are you saying he might molest her?"

"Nossir. Might *eat* her, though."

7.

Cricket peeled open eyes heavy with grit. She could feel their red rims burning. Pop knelt beside her, his hand on her forehead like cool mist. Beneath her, Rob's thin groundsheet and blanket did nothing to soften the knees of the oak that held her.

"Pop, when did you get here?" Her voice was a croak that tore her throat as it freed itself.

She didn't know where *here* was, only that she and Rob had walked all night, and that sometimes the big man had carried her. For a while, the rain had fallen in long, stinging shards so that she could barely breathe. They had scrambled through the fern and laurel in the moonless dark until she lost all sense of time and direction, and floated in a dream of flight through chilly palaces of trees. Finally, they had come to this place, where the trees held troll-like hulks of stone in their root-fists – the rock fissured and hollowed by the pressure – and had crawled into one of the shallow caves. Rob had built a fire, and they squatted over its wild pungency and gobbled cold hotdogs straight from the pack, too hungry to do more than pass them through the flames. The fire no longer burned, but Cricket could still smell it. Her stomach rolled, and she moaned.

"This girl is sick," Pop said, turning toward Rob. His voice was low and lethal. "You've left her to sleep on the cold ground in her wet clothes."

Rob sat on his heels by the dead fire, and stared at Cricket. His gaze never wavered, and Cricket wondered if he'd even heard Pop. "Fever," he muttered, speaking to himself. He reached out and found her backpack. His hand stirred the things inside it and came out with the bottle of aspirin. He dropped two of the tablets into a tin cup and crushed them with his thumb. In one lithe move, he was beside her, displacing an outraged Pop. He poured water from his canteen into the cup and stirred the slurry with his finger.

"Drink this, Bug. All of it." He lifted her against him and held the cup to her lips.

The potion was bitter and choking. Cricket gulped it down, and Rob gave her more water to rinse the taste from her mouth.

"You're sick," he said. "I'm sorry."

"It's not your fault, Rob – "

Pop interrupted. "Yes, it is. She's not a great, strong beast like you, Robert Dark. I should think you'd take greater care with your queen."

Rob stroked her hair from her flushed face. His brown eyes held worry, but beneath it, they were as calm as always. Cricket relaxed against the immense heat of him, and he shifted so she lay in his lap.

"He can't see or hear you, Pop," she sighed.

"Pardon me for contradicting you, Your Majesty, but he can and does. He is simply impudent enough to ignore his betters."

She looked up at Rob and caught the glitter of anger in his eyes, there and gone like a darting fish. "Sleep," he whispered, holding her like a baby.

The second time Cricket awoke, Rob was gone. She started up in alarm. Pop, hunched over a paper he'd spread in the shadows, looked up at her. His glasses were gone, and his face seemed hardened into an expression of authority.

"Robert is scouting," he said. "We are very close now, Your Majesty. How do you feel?"

"Better," she lied. If anything, she felt as though hot stones had been tied to her limbs. She had never lied to Pop before, and didn't know if it was possible, but he only nodded in a distracted way and resumed his study of the paper.

"You look different," she said, and was ashamed at how accusatory her voice sounded. "You aren't wearing your glasses."

Pop sat back on his heels and regarded her with keen grey eyes. His gaze reminded her of that of a hunting hawk, fierce and sharp. "As I said, we are very close to the crossing. Many things will be different, even your loyal dog." He appeared at her side, and laid the paper in her lap. It was the map of Ever After, and the ford of the nameless creek glowed as if drawn in fire. "Look. We are here," Pop said, pointing. "There is less than two miles distance between the crossing and us. But, I fear it won't be an easy trek."

Cricket looked up from Pop's finger on the map and noticed with a shock that he no longer wore his usual trim button-down and houndstooth vest. In their place was a black shirt of some fine woven fabric and a scarred, leather corselet. His soft wool slacks and gleaming Oxfords had transformed to leather breeches and boots. Even his skin, which had always gleamed with a librarian's pallor, was nearly as tanned as Rob's.

Cricket's head thumped. "Who are you, Pop?"

"Your good and humble servant, my queen. I'll be going on ahead to open the way." He went out into the sunlight that no longer made a phantom of him. Cricket watched as he buckled on a sword, his hands sure and steady. "Be quick and keep safe. I'll meet you at the crossing."

He was gone before she could speak, and the hazy morning light fell on the place he had stood. Cricket rose on wobbly legs and crept into the warmth. She wondered if she could walk two miles, or even a quarter of that distance. As she contemplated the possibility of staying another night in the hollow rock, Rob burst from the undergrowth.

"Leave your things, Bug. Time to go." His voice was composed, but his eyes had kindled to an amber glow. A violent energy hummed around him.

"What's wrong?" she cried.

"They're close enough to smell. They brought dogs," he growled. "Listen."

She tried to make her ears as sharp as Rob's, and soon she heard a sound drifting over the woods, falling into their little camp with soft, terrifying promise. It was the throaty baying of a hunting pack.

8.

They ran. Fear lent Cricket strength, and when she flagged, Rob scooped her up and raced like a deer through the woods. They burst out of the thick growth into a sun-dappled grove of river birches, and he zigzagged through ferns as high as his knees. Ahead of them lay the bright shimmer of the creek through the trees, but the dogs had seen them. They closed the gap, howling in triumph. Cricket, clinging to Rob with arms and legs, saw their bounding figures through the ferns. The pack opened and swung to either side of them. They were big dogs, a rangy mix of hound and shepherd with long, red jaws full of gleaming teeth. She squeezed Rob, and shouted in his ear.

"They're going to catch us!"

Rob peeled her from his body in mid-stride, and dropped her gently into the sweet-smelling foliage. He pivoted on the ball of one foot, his arm coming up in time to block the leap of the pack leader. The dog fastened its teeth in Rob's forearm. Cricket screamed as the blood leaped out, but Rob continued to turn, slinging the dog into the forest with a mighty heave. Rob's eyes gleamed wolfish gold. His body hunched forward, and his shaggy hair flowed along his neck like the raised hackles of the dogs. Another hound leaped. Rob swatted it against the trees with a savage snarl. The third, he unzipped from throat to groin with a hand twisted into a claw. Cricket covered her head with her arms, as terrified of this new Rob as she was of the dogs. The sharp report of a rifle brought her head up. She leaped to her feet, and Rob snatched her from the ferns, bending his body around her. Another shot rang out, she heard him gasp, and then he lifted her and sprinted for the creek.

"Hold your fire, you damn fool," someone shouted. More men raised their voices, calling for Rob to stop, to bring back the girl. Cricket clung to his great, trembling frame, afraid to look at his wild face. Something hot had blossomed under his shirt, and she looked at the red painted on her hand.

"Rob, you're shot! Put me down."

He checked his flight, skidding on the smooth stones at the creek's edge, and set her on her feet. She swayed backward and sat down in the shallows, still staring at her hand. She held it out to show him.

"Get across," he said in a rough voice.

She looked at the stones that peeked out of the boil of fast-flowing water. They were green and slick with streaming floss. Where they broke the surface, moss clung to them like footprints. They meandered along the edge of a steep fall, at the bottom of which the water turned powerfully back upon itself, forcing what fell into it to the creek bottom and holding it there. She rolled to her hands and knees, feeling sick and weak, and crawled onto the broad, flat back of the first stone. The opposite side looked miles away, swathed in fog the sun hadn't yet burned away. The next stone was smaller, and she stood shakily, reaching for it with her toes. The angry creek drenched her shoe, but she hopped forward, windmilling her arms for balance. She glanced up. The fog began to part a little. She stretched for the next stone.

"I told you, dummy. I told you'd we'd talk again." Dean's voice cracked out like a whip. Cricket, straddling a perilous white froth, looked back to see her uncle emerge from the birches, his rifle leveled at Rob. "Don't you go no further, kid. I'm gonna come get you," he yelled.

Cricket teetered on the two stones. Closing her eyes against the vertiginous fall, she pulled herself forward and, brave with momentum, leaped to the next stone. She was nearly halfway across, dizzy, sweating, and shivering at the icy bite of the water that drilled her bones to the marrow. Her vision blurred, and she thought she heard Dean and Rob fighting. There was a sound like a firecracker going off. The fog on the opposite shore swirled away, and Pop was there, holding out his hand toward her. In the distance behind him, she saw the castle with its snapping banners emblazoned with a golden fox and crown. For a moment, there was no sound, and then she heard Pop shouting.

"Come to me, Your Majesty. You must cross the bridge yourself. I cannot leave this shore."

She looked back. Dean lay on the pebbled bank, unmoving. Rob, on the first stone, staggered and fell into the water with a groan. She turned to go back.

"No! No, Your Majesty, you must not." Pop's voice froze her. "Gods, you're so close. You must not go back. I cannot hold the way if you return."

More men stepped from the birches. She looked at Pop with tears in her eyes. "Rob's hurt. I can't leave him."

As she hesitated, Rob stirred. He stood, one arm hanging limply at his side, and lurched onto the stone bridge. One of the men raised his gun and fired. The shot struck the water by Rob's foot, making him flinch. Grimly, he hopped to the next stone, his feet agile despite his wounds. Cricket turned and skipped over the bridge, putting her sneakers on the moss footprints, with Rob close behind her. She thought of Gran, waiting for her in the castle, and of Pop, whose anxious face urged her forward. The farm, her father and his wife, the threat of Eastlake Girls' Academy, all receded like dissipating wisps of dream. Ever After shone before her. She felt its loving embrace.

The thunder of the gun was like the distant rumble of the previous day's storm. It didn't seem important. It was far away, and Pop was reaching for her. It didn't seem important, yet still Rob fell. First to his knees on the slippery stone, and then over and away. Cricket screamed. She reached to catch at him, but Pop lunged onto the last stone and swung her to the bank. For a blink before the fog swirled between them, she saw him standing on the bridge, with her other father behind him at the far edge of the creek. The black thread of sorrow lay under their boots, a shadow cast long through the Johns Woods.

ABOUT THE AUTHOR

Elizabeth Yon is the author of *Wilderness: A Collection of Dark Tales.* Her stories have appeared in the anthologies *Echoes in Darkness* (Bannerwing Books) and *Precipice,* Volumes II and III (Bannerwing Books). More of her work can be read on her blog, The Palace of Night.

www.elizabethyon.com

www.amazon.com/Elizabeth-Yon

Also by Elizabeth Yon

Books

Wilderness: A Collection of Dark Tales

Stories

"Love Apples" in the collection *Echoes in Darkness*
"Queen and Knave" in the anthology *Precipice, Volume II*
"Lake Effect" in the anthology *Precipice, Volume III*

Made in the USA
Middletown, DE
21 March 2015